A Spring Deception

(SEASONS BOOK 2)

By

USA Today Bestseller
Jess Michaels

A SPRING DECEPTION
Seasons Book 2

Copyright © Jesse Petersen, 2016

For more information, contact Jess Michaels
www.AuthorJessMichaels.com

To contact the author:
Email: Jess@AuthorJessMichaels.com
Twitter www.twitter.com/JessMichaelsbks
Facebook: www.facebook.com/JessMichaelsBks

Jess Michaels raffles a gift certificate EVERY month to members of her newsletter, so sign up on her website:
http://www.authorjessmichaels.com/

DEDICATION

*This book is for everyone who ever felt
like they didn't "fit".*

*And for Michael,
who does all the heavy lifting.
Thank you baby!*

CHAPTER ONE

February 1811

John Dane pulled his horse up in the circular drive and looked up and up and up at the castle before him. The stone fortress was an ostentatious display of a man's power if he'd ever seen one, and he had seen *many* in his thirty-two years.

Of course, power hadn't helped this particular man much. In fact, quite the opposite.

As he swung down from his mount a young man rushed through the imposing front doors and down the steps to greet him. "Good evening, Mr. Dane," he said.

He sent the man a sharp look. "What have I told you, Corbett? There's no mister. Hell, there's hardly a Dane."

"Of course, sir, I-I'm sorry," Corbett stammered, motioning up the stairs to the entryway. "Lord Stalwood is waiting for you."

Dane pursed his lips. He was not looking forward to this. "Lead the way."

Corbett nodded and did just that, scuttling back up to the house with Dane on his heels. He was engaged in a ceaseless stream of chatter as they walked, but Dane blocked it out. He preferred to determine facts by his own senses, not through someone else's perceptions. Especially someone so young and inexperienced as Corbett.

Inside he let his gaze dart around as his companion led him

through dark, twisting, gloomy halls. It was certainly an interesting aesthetic, like something out of a gothic novel. Or a nightmare.

"...here." Corbett finished whatever he was saying and smiled before he pushed open a large door and indicated that Dane should enter.

He forced himself to focus back on the man before him. "Thank you, Corbett."

The thanks seemed to light up Corbett from the inside, and he grinned. "You're welcome, sir. Anything I can do, I'm happy to serve. You're a legend, you know."

Dane arched a brow, uncertain if he should show gratitude for the praise or mistrust it. His first reaction was generally mistrust, though he sensed nothing false about Corbett.

The young man blushed. "A-and now I'm off to help the boys outside."

He took off like a puppy who hadn't quite grown into his legs. Dane shook his head. The young ones were always like that. Thrilled by the hunt, he supposed. Though he didn't recall ever being so eager. Of course, his background was likely far, far different from Corbett's and he'd come to this place with a much different view of it.

He pushed the thoughts aside, drew in a deep breath and entered the room. It appeared to be a library, with tall shelves brimming with books. A bright fire was burning in one corner of the room, and unlike the rest of the dark, moody house, lanterns and candles brought significant light to the chamber.

Behind a settee with a high back, a man stood, and his presence elicited the first hint of a smile on Dane's face.

"Hello, Stalwood," he said.

Stalwood looked up, and his wrinkled face brightened with his own smile. "Dane. Thank you for coming so swiftly. We were lucky you were close by."

Dane took a breath. He could smell it now. The metallic tang of blood that filled his nose and brought back memories of many a terrible day. He moved forward and around the settee.

And there it was. The body. A man, lying in a huge pool of blood. His face was twisted in pain and fear. Dane had seen the dead many a time before, but it remained a jarring experience. He often wondered what their last moments had been like. What they had thought of as they struggled to stay alive, then realized that struggle would be in vain. What did a man wish for in that moment?

As for the man lying before him, Dane couldn't believe many thoughts had plagued him, at least at the very last moments. The victim's head had been crushed by some kind of bludgeoning weapon. Probably the fire poker that lay beside him, caked with blood and slightly bent from the force of the blows it had struck.

"A weapon of opportunity," Dane said softly.

Stalwood glanced up at him with a nod. "Yes, I thought the same. It leads me to believe his attacker might not have intended for this outcome tonight."

"All the better for us if the murder wasn't planned. There are more chances that the perpetrator left traces of himself behind. And who is the victim? I assume the War Department wouldn't be involved if he weren't important."

Stalwood nodded slowly. "Oh, yes, he is very important. This is…or *was*, I suppose, the Duke of Clairemont." Dane's eyes went wide as he jerked his face toward Stalwood. The earl nodded. "You know the name."

"Everyone in the game knows that name. I've seen it in a dozen reports. Clairemont has been long suspected of involvement in weapons trade with France, behind war lines, a direct violation of embargo and an act of treason. And worse, the man has been trading in information. When Smith was unmasked and executed in Napoleon's court, wasn't that rumored to be Clairemont's doing?"

Stalwood's face grew grim. "Indeed, it was."

"Then someone has done the War Department a favor, it seems," Dane said, glancing over the dead man again, this time with more disdain than pity. How many lives had Clairemont cost, either by providing instruments of death or information to the enemy? A bludgeoning seemed too good a fate.

"Not much of one," Stalwood said.

"What do you mean?"

His superior motioned Dane to a desk beside a window. A thick book of poetry rested there, opened to reveal a hidden chamber within the tome. It was filled with letters.

"Ah, so His Grace wasn't as much of a reader as he might have seemed," Dane said. "At least not of books."

Stalwood shook his head. "No. Once we clear the body away, we'll have half a dozen agents searching through every book looking for more hidden correspondence. Right now, though, what this tells us is that Clairemont was involved in a great many dealings with a great many people. Even more connections than we thought. And certainly, though he was a villain, there are many branches to this poisonous vine, and cutting away one piece will do us little good."

Dane nodded, understanding. "You need the root."

"Yes. And alive, Clairemont might have helped us with that, whether willingly or not. But now…"

Dane clenched his fists. "Yes, I see. Do the servants have any information?"

"They are gathered away in the kitchen, but after a brief interrogation I would say no. Clairemont was secretive and he had only three servants."

"Even in this castle?" Dane said in disbelief. "It's huge."

"Apparently most of it was closed off years ago. Those who serve here are overworked and abused, it seems, with no love for their master, especially the maid and the housekeeper. They say Clairemont was not expecting anyone they knew of last night, but that he ran his own schedule, keeping them away from his plans. He didn't employ a butler and managed his own correspondence."

"And you believe them?"

Stalwood inclined his head. "You may speak to them, of course—in fact, I very much want you to. I trust your instincts, you've always been able to smell a liar. But I have some small skill in that area, myself, and I have no reason to doubt them, especially given their abject terror at what transpired here tonight."

Dane moved toward him. "My lord, I was not implying—"

"Of course you weren't, my boy." Stalwood smiled, and it was a genuine and warm expression. "I take great pride in your mastery of this work. I'm very happy to have you surpass me in skill."

Dane let out a burst of laughter. "No one shall ever do that, my lord."

Stalwood shrugged, but his smile faded. "I was very pleased to have you close by, but not only because you are my best spy, Dane. Have you looked carefully at the man on the rug there?"

Dane turned and glanced at the body again. "I haven't taken a huge amount of time, but I have my impressions, yes."

"Have you taken note of Clairemont's appearance?"

Dane wrinkled his brow and took a few steps toward the fallen duke. "I see that the blows were struck on both sides of the head, indicating a swinging back and forth. There was a great deal of force, there—"

"Not that. His face." Stalwood tilted his head. "Who does he look like?"

"Hard to say with half his head bashed in," Dane said with a shrug.

Stalwood sighed and motioned Dane out of the room. He was just as happy to leave the bloody scene behind him. Yes, he had been trained for such things, and in his life he'd seen a great deal of death, both violent and otherwise. But it wasn't an enjoyable aspect of his occupation as a spy in the War Department. He much preferred investigating, becoming another person, needling into a situation until all the facts became clear.

Stalwood stepped into a long hall where pictures had been hung. He caught up a lantern from the wall and moved to one of them, lifting his light up to the face depicted there.

"Our victim," his mentor said.

Dane stared but could see nothing unusual about the appearance of the man who lay dead on the floor. He had dark blond hair, light eyes and an entirely arrogant expression that made Dane even less sorry for the bastard's bitter end in the library.

"Looks like a prick. What of it?"

"You don't see it, which is fascinating considering your attention to detail." Stalwood shook his head. "Very well, I shall guide you until you do. You two do not look dissimilar, Dane. Surely you must see the resemblance."

Dane stepped back in surprise at that statement, his eyes going wide. He stared again at the portrait and tried to compare it to the dead man in the other room.

"I...*suppose* we are alike in that we are both men and under five and thirty," he conceded slowly, reluctantly. "And our hair is somewhat alike in color."

"And your eyes. This portrait does not do him justice, and the light is out of them in the other room. But they are very close." Stalwood folded his arms, and suddenly he looked very smug.

"What are you getting at?" Dane asked, his hackles up and the little hairs on his neck at attention. This was danger. He knew the feeling well, though he'd hadn't felt it coming from Stalwood in years.

"I said earlier that if Clairemont were alive he might be of some use to us," Stalwood said.

Dane glared at him, trying to ignore the rising sense of dread in his chest. "Well, I've no magic to bring the man back to life."

"You've more magic than you think, *Your Grace*."

Dane shut his eyes. Over the years he'd served this man, he'd gone all over the empire, serving his king and country. He'd played many a role in those years, rich and poor, but never titled. Never a duke.

The very idea chafed at him.

"You want *me* to take over as Clairemont," he said softly. Stalwood smiled. "There it is. Yes, I do. Imagine if we were inside that world. You'd be reading Clairemont's letters, seeing everything he does from his eyes."

"The only problem with that plan is that Clairemont's eyes are glassed over in the middle of a pool of blood in his library," Dane said, motioning wildly toward that room in the distance. "And people know it."

"Three servants and half a dozen agents to the crown known it," Stalwood corrected him. "And, I suppose, one murderer. Otherwise, there has been no announcement, no scandal, no information spread far and wide. To almost all of the world, the Duke of Clairemont is *not* dead on a library floor—he is sleeping peacefully in his own bed. He could stroll into a ballroom in London at any moment and no one would blink about it."

Dane drew farther back, as if stepping away would cease this foolish notion. "I might look something *vaguely* like the man, but it seems what you are suggesting is that I go into the bright light of Society and play the part. Surely dozens of people will mark me immediately."

"Oh, but they won't."

"In my duties as spy, I've met some of these people I'm certain to encounter," Dane insisted. "Someone might recognize me from a prior case."

Stalwood seemed to contemplate that. "You have. But often in physical disguise. You're my best agent—there is a reason that up until now I've not asked you to play a role without some kind of camouflage to protect you."

Dane gritted his teeth. Stalwood did have a point. But it made him no more excited at the prospect. "And what of Clairemont's friends and family? Certainly they'll look right through me if I'm pretending to be him."

Stalwood smiled slightly. "You said you've heard something of this man's involvement in criminal enterprise, but have you ever *seen* him?"

"I don't move in those circles outside of in the confines of a case, Stalwood, you know that," Dane snapped, sharper than he would normally dare be with the man who had rescued him off the street and trained him not just for this life, but to be the man he was now.

Stalwood nodded. "Well, I *do*. No one will mark you as a fraud because Clairemont has been a hermit for over a decade. *No one* we can find has seen him aside from his servants."

Dane blinked in confusion. "What?"

"His father died during Clairemont's time at school and he moved straight into his dukedom. And though he kept up a robust correspondence, he did not maintain *any* known friendships in person." Stalwood leaned back and folded his arms, looking very self-satisfied. "As far as anyone in Society knows, he could be anyone."

"Me, you mean," Dane said softly. "He could be me. Or I could be him, I suppose. Only I have no idea how to behave as a duke."

"You will learn," Stalwood assured him. "We'll have at least two months until the Season begins and it would even make sense to send you to London."

"And the murderer who cut this man down?"

"Can you imagine his confusion, his anxiety as days and weeks and months stretch by with no announcement of the death of the Duke of Clairemont? By the time you arrive in London, he will be on the edge. Dangerous, yes, but just as much to himself as he is to anyone else."

"At the minimum you hope to sniff him out," Dane said with a shake of his head.

"And while you train, we'll come up with a list of suspects in regards to who Clairemont was working with. London will give you ample opportunity to evaluate them." Stalwood came closer. "Dane, I know this isn't the kind of assignment you relish, but it *is* important. As you said, one of our agents is already dead because of this man and his cohorts, and untold numbers of soldiers have likely already been endangered. This is *good* work, important work."

Dane couldn't help but smile. Good work. That was what Stalwood had once said to him, years and years ago, when the earl was trying to recruit him off the street. Good work had appealed to Dane then.

It appealed to him now.

"Very well," he muttered, pushing down the swell of doubt that rose in his chest again and again. The one that said he was nothing but a street tough, a no one who would never fit in as a duke, hermit bastard duke or not.

Stalwood smiled. "I'm pleased you agree. Otherwise I would have had to pull rank."

Dane motioned Stalwood back toward their murder scene. "You know I don't give a damn about rank."

"When you're a duke you'll be above me, if it helps."

That elicited a laugh Dane couldn't contain. "Actually, that's the best reason I've heard yet to do this foolish thing. Outrank the Earl of Stalwood? I cannot wait."

But deep in his heart, Dane knew that was a lie. A bitter lie at that. He was not looking forward to this. But he knew his duty and he would serve his king with all the honor he'd been trained to uphold.

CHAPTER TWO

April 1811

Celia Fitzgilbert sat at the pianoforte, letting her fingers dance over the keys as she played out a mournful song. Her sister, Rosalinde, preferred a happier tune, but tonight Celia could not manage it. Her heart hurt too much not to express it with the music she played. The loss was too great.

As if on cue, Rosalinde stepped into the room. Her sister's beautiful face was lit up with pure happiness, her blue eyes aglow with what Celia knew was deepest love and joy. And why wouldn't she be so happy? Her marriage less than six months before was one filled with love and passion.

After all they'd been through in their lives, Rosalinde's contentment was wonderful to see. But it was also isolating. Celia had spent so much time telling herself that she didn't need those things, now being in such close quarters with Rosalinde and her husband, Grayson Danford, slapped her in the face with reality. In truth, she longed for such a deep connection as they shared.

Her fingers faltered on the keys and she stopped playing with a sudden, incongruous note.

Rosalinde stepped forward with a shake of her head. "Oh, please don't stop playing. I love to hear you."

Celia forced a smile to her face and looked up at Rosalinde.

"I'm afraid I *must* stop playing. After all, we should leave for the ball soon."

Her sister slipped a gentle hand to her shoulder and squeezed lightly. "You sound anxious."

Celia shrugged. "It is only the second ball I have gone to since our return to London last week. I cannot help but remain nervous."

Rosalinde shook her head. "But there has been no scandal following you after your broken engagement. From what I've seen at every event we've attended, there are a few whispers, but the overall response is positive."

Celia held back a sigh. Just a few months before, she had been pledged to marry the Earl of Stenfax, who was the brother of her sister's new husband. It had been a loveless match, to be certain, and one that had been fought strenuously against by her new brother-in-law and eventually, her sister, though they each had very different reasons.

Breaking the engagement *should* have destroyed Celia in the eyes of Society. But it hadn't.

"You and Gray saved me from the worst with your true love story. The idea that I would step aside so you could marry into the family for love made both Stenfax and I look like heroes. So no, it has not been unpleasant. But it's an adjustment, regardless."

"What has been an adjustment?" Gray asked as he entered the room.

Rosalinde's face brightened immediately and she all but glided toward him. The expression on his hard face softened as she straightened his cravat, and Celia had the very strong impression that had she not been standing there, the two might have kissed. Not that her being there stopped them every time. They were enjoying what was obviously a very happy honeymoon period. Some nights there was no denying it at all.

She cleared her throat as heat filled her cheeks. "Rosalinde and I were talking about my nervousness about the ball tonight."

"Ah," Gray said as he stepped away from Rosalinde and

toward Celia. He held out a hand and she took it. "What can I do to help?"

Celia stared up into his face and smiled. It was strange that such a short time ago she had despised this man. He had been working to break up her engagement to his brother— he had thought her nothing more than a title-grabber. But since he had married Rosalinde, Gray had been very kind to Celia. They had developed a budding friendship, in fact. One she could tell would grow and deepen over the years. She never would have guessed that could happen, even in her wildest dreams.

"Nothing, Gray," she said softly. "Thank you, though. Your being there will be comfort enough."

At that sentence, Gray's hand dropped away from hers and his smile fell. "I'm not certain I am there enough, for *either* of you. I have something to tell you both."

Rosalinde moved forward and wrapped an arm around Celia. Celia felt her tremble slightly and she couldn't help but do the same.

"Is it about our father?" Celia asked.

Gray's face told the story even before he said a word. Since their marriage, he had been searching out information about Celia and Rosalinde's father, a servant who had lost them when their powerful grandfather snatched them away after their mother's death. The two women had been lied to their whole lives about his identity, his whereabouts. Only when their wicked grandfather had wanted to blackmail Celia into marrying a title to satisfy his ambition had he dangled the truth of the man before them.

And Celia did so *desperately* want to know who he was. She'd been ready to go through with a loveless marriage for that information. To bargain with her grandfather, a man who had once tried to kill Rosalinde.

"Please tell us," she whispered, her voice breaking.

Gray dropped his chin. "I'm sorry. I thought I had a promising clue, but it has led to nothing yet again."

Rosalinde pulled from Celia's arms and Celia watched as

she went to Gray for comfort. Alone, she moved to the window and stood to look into the dark with unseeing eyes.

Her father was a missing piece in her life. Unlike Rosalinde, she had nothing else to fill that hole. Celia wanted to know him so very much. To have the whole truth of who she was.

She turned back and could hear Rosalinde's soft whispers to Gray, his murmurs of comfort and apology. She flinched at the intimacy of that moment and forced a serene expression on her face.

"Thank you for trying, Gray," she said.

He looked at her at last. "I won't give up," he vowed. "I will continue to search with all my resources."

But she could see that those resources were wearing thin. Gray didn't think he would ever find the answers she needed. Which meant the only person with any information was her grandfather. The man she had not seen since he tried to choke the life out of her sister in a parlor months before. A man who wanted her to marry a title in order to share the particulars of her family.

She pressed her lips together. "Come, we should go. I don't want to be more than fashionably late."

"Yes," Rosalinde said, linking arms with Gray. "We should forget our troubles for now. You never know what the night will bring."

Celia smiled for the sake of Rosalinde, but as the couple exited the room, that smile fell. It seemed whatever the night would bring would not be enough. But she would put on a falsely happy face regardless and see if any opportunity might present itself.

Celia sighed as she looked out over the dance floor and watched Gray and Rosalinde swirl by in the crowd. Gray's hand was firmly pressed into Rosalinde's hip and their gazes were locked on each other, proof once again of their loving bond.

"She *does* look happy."

Celia started and looked at the two young women who had stepped up beside her. She'd known Miss Tabitha Thornton and Lady Honora for as long as she could remember. They were old friends and ones who had stood staunchly beside her before, during and after her ill-fated engagement. She appreciated that beyond measure.

"She does," Celia said, addressing Honora, for it was she who had made the statement. "She is. Lucky her."

"Indeed, for Mr. Danford cuts a fine figure," Tabitha sighed. "And I've heard he's worth a fortune, even if Father *does* turn up his nose that he made it all by work and *not* inheritance."

Celia shrugged. "I don't care *what* he does to earn his keep, as long as he takes care of my sister. Which he does in spades."

"So you don't regret breaking your engagement to Stenfax at all?" Tabitha asked, curling a loose blonde lock around her finger.

Celia pursed her lips. Her friends had kindly danced around that subject since her return to London a week before, but here it was. She found herself searching through the ballroom and found the tall, stern figure of the Earl of Stenfax. He was standing in the corner, talking to his sister, Felicity. When they saw her looking their way, both raised their hands in a friendly hello, which she returned before she sighed. Stenfax was very handsome, of course, but he had never moved her, nor had she moved him.

"I do *not* regret it," she said, and meant it. "Things have worked out exactly right." She cleared her throat and looked around. The women who were not dancing were all gathered in clumps, it seemed, and there was a crackling electricity in the air that made no sense to Celia. "Why is everyone so odd tonight?" she asked, hoping for a change in subject since the topic of her former fiancé was uncomfortable to say the least.

Honora grasped her arm in both hands, her face lighting up in excited pleasure. "You mean you haven't heard?"

"Heard what?" Celia asked, shaking her head. "What is there to hear that would inspire *that* expression?"

Both women leaned in and Honora whispered, "The Duke of Clairemont is making a return to Society tonight."

Celia wrinkled her brow. "The Duke of Clairemont. I vaguely recognize the title, but why does *that* matter? We've a room full of stuffy old men as it is. One more boring duke is hardly any matter."

"Oh my Lord, she doesn't know!" Tabitha squealed, and now Celia was being held by both her arms, one for each friend. She rather hoped they didn't try for a tug of war.

Honora all but bounced. "His Grace is *not* an old man," she said, trying for a whisper but not really accomplishing it in her excitement. "He is *barely* above thirty and rich as Midas, himself!"

Tabitha tugged on Celia's arm none too gently. "His father died a decade ago and he took the title, but since then he has been a recluse, hiding away in his country estate, Kinghill Castle. No one has seen him in years and years."

"There are so many rumors about why he hid so long, Celia," Honora continued, pulling Celia back to her side. "Some say he was scarred in an accident—"

"A fire!" Tabitha said. "I heard it was a fire."

"Whatever it was." Honora shrugged. "Or that he was driven mad over his father's death."

"Oh there are a dozen stories or more," Tabitha said. "Whatever the truth is, *everyone* is agog over his return. He is quite the catch."

"Despite being horribly disfigured or mad? Or both?" Celia asked mildly.

Honora let out a huff of breath. "He's *titled* and *rich*—did you not hear that part?"

Celia held back a sigh. She hated to be mercenary, especially after all she'd gone through breaking her engagement to Stenfax, but the idea of this duke's title *did* appeal to her. Since Gray had had little luck in finding out her father's identity, she couldn't help but wonder if her grandfather might consider honoring his original bargain with her.

Marry a title to satisfy him and receive the information that was so well hidden. Rosalinde would hate that. She wouldn't want Celia anywhere near the old man.

But Rosalinde didn't need the truth as much as Celia felt she did. It didn't eat at her at night, it didn't haunt her every time she looked in the mirror and wondered if she had her father's nose or chin.

"Are you well, my dear?" Tabitha asked, tilting her face to get a closer look at Celia. "You have gotten very pale."

Celia shook her head. These were not thoughts she should entertain. Likely when this mysterious duke arrived he would not be interested in her at all. He would probably be a boring, fat aristocrat who already knew exactly what family he would merge his own with. There was no use getting one's hopes up over a mirage.

"I'm fine, I was woolgathering," she said with a smile to reassure her friends.

Tabitha didn't look certain, but before she could follow up with more questions or concerns, the crowd in the room began to titter and shift. It seemed everyone in the room turned toward the door at once as the servant there made some muffled announcement.

Celia turned with them, lifting on her tiptoes to see who had caused the commotion.

"It must be him," Honora breathed, her hand coming up to fluff her hair. "It *must* be!"

Celia supposed her friend must be correct, for this mysterious duke was the only addition to Society that would cause such a stir. The crowd began to part, splitting apart like a torn seam, and then the few people before her stepped aside and she caught her breath.

An impeccably dressed man now stood not three feet from her. And he was utterly beautiful, with dark blond hair and steely gray eyes that swept over the room. He had an angled face with a strong jaw and a slightly imperfect nose, like he had broken it at some point during his life. But the imperfection only made the rest of his face that much more striking.

He shifted slightly, revealing some discomfort on his handsome face. And something else, too. Sadness. There was a sadness in his eyes that spoke to Celia in a visceral and immediate way.

"*That's* him?" she breathed, unable to take her eyes off of him. Tabitha and Honora nodded mutely. "He certainly isn't scarred."

"Or fat," Honora added. "Or hideous."

"No," Celia whispered as he turned away and smiled as their host and hostess, the Marquess and Marchioness Harrington, rushed to greet their coup of a guest. He was led off into the crowd and it felt like the air had been let back into the room. Celia sucked in a gulp of it with a shiver.

She had never had such a strong reaction to a stranger before. A man. It was like her whole body was tingling and her heart pounded so loudly in her ears that the rest of the sounds in the room were muffled by the rush of blood.

"I think he'll be even more of a catch now that we've all seen him," Tabitha said with a sigh. "The Diamonds of the First Water will wrestle for him and some lucky girl will land him before the summer, I can almost guarantee it!"

Celia blinked as those words sank in. Of course that was true. The mamas would swarm on their newcomer before he could settle in for five minutes, and he would be the focus of their manipulations until someone had landed him.

Someone who would almost certainly *not* be Celia Fitzgilbert. She turned away from where the duke had stood and took a few more deep breaths. It was foolish to be swept away by the appearance of a handsome face. And if she were smart, she'd just forget about the man.

Only she didn't think that would be so easy to do.

CHAPTER THREE

Dane stood with the Earl of Stalwood, staring out at the swirling crowd of dancers. It seemed every time a pair passed him, they whispered to each other and stared pointedly in his direction. He shifted with discomfort at the unexpected and utterly unwelcome attention.

"So Clairemont, what do you think?" Stalwood asked, breaking through the cloud of his thoughts.

Dane blinked a few times. *Clairemont*. He was Clairemont now, and he had to *think* of himself that way so he didn't slip up in his duty.

"It seems a perfect place to find our marks," he said slowly, speaking with the more formal accent he had been perfecting for two long months. It came naturally now, even if it still sounded foreign to his ears.

Stalwood nodded as he surveyed the crowd around them. Unlike Dane, there was no discomfort or feeling out of place for the earl. "Indeed. The duke might not have met with people in person during the past decade, but his correspondence included a great many of those in this room." Stalwood's tone grew hard. "Likely one or more of them were involved in his schemes. One may have even killed him."

Dane…no, *Clairemont*—now more than ever he had to immerse himself in his role so that he never slipped—shifted with discomfort.

"My appearance here has created a great deal of attention,"

he mused, trying not to chafe at the continued stares and whispers.

"More than we anticipated," Stalwood agreed. "Though I suppose it shouldn't be so surprising. There are only so many titles in our world. When one comes out of hiding, it is bound to cause a splash."

"I've been accustomed to simply fitting in," Clairemont explained. "To becoming invisible in whatever role I take in the organization. Blending in makes investigation smooth. But this focus will make my job all the harder."

Stalwood nodded, his face suddenly grim. "That is likely true. Unfortunately, you'll have to work around it, at least until the interest fades in a few weeks."

"A few *weeks?*" he repeated, and his stomach roiled as he let his gaze slide around the room once more. The crowd with their finery and their foolishness did nothing for him. "These people," he murmured. "How in the world shall I ever keep track of them?"

Stalwood arched a brow. "If you let you prejudice guide you, you won't. So figure it out, Clairemont." He stopped for a moment, his gaze shifting over Clairemont's shoulder. "And do it quickly. Here come the mamas."

Clairemont stiffened and slowly turned. Sure enough, there was what felt like a gaggle of middle-aged women moving across the floor to him. Some had young ladies in tow, others came alone. But all had the same predatory look in their eyes.

His mouth went dry. He'd spent decades being the hunter. Now he was the prey.

And for the first time since he was a pup in training, he had no defense against the attacks about to come. So he clenched his fists behind his back and muttered, "Shit."

Celia stood on the terrace in the shadow of the great house

and stared up at the waning moon above. Even though it wasn't quite full anymore, it had a beautiful glow about it that filled her with happiness. She'd always enjoyed the many faces of the night sky.

And tonight she needed them. The ball was stuffy and crowded and she was out of sorts.

She had tried to explain away the discomfort in her chest with thoughts on the scandal she and Stenfax had caused with their broken engagement, but that wasn't it. Very few had rejected her due to that decision. Those who had were inconsequential.

No, she felt odd for another reason. And when she was honest with herself, the reason was the entry of the Duke of Clairemont. It had been such a strange thing to look at that man, that stranger, and feel such a strong and instant connection to him.

"What a handsome face will do," she muttered to herself, ignoring the fact that she'd known many a handsome face, including that of her former fiancé, and she had never been so moved by one before.

Clairemont was a confusing one, that was true enough. Perhaps it was the mystery of his being hidden away for so long. Perhaps it was the air of sadness she had noticed in his gray eyes. Perhaps it was the piercing glow of those same eyes. Whatever it was, it was entirely distracting.

She sucked in another cool breath of air and sighed. She should go back inside before Rosalinde and Gray noticed her absence and became worried. Worse, before they both began to question her and coo over her like she was a broken thing that needed fixing.

She was about to do so when the terrace door flew open and a figure strode out, slamming it behind him. He rushed toward the wall, gripping it with both hands and sucking in a few long breaths of air as he lifted his face toward the moonlight, just as she had done a moment before.

Her breath hitched. The man who had invaded her sanctuary

was none other than the one she had been musing upon. The Duke of Clairemont. And he looked mightily upset.

She hesitated. In the shadow of the house, he didn't appear to have noticed her yet. She supposed she could slide along the wall and simply go inside as to not interrupt him.

But she didn't. Instead she took a long step toward him and exposed herself to the light.

"Good evening, Your Grace," she said.

He spun toward her, his eyes wide and his stance one of defensiveness. When he saw her he relaxed, but not entirely. "I didn't see you there," he said with a shake of his head. "I must be slipping."

She smiled. "You were distracted, it seems."

His eyes narrowed. "I must never be so distracted as to not notice someone at my back."

He sounded so serious that she couldn't help but laugh. "A threat, you mean?" she asked.

"Yes," he said sharply. Then his gaze flitted over her from head to toe. His expression was unreadable, so she had no idea what he thought as he looked at her. "Well, *no*, I suppose not in this case," he finally conceded.

"You suppose correctly," Celia said, moving a little closer. "I have no weapon, I assure you. I'm not sure where I'd put it in this ridiculous dress."

She motioned to herself, to the green gown that clung to her breasts before cascading in a flow of silk and lace. He followed the motion, but his eyes didn't seem to find their way past her bosom. And it was a heated gaze at that. One that warmed her in the cool night air.

He blinked and jerked his gaze back to hers. "You'd be surprised," he said, and his voice was rougher.

Celia shifted her weight on her feet. Suddenly this conversation felt very inappropriate. She changed the subject with a blush. "The ballroom is very hot. I don't blame you for needing air."

His shoulders relaxed a fraction and he glanced back up at

the moon. "It is stifling. Why in the world do they invite so many people? My feet have been trod upon at least ten times—the dance floor can only laughably be called such. And you can hardly hear yourself think, let alone have a proper conversation with those around you."

She examined him carefully. Great God, he was even more handsome when she was nearer to him. She edged even closer and caught the faintest whiff of pine and something smoky. She wanted to lean into it, to lean into him. But she managed to avoid doing something so foolish.

"W-Well," she stammered. "I'm not certain conversation is the purpose of these events, in truth."

He turned to face her and those pale gray eyes caught hers. "Then what *is* the purpose? I cannot seem to divine it, no matter how intently I study the problem."

She felt speared in place by his attention, his focus. She blinked up at him, mesmerized in a way she'd never experienced with another person on this earth.

"To show off," she said when she could find her voice. "To prove that this host and hostess are more popular than the last. And since *you* agreed to come here tonight, to flaunt that they have pulled off the coup of the Season by bringing you here."

He tilted his head at her candor. "Interesting. That explains all the attention, I suppose."

She smiled. "You've been away a long time. I can guess how uncomfortable all this must make you."

He shrugged. "I don't belong here. No matter what the title says."

"Do you really feel that way?" Celia asked, narrowing her eyes.

He hesitated a moment, staring at her like he was truly seeing her for the first time. It seemed he might say something important, something sincere, and the moment hung between them like a heavy curtain waiting to be peeled away to reveal the truth.

But then he shook his head as if clearing it, and smiled. "I'm sure it will pass. After all, *this* was what I was raised to do, isn't it? My duty is here and I will do it."

Celia nodded, but there was disappointment heavy in her chest. As if something important had just been taken from her. She shrugged off the foolish reaction and moved another step closer.

"I realize we haven't formally met. Though this isn't exactly the proper way to do it."

He inclined his head. "Yes, I should be introduced to you by our hostess or some other mutual acquaintance. And yet here we are, on a terrace, unchaperoned. That is dangerous, isn't it?"

"Only if we intend to hurt each other," Celia said. "I know I do not. Do you?"

He held her gaze steadily. "I have no intentions of hurting you, miss."

"Good. But you see, I am at an advantage over you that I think is unfair," she said. "After all, I know who you are, Your Grace."

"Have we met before?" he asked, suddenly stiffening.

She frowned. It seemed after all their banter that he would know they hadn't, especially since he had been holed up in the countryside for years. But then, maybe he secretly brought women there, looking for a bride or just a companion to warm his bed. Perhaps they were forgettable, and she would be too, despite the connection she felt in their conversation.

"No, we've never met," she said slowly. "There is just a buzz about you in the room tonight, so I was informed who you were by friends."

Now it was he who took a long step toward her. She could feel the faint warmth of his body heat now.

"Who am I?" he asked, his tone once again the rough version that seemed to ripple through her and settle somewhere in her lower stomach.

"You are the Duke of Clairemont," she breathed.

"And who are *you?*" he pressed, his gaze now locked with hers.

She swallowed. There were a dozen inappropriate answers that flowed through her head, but she didn't say any of them. "I'm Celia Fitzgilbert."

"Miss?" he pressed.

Her breath caught. He wanted to know if she was married. "Yes, *Miss* Celia Fitzgilbert."

"Well, *Miss* Celia Fitzgilbert, it is a pleasure to meet you, unorthodox as this introduction is." He leaned in and took her hand, lifting it to his lips. Through the thin fabric of her glove, she felt the swirl of his breath and a tingle made its way through her.

He lifted his eyes as he remained bent over her hand, and her own breath hitched. She'd never felt so out of sorts with a man before. Never felt confused and drawn, hot and shivery, all at the same time.

He released her hand gently and straightened up, but he didn't step away from her. And he didn't look away. Heat flooded Celia's cheeks at the intensity of his stare and she found herself backing up, even though what she truly wished to do was step even closer. But that was not what ladies did.

"I-I should probably go back inside," she stammered. "My sister and brother-in-law will be looking for me."

He arched a brow. "And who are your sister and brother-in-law?" he asked.

"Mr. and Mrs. Danford," she explained.

The slight smile on Clairemont's face fell and he took a sudden step back. "Grayson Danford?"

"Yes, Grayson Danford," she repeated slowly. "He is the Earl of Stenfax's younger brother. My sister is his wife, Rosalinde."

The warmth that had been on Clairemont's face disappeared entirely, and he swallowed. "Ah, I see. Well, I should not keep you. Good evening, Miss Fitzgilbert."

He gave a stiff, formal bow and turned on his heel to stalk back into the house. Celia stared at his retreating back in shock and embarrassment. He had dismissed her.

But why? Gray and Rosalinde were well liked in Society, there could be no reason why their names would inspire such a quick retreat. Unless…

Her breath caught. Was it possible that even in his hermitage the Duke of Clairemont had heard of Celia's broken engagement? That he judged her for it, as a handful of people did? Perhaps until he heard Gray and Rosalinde's names, he hadn't recognized her for her role in that minor scandal.

But once he did, he had retreated immediately, not wanting to sully his good name by associating it with her.

Tears stung her eyes and she blinked at them. It was a foolish reaction, for she had been well-aware there would be censure in some corners of Society, even if the romantic version of why the engagement had been broken appeased the majority.

And it wasn't as if she knew this man or had any connection to him. He was handsome and had turned her head, he was charming and she'd been charmed. But if she never saw him again, it wasn't as if she'd lost anything.

But as she reentered the ballroom and slowly crossed the floor to rejoin Gray and Rosalinde, she felt like she had. And it brought a terrible heaviness in her chest that made the ball seem a little less gay, the colors less bright and the night far less successful than it had been before.

CHAPTER FOUR

Clairemont paced across the parlor floor, his blood pumping and his heart racing, though he could not lie to himself and say it was the thrill of the hunt that caused those reactions. No, it was something else. Something he had to squash as swiftly as possible so he could refocus on his duty.

"Explain why you are so worked up," Stalwood said as he poured Clairemont a drink from their host's sideboard and held it out.

Clairemont waved the offering away and continued to pace, but his restlessness didn't abate even a fraction. "I thought I had made it perfectly clear. I found myself out on a terrace alone with *Celia Fitzgilbert*, the sister-in-law of Grayson Danford. In case you have forgotten, the man is one of our prime suspects, Stalwood."

The earl nodded. "Indeed, he is, and it *is* an interesting development, but you are flushed and distracted and that isn't at all like you."

Clairemont stopped and gathered himself quickly. Showing emotion or weakness was not a good thing, not in his world, and he had to stop doing it immediately. He took a deep breath to calm himself, stuffed his emotions down deep and faced his mentor again.

"I'm not distracted," he explained, hearing the peevishness in his voice that belied his words. "It is simply an unexpected and...*interesting* development."

Interesting. No, his encounter with Celia on the terrace hadn't been interesting. It had been…remarkable.

Oh, she was lovely, there was no denying that. What man would not be attracted to her dark hair and startlingly bright blue eyes? What man could resist the cheerful and lovely face that was so quick to smile and laugh? And what hot-blooded man wouldn't notice her perfect figure, from her full breasts to her slender waist to the slight flare of her hips that teased beneath her gown?

And yet it was more than those things which had drawn him to her. From the moment she stepped from the shadows behind him, he had felt almost as if he had known her before. Like they were connected on a level that he never allowed, not even with friends and colleagues. Relationships were fleeting. They could end in a heartbeat.

He didn't make them, beyond perhaps his long friendship with Stalwood.

"Are you listening to me, Clairemont?" Stalwood asked, his tone even and almost placating.

Clairemont drew himself away from his troubling musings and nodded. "Of course I'm listening. But are *you*? You don't seem to understand that I've just made an accidental connection to a relative of one of the men we suspect of helping the real Clairemont in his dirty doings. This was not part of our plan and it means we must rethink our methods."

Stalwood sighed. "There were many pieces of correspondence between Danford and Clairemont, yes. And Clairemont is heavily invested in a great many of Danford's moneymaking schemes. The man is on the cutting edge of industry—it is not out of the question that he may very well be involved in nefarious elements. Grayson Danford must be investigated. But I'm telling you that this interaction with his sister-in-law tonight doesn't hinder that investigation. In fact, it may be an excellent way to further it."

Clairemont wrinkled his brow. "You don't think it was a mistake to approach her? After all, if Danford is a part of this scheme it might chafe him that I spoke to her before I came to him."

Stalwood paced the room, his expression one of careful consideration. "Perhaps, but perhaps not. After all, the attention heaped on you tonight is something that might hold us back. But if you were to begin to show interest in one person in particular…"

He trailed off, and Clairemont blinked. "What are you asking of me?"

"The girl, Celia, she is just returning to Society after a broken engagement. Oh, the scandal was minor at best, but she is not in a perfect position. If a duke were to pay attention to her, I don't think her brother-in-law would be unhappy about such a match. Especially since he already feels he knows the Duke of Clairemont, at least on some level."

"Are you saying I should pursue an interest in Celia Fitzgilbert?" Clairemont asked blankly, his traitorous mind taking him back to the moment when he'd held her hand in his, looked into her face. He'd wanted very much to draw her into his arms, to kiss more than her gloved hand.

It had been a shocking desire, and one he had used all his strength and training to bury.

"Did you flirt with her on the terrace?" Stalwood asked benignly.

Clairemont froze. His mentor knew him well. He knew Clairemont was no monk. He liked his pleasure as well as the next man, as long as it didn't interfere in his work.

"I suppose I did," he admitted. "Before I knew who she was."

"I'm not saying you should get engaged to the girl," Stalwood said with a shrug.

"I would hope not," Clairemont said, and a great shudder worked through him at the thought of even a pretended engagement or marriage. That was not in his future. Better for everyone.

"But what harm could come in showing her a little extra

attention?" Stalwood pressed. "In the interest of getting closer to Danford and in the interest of fitting into Society a bit more smoothly?"

Clairemont considered it. Talking to Celia had been very easy, comfortable even, unlike every other tedious conversation he'd been forced to have earlier in the evening.

"You *can* do this can't you?" Stalwood asked. "You have no gentlemanly objections?"

Clairemont straightened and met the earl's gaze evenly. "I am no gentleman," he said, hardening himself to any objections he might, indeed, have on his own behalf or on Celia's. This was for king and country. "I know my duty."

"Good," Stalwood said with a slight smile. "Then we should return to the ballroom."

His mentor led the way from the parlor and Clairemont followed, trying to tamp down all his reasons not to do exactly as Stalwood said. Trying not to relive every moment on the terrace with Celia Fitzgilbert. She was a means to an end now. He could not make her any more than that.

"What is wrong?"

Celia flinched as she slid up next to her sister. Damn Rosalinde for knowing her so well. She forced a smile. "Wrong? Nothing at all. I just needed a bit of air," she lied.

Rosalinde sent Gray a look and then examined Celia more closely. "You look upset, Celia. Are you certain nothing is wrong? We saw the Duke of Clairemont go out onto the terrace after you did."

Celia felt the blood drain from her face. "You did?"

Rosalinde nodded. "Perhaps I should have followed. He wasn't untoward with you, was he?"

Celia's lips pinched as she recalled her few moments with the duke on the terrace. Untoward? Not exactly. Perhaps a bit flirtatious, at least until he realized who she was.

"No, he was...*fine*. We—we talked, actually," she said, again casting a glance at Gray. Although they were finding a better relationship now, it still felt odd to talk about something so personal in front of him.

As if he sensed her discomfort, he turned away slightly, to give Rosalinde and her at least the illusion of a moment of privacy.

"You talked," Rosalinde repeated softly. "And it didn't go well?"

Celia shrugged. "At first it was fine. He was charming and I was...I suppose I tried to be charming—"

"You are always charming, go on," Rosalinde encouraged.

"And then I mentioned you and Gray, and he realized who I was. His demeanor changed and he gave me what amounted to a very gentle set down and walked away." Celia cleared her throat so her sister wouldn't hear the lingering emotion that accompanied those words. "It makes me wonder if the broken engagement with Stenfax has hurt me more than we realized."

Rosalinde folded her arms. "I can't imagine that is true," she said. "There are only a handful of people who seem troubled. Stenfax has said as much, himself. If Clairemont would judge you for that, it seems he isn't much of a man, himself."

Celia let out a breath on a laugh. Leave it to Rosalinde to dismiss anyone out of hand who didn't like Celia. It was harder for Celia to do the same. Especially when the duke had inspired such...*interesting* reactions in her body and mind.

"You liked him," Rosalinde whispered.

Celia met her gaze carefully. "I did, actually. He really is very handsome and there was something about him...I can't explain it." She sighed and shook her head slowly. "But it doesn't matter, does it? His Grace has made it clear that he is not interested and that is the end of the conversation, I would assume."

"Perhaps not." Celia turned and found Gray inching back toward them. "I'm sorry, Celia, I realize I was not invited to this particular conversation, but I overheard it regardless. You assume the duke walked away because of your past, but that might not be true."

Celia pushed aside her embarrassment at Gray being so aware of her awkward conversation with the duke and clung to the possibility he now presented. "Why do you say that?"

"The Duke of Clairemont and I are of an age. Stenfax and I were in school with him a very, *very* long time ago. We lost touch for years, but after I inherited and began to invest, Clairemont wrote to me. He was interested in my dealings and connections. He has long been invested in my businesses. You said he turned away when you mentioned my name, didn't you?"

Celia nodded. "Yes."

Gray smiled as if he were more certain of what he was saying than before. "It may be that Clairemont was more concerned with the potential complications to our business relationship by talking to you without a chaperone or a proper introduction than he was worried about your broken engagement."

Celia moved closer, hope flaring dangerously in her chest. "Do you think so?"

"His correspondence is…" Gray pursed his lips. "Well, he is a meticulous man, we'll say. And quite concerned with managing his business relationships closely. I would say it is a good possibility."

Rosalinde slipped an arm around her. "You see? You jumped to a conclusion that may not be truth after all."

Celia let out a sigh of relief. "I hope what you say is true, Gray."

He cast a quick glance at Rosalinde before he said, "Well, there is one way to find out, I suppose. What if we invited him for supper?"

Celia's eyes went wide. "Do you think he would come?"

"Why not? A party like this is too difficult to truly talk to anyone. And I get the feeling the man is slightly overwhelmed by his return to Society after so long away."

"Yes," Celia agreed. "On the terrace, he seemed out of sorts."

"I'm certain he would jump at the offer of a quieter gathering," Rosalinde said with a wide smile for Gray. "And then we could ascertain with certainty why the man walked away tonight *and* if he's worth all this anxiety on your part."

Celia couldn't help her broad smile. Rosalinde was right that a more intimate setting would give her a chance to read Clairemont better. But then again, if he didn't want to know her better, if her past did cut off a chance of a future, it would be a rather embarrassing night.

But if that happened, then she'd feign a headache and simply vow to avoid him for the rest of her life.

There, it was decided.

"If you have other business with the duke, I think inviting him to supper is a fine idea," Celia said, trying to sound like she wasn't fully invested in whatever Gray did. "As I said, I got along with the man insofar as we talked. I wouldn't mind seeing him again."

Gray nodded, though the look he and Rosalinde exchanged wasn't subtle to say the least. "Excellent. Then I will send an invitation tomorrow morning for supper the night after. Now, Celia, would you like the dance?"

Celia smiled at her brother-in-law and took his hand to go to the dance floor. But as they moved into the allemande together, her mind spun on thoughts of the Duke of Clairemont. A night together in the company of her sister and brother-in-law would allow her to see him again, and perhaps even test a little more of the connection she had felt with him outside.

After all, what harm could it do?

CHAPTER FIVE

Clairemont had always prided himself in his ability to plan. No one in the War Department was better than him at orchestrating the accidental meeting or the carefully handled conversation that would casually lead to real information.

But after the Marquess Harrington's ball, he hadn't been forced to arrange such a casual way to come face to face with Miss Celia Fitzgilbert and her family. An invitation had arrived the next morning in Grayson Danford's neat, even handwriting that Clairemont had come to know so well during the course of his investigation.

I'm sorry the crush of the ball prevented us from speaking. Won't you join my family for supper tomorrow night?

Clairemont had read that note over and over, trying to find every nuance, trying to ascertain guilt or innocence in the turn of the phrases, the hand. But he had discovered nothing. Still, it was a good opportunity to meet privately with the man.

And a better opportunity to see Celia. He hated to admit it, but although he should have put more focus on Mr. Danford, *she* was more on his mind.

Now he stood in the parlor of Danford's London home, waiting for the arrival of his hosts. He took the opportunity to make some observations. The chamber was small, but beautifully appointed. As Clairemont paced the perimeter of the room, he took note of expensive furnishings and decoration. The man was making money, everyone knew that.

But how much of it was legitimate, and how much was taken from the broken backs of spies and soldiers?

His spine stiffened at that thought, and he refocused away from Celia's charms and back to the matter at hand. He was here with a purpose, and it wasn't the lovely Miss Fitzgilbert. If he pursued Stalwood's suggestion, she would only be a tool for him, a means to the end of discovering if Grayson Danford was involved in either the real Clairemont's traitorous dealings or his death.

Clairemont had firmed his resolve to the best of his ability when the parlor door behind him opened. He turned to face the door and caught his breath. It was not Danford or his wife who entered, but Celia, herself.

Tonight she wore a pale blue gown which matched the color of her eyes to perfection. Her hair was done simply, but little tendrils framed her face, drawing his attention to her smile. Well, her lips. Kissable lips.

He blinked. "Miss Fitzgilbert," he managed to say, perhaps too loudly for the small room. "Good evening."

He thought she frowned just slightly when he said her name, but she entered the chamber nonetheless.

"Hello, Your Grace," she said, motioning him toward the chairs before the fire. "I've been sent to greet you in my brother-in-law's stead. He and my sister are running slightly behind, but they will join us shortly. I hope you aren't too disappointed."

"With you as company?" he drawled, allowing her to take a place in front of the fire before he joined her. "How could I be?"

Her cheeks brightened with the slightest color and she smiled. "You and Gray know each other through…business, isn't it?" she asked.

Clairemont stiffened ever so slightly, watching her carefully. He hadn't before thought that perhaps Celia and her sister might also be involved, or at least aware, of anything untoward that Danford was involved in. Now that she had broached the subject of his involvement with her brother-in-law, Clairemont had to at least consider the possibility that she had been sent to the room in first as a spy of sorts. Or at least a distraction.

"We met in school a very long time ago," he responded, easily finding the information that he had been memorizing and internalizing for months. It was remarkably easy to make another man's story his own. Especially when his own past was something he liked to forget. "But our current relationship was developed around Mr. Danford's success, yes."

Celia nodded, but there was no real interest regarding the subject in her eyes. She seemed to be making simple small talk rather than digging for information, for which he found himself happy.

"He married your sister about six months ago, did he not? And you have lived with them in the North Country ever since?"

Once again, her face pinched ever so slightly. He could tell this was not a topic she enjoyed discussing. He found himself leaning forward to read her better.

"I think everyone knows that story," she said with another fetching blush. "At first I was meant to marry Gray's brother, the earl. It was an arranged union. But when Gray and Rosalinde fell in love, Stenfax and I set our engagement aside so that they could wed instead."

Clairemont had known the particulars of that story, thanks to Stalwood. But now he frowned. Celia didn't seem very happy about the broken engagement. Had she cared for her fiancé? He didn't like that idea.

"You gave up being a countess? Why would you not marry Stenfax regardless and have two sisters in the same family?"

She shifted and her gaze flitted away. An indication of discomfort...or a lie about to be told.

"My—my grandfather has ambition, I'm afraid," she said, her voice suddenly low. "He wanted us to marry into two different families in order to increase his connection, his power. I didn't want Rosalinde to lose a chance at love, so I stepped aside to appease him."

Clairemont clenched a fist on his thigh. There was *some* truth to what she said. But also a great dose of falsehood. And yet he didn't sense any of it had anything to do with his case. It was a family drama, nothing more. He should dismiss it and dig into something more vital.

Instead, he found himself wondering at the truth, at why Celia Fitzgilbert's gaze was so sad at this subject. Worse, he found himself wondering how to ease that sadness.

Her gaze flitted back to him. "I-I…" She trailed off and got to her feet, pacing away from him.

He stood out of propriety and watched her. "What is it?"

"Nothing," she said, casting a quick glance at him. "I had a question that was inappropriate. I shouldn't have even begun to ask it."

He moved toward her, unable to stop himself. "Ask your question, Miss Fitzgilbert."

She turned toward him, lifting her chin as if to steel herself to whatever would come next. "I-I thought perhaps my broken engagement was why you departed the terrace so swiftly the night of the Harrington ball."

He wrinkled his brow in confusion. "Why would your broken engagement mean anything to me?"

She hesitated before she whispered, "It could be seen as a scandal, something to be judged upon."

He considered his response carefully. "It *seems* as if you committed a selfless act for your sister's happiness. If anyone were to judge you harshly for that, I would say they were not worth your time."

She swallowed hard, but a light of happiness brightened her face. He almost withdrew from it. His opinion actually mattered to her. Which meant the unexpected connection he'd felt on the terrace had not been entirely one-sided. He couldn't deny the thrill that gave him.

"Thank you," she said softly.

He stepped a little closer and words he hadn't meant to say

fell from his lips. "I *do* find myself pleased you are no longer engaged, Miss Fitzgilbert."

She flinched a second time at the use of her name. "Won't you call me Celia, at least in private? I do despise the other name."

He drew back in surprise. He'd spent the past two months brushing up on every bit of propriety in interaction he could learn. This request of hers was certainly not proper. And yet it was very real, very straightforward. He had never expected such a thing from a woman of her rank.

"If you would like," he said, just barely containing the urge to take her hand. "And you should call me—"

He didn't get to finish that sentence before they were interrupted by the arrival of Danford and his wife.

"Clairemont," Danford said as he entered the parlor and crossed the room in a few long, confident strides. He extended a hand, which Clairemont took even though he found himself incredibly irritated at being interrupted in his private conversation with Celia.

"Mr. Danford," he said, his voice sounding tight to his own ears. "Thank you again for the invitation."

"I was pleased to make it," Danford said, and motioned to the lady at his side. "This is my wife, Rosalinde. May I present the Duke of Clairemont?"

"Mrs. Danford," Clairemont said, bowing toward her.

She smiled, and Clairemont took her in with a sweep of his gaze. She and Celia had similar coloring and features, but Mrs. Danford did nothing for him. She didn't seem to have the same spark as her younger sister.

"And of course you've met Miss Fitzgilbert," Danford continued, smiling at her.

Celia returned the expression, though there was a shaky quality to her expression that Clairemont couldn't help but take triumph in. He affected her.

He *liked* affecting her. He also liked reading her. She was complicated and it fascinated him. Intelligent but a little guarded. Sad but also direct. And lovely. So lovely that when he looked at her, it hurt. She surprised him, both with her direct question about his behavior on the terrace, but also with her request that he call her by her given name if they were alone. She hated her grandfather's name and he wondered why.

"It's good to see you," Danford said, pulling Clairemont's attention away from his musings on the charms of Celia and back to the matter at hand.

"And you," Clairemont said carefully.

Mrs. Danford smiled. "You and Gray went to school together, did you not?"

"Indeed, we did," Clairemont said, once again accessing the details of a past that was not his. "I was a little ahead of him and slightly behind Stenfax, so we were friendly. But when I inherited my title, I'm afraid the majority of my friendships went by the wayside."

Danford nodded. "You *did* fall off the map a bit. I kept waiting for you to show up in London, at least to perform your House of Lords obligations."

Clairemont forced a smile. "I've never been much interested in that duty."

He held Danford's stare, trying to see if that remark would inspire some kind of response. While reading Celia had been an interesting exercise, reading her brother-in-law was much harder. On the surface all Clairemont could see was intelligence, a great love for his wife and an affection for Celia. Protectiveness, perhaps, judging from the occasional look toward his wife. Nothing that would lead him to believe Danford was a mastermind, or even a co-conspirator.

But that didn't mean he wasn't. And if his wife and her sister were in the dark about his true nature, it might take a private meeting to determine the full truth of this man.

"Speaking of duty," Mrs. Danford said. "It is mine to tell you that Greene has just given me the signal that supper is ready. Shall we continue this conversation there?"

Clairemont inclined his head in the positive and watched as

Danford offered an arm to his wife. She smiled up at him, and there was an intimacy that flowed between them, a connection that was difficult to ignore. Whatever Danford was, he and his bride truly adored each other.

Clairemont had never been so close to such a connection before. He found himself wanting to turn away from it. When he did, he came face to face with Celia. She smiled at him, but her lips trembled. Her gaze flitted to her sister and brother-in-law.

"Shall we follow?" she asked, her expression one of anticipation.

He shook away his reaction and recalled his manners. He offered her an arm and she hesitated just a fraction before she took it. Her delicate hand folded around his bicep and he stiffened. This was the first time she'd touched him, and it triggered awareness in every part of his body. Especially his cock, which began to remind him exactly what he would like to do with the lady at his side.

He ignored it as best he could, hoping it wouldn't take on a life of its own, and stepped out to lead her behind Mr. and Mrs. Danford.

"I see why you gave up your future as a countess for them," he said softly.

She jerked her face toward his. "Do you? Oh, you mean their connection. Yes, it's quite something isn't it?"

He nodded. "Indeed. You rarely see that in Society."

"They are, well, they are remarkable, I suppose." She looked toward them again, and even in profile he saw a bit of longing on her face. "It makes one believe in fairy tales."

"Fairy tales," he repeated, keeping an eye on her even as he guided them closer to the dining room where Danford and his wife were entering. "Are you saying you'd like to be rescued from a tower by a prince?"

A pink blush filled her cheeks, but she lifted her chin. "I suppose it would depend on the prince, Your Grace."

He couldn't reply, for they entered the room and he was forced to release her so they could sit. But as he settled into his chair across from her, he had ample opportunity to look at her lovely face. She was right about her observation. The wrong prince could be worse than no prince at all.

And he was most definitely the *wrong* prince.

Celia looked at her half-empty plate and sighed. Supper had seemed to fly by, and now it was nearing an end. She didn't like that, for she was having a very good time

Since coming to stay with her sister months ago, she had often felt like an extra, unneeded wheel. Gray and Rosalinde were so young in their marriage and so passionately in love. They didn't mean to exclude her, but there were times when they exchanged glances and unspoken communication over her head that shut her out.

But tonight was very different. Clairemont's presence made the night more interesting, indeed.

Perhaps because *he* was interesting. He could easily speak on matters of politics and literature, business and nature. He was intelligent, but it was a quiet kind of intelligence, not the arrogant boasting she sometimes saw men of his rank display.

Beyond that, he actually seemed interested in *her*. He'd encouraged her to participate in their conversations, even leaning forward when she spoke, as if he hung on her every word. Between that and their encounter in the parlor, she couldn't help but feel that they were beginning to create a connection.

There was a thrill low in her belly when she allowed that thought to settle into her body.

The servants came in and took the empty plates, and Gray rose. "What say we take a glass of port in my office?" he said to Clairemont. "We can rejoin the ladies in a short while."

Clairemont got to his feet with a nod. "I would like that." He inclined his head toward Rosalinde. "Ladies."

He turned his attentions toward Celia, and she froze as his gray gaze held hers. She felt pinned in her spot by it, held steady by his even regard. The breath left her lungs and her head spun a little. She was only set free when he turned away and followed Gray from the room.

She sucked in a breath once he was gone, and leaned back in her chair. She felt Rosalinde staring at her and knew she'd have to look at her sister at some point, but she was so out of sorts that she could hardly do it.

"Well, well, well, Miss He-May-Judge-Me-On-My-Broken-Engagement," Rosalinde said with a laugh. "It seems you read *that* situation entirely wrong."

Celia at last allowed herself to look at Rosalinde, and couldn't help the wide smile that broke across her face. "Yes, it seems it didn't matter to him in the slightest. He even told me that if someone would judge me for such a thing, he didn't think they would be worth knowing."

Rosalinde tilted her head in surprise. "You brought up the subject?"

"I took a page from your book," Celia said as she got to her feet and smoothed her hands along the front of her gown reflexively. "You've always been so honest with your feelings, so open—I thought it wouldn't hurt to try the same in this instance."

Rosalinde also rose and moved toward her. Celia could feel her sister trying to read her, trying to see deeper into her soul. There was no locking her out, they were just too close. And Celia didn't particularly feel as though she had anything to hide.

"I'm glad you took a risk," Rosalinde said at last, then slipped her arm through Celia's as they exited the dining room. She took them down the hall to a parlor where the men would join them later. "He is an interesting fellow, isn't he?"

Celia nodded, releasing her sister's arm and pacing around the room restlessly. Thoughts of Clairemont seemed to inspire that in her. Rosalinde sat and watched her, a soft smile on her face.

"Oh, he is," Celia agreed. "Very intelligent, don't you think?"

"He seems very intelligent," Rosalinde agreed.

"And handsome." Celia thought of his full lips, his expressive face. "Quite possibly the most handsome man I've ever seen."

Rosalinde laughed. "There I cannot agree with you, but to each her own."

"But I'm ahead of myself, aren't I?" Celia asked, facing Rosalinde. "I've only just met him, and he came here to meet with Gray, not to see me. I'm reading too much into a simple supper. I'll get my hopes up and they'll be dashed."

Rosalinde frowned. "My dear, while I certainly wouldn't start buying your wedding trousseau quite yet, I think you are not entirely unfounded in your excitement. It's clear you like this man, for I've never seen you so aflutter. But it's also clear that he likes you. He was attentive at supper, he watched you even when you were not looking at him—there is much evidence that his coming here was guided by you as much as Gray."

"Do you think so?" Celia asked, clasping her hands together. "I fear I'm badly influenced by you."

Rosalinde shook her head. "What do you mean?"

"It's almost impossible to live in the same house as you and Gray and not be inspired by your affection for each other. I fear I may be looking for something that might not exist, at least not for me."

Rosalinde got up and came to her, wrapping her arms around her waist as she met Celia's gaze. "Now you *are* ten steps ahead of yourself. Do you like this man?"

Celia nodded. "I do."

"Then that is a fine start. Whatever comes next will happen naturally." Rosalinde kissed her cheek. "And you deserve a great deal of happiness, so I will intervene if I feel you won't receive it."

"Big sister to the rescue." Celia laughed. "Good, I will trust you to steer me correctly."

Rosalinde broke away with her own laugh and both of them took a place on the settee this time. Celia sighed as her thoughts moved from ones of Clairemont to the further reaching consequences if their new connection did blossom.

"He's a duke," she said softly.

"He is," Rosalinde said. "Would you ask me to curtsey when I meet with you if you were to marry him?"

"Of course not." Celia didn't laugh at her sister's teasing, but shifted. "I-I was just thinking that Grandfather would be very happy if I were to wed him. A duke, and one with money and power, is a far better catch in his eyes than the earl he despises me for breaking with."

Rosalinde stiffened and one of her hands lifted to her throat. Celia flinched at the instinctive action. The last time either of them had seen their grandfather, the man who had raised them, was just before Rosalinde's wedding. He had attacked her, trying to choke her to death. He might have succeeded too, if it weren't for Gray's violent intervention.

Neither woman had heard a peep from him since. Not a threat. Not a conciliatory apology. Not a holiday wish. He was in London, of course, but he hadn't tried to come in contact with them since their recent arrival.

"Do you *care* what Grandfather thinks?" Rosalinde asked softly, her voice catching just a touch.

"No," Celia said. "I despise him for what he did to you, for his attempt at blackmailing me into wedding a title for his ambition. But Rosalinde, Gray's attempts at uncovering the true identity of our father have been unsuccessful. The only man with that information seems to be Grandfather. If I were to be pursued by a duke, it *could* give us a bargaining chip for that information."

Rosalinde recoiled, as if Celia had suggested they invite a poisonous snake to sleep in their beds. She supposed that was exactly what she was doing, in a way. But the facts were the facts, unpleasant as Rosalinde might find them to be.

"You cannot mean you would actually involve him in your

43

future," Rosalinde said. "Not after what he did, what he is capable of doing."

"Don't you want to know about the man who sired us?" Celia asked. "Because I do! I dream of him at night, I wonder about him almost daily. Who was he? Did he care for us? When our mother died, did he grieve? When Grandfather took us, did he fight for us at all?"

"I *do* wonder those things," Rosalinde said. "But I still think we are better off continuing to look on our own, rather than making yet another twisted bargain with Gregory Fitzgilbert."

"Rosalinde—" she began.

Her sister caught her hands and stopped her by saying, "Please, Celia. Enough! I don't wish to discuss this subject any further."

Celia let out a great sigh. She couldn't blame her sister for her strong feelings on the matter, given what she'd endured not so long ago. But Celia feared Rosalinde wasn't seeing the whole picture. Or perhaps her picture was just different. Rosalinde could make peace with not knowing.

Celia couldn't.

But there was no use upsetting Rosalinde further. At least not yet. But she wasn't going to put aside the idea of using her grandfather to get what she wanted.

Especially if a good opportunity was provided by the duke who would rejoin them soon.

CHAPTER SIX

Clairemont folded his hands on his lap and smiled as Danford poured him another drink. So far their conversation had been little more than small talk, a continuation of supper's topics of discussion.

But Clairemont was about to make a move.

"I suppose I should thank you," he said.

Danford laughed. "For supper? We were pleased to have you join us."

"Not for supper, though it was delicious and I more than enjoyed the company," Clairemont said, trying to push aside thoughts of Celia which kept infecting his mind.

Danford's eyebrows came up. "Then what?"

"My investments in your ventures have paid off very well," he said. "I have no illusions that it isn't from your keen mind that all these things flow."

Danford brushed off the compliment with a shrug. "I think any man who recognized the potential for the canals, for steam engines, for all these things that will lead our country into the future, would have done just as well as I have."

"I'm not certain that is true. To succeed you must have a vision for the future," Clairemont insisted.

He nodded. "I suppose."

"And what is yours?"

His companion seemed to ponder his answer for a moment before he responded, "I think industry is the future. Building, inventing, expanding."

Danford's eyes lit up as he spoke, perhaps not with the same passion that he showed when speaking of his wife, but some small version of it. It was clear he was enthusiastic about his ventures. But what was he willing to trade for that zeal?

"Does the war not make it more difficult?" Clairemont pressed, careful now. The correspondence between the real duke and this man had never blatantly addressed the issue of the war, the embargo, the information and weaponry being traded at the expense of the effort.

But there had to be a reason the dead duke had filed Danford's letters in hidden places just like he did with more incriminating papers.

Danford dipped his head, and Clairemont leaned forward as he awaited the answer. He wanted to see the body language, hear the tone, as well as analyze each word.

"The war is difficult for many reasons," Danford said, his tone suddenly rough. "Trade is impossible in some ways, which makes *any* business more complicated. Some of the effort that could go to building must go to defense. But I think I see the results more in my workers."

"How so?"

Danford frowned. "Many of their relatives are enlisted men. They are dying, and it breaks the spirit. There is discontent and I can hardly blame them for it."

Clairemont nodded, but his heart rate had increased with that statement. Turncoats on the inside were said to be breeding the very discontent in the populace that Danford referred to. Was he part of that treasonous effort or just commenting on it?

"You think they should hate our leaders?" he pressed, trying to maintain a disinterested tone.

Danford shrugged. "I think it's hard *not* to blame the leadership when you are scraping for bread and burying your brothers. I try to provide a good and safe environment for them and pay them fairly. It is the best I can do for crown and country, I suppose."

Clairemont pondered the answer. Those were not the words of a traitor, but of a fair and decent employer. A man of principle who could see the feelings of his workers and tried to better them. Perhaps even tried to calm them for the sake of his king.

Danford rose to his feet and set his empty glass aside. "Two lovely ladies are awaiting our return in the parlor," he said. "Shall we set aside these less than pleasant topics and join them?"

Clairemont nodded, perhaps more enthusiastically than he should, for he was pressing his finger on the topic he needed to explore most. But right now he wanted so much to put duty aside and spend a little time with the very interesting woman in the parlor.

He placed his glass next to Grayson's and followed him into the hall. "Miss Fitzgilbert was engaged to your brother once, wasn't she?"

Danford sent him a side glance, and in an instant their positions were reversed. Where Clairemont had until this point been investigating him, he now felt Danford searching *him*. He was protective of Celia, and there was a part of Clairemont that appreciated that.

"She was," Danford said slowly. "An arranged union, as many are. She and my brother were kind enough to step aside from it when they realized Rosalinde and I had fallen in love."

"To appease her grandfather, so she said," Clairemont mused. "But you do not see the man now, do you?"

Danford's body language transformed to an angry tension, coiled and ready to strike. "He was not appeased, unfortunately. But it is for the best. Celia is better off with us."

Clairemont tilted his head. There was more to this story. He had sensed it before, but now he was certain. And though he doubted it had anything to do with his case, he found himself wanting to understand the truth.

"Here we are," Danford said, his tone still taut as he opened the parlor door. But the moment he stepped inside, his body language changed. Clairemont watched as he strode across the room to his wife and took her hand as if they had been separated for days rather than less than an hour.

He found his gaze shifting to Celia. She, too, watched the almost intimate exchange, and when her eyes moved to him, she blushed.

He moved toward her and smiled. "What is it that ladies discuss when the gentlemen leave the room?" he asked. "I've always wanted to know."

He expected her to smile at his teasing, but instead her face fell a fraction. Whatever she had discussed with her sister, it hadn't been a happy topic. The tension in the room was now palpable.

"Celia?" he asked, dropping his tone so the other two wouldn't hear the familiarity of his address. "What is it?"

Celia blinked. Was she being so obvious in her feelings regarding her conversation with Rosalinde? She must be, for Clairemont seemed to recognize them effortlessly.

She dipped her head. "Why, we discuss the gentlemen, of course," she said, trying for a teasing tone that would hopefully distract him.

He pursed his lips as he looked at her, then turned toward Rosalinde and Gray. "It is a mild night," he said. "Might I have your permission to take a turn around the terrace with Miss Fitzgilbert?"

Rosalinde arched a brow and exchanged a look with Gray. He stepped forward. "If it is what Celia would like," he said.

"Miss Fitzgilbert?" Clairemont pressed, his gray gaze flitting over her face with rapid, reading focus.

She nodded. "Of course. I would very much enjoy that."

She said those bland words, but inside her heart was beating rapidly. Her hands were shaking at her sides. He *liked* her. And she liked him.

Rosalinde moved to the bell at the door and asked the servant who appeared for Celia's wrap. There were a few moments of mindless small talk as it was fetched, but Celia hardly heard the exchange between Clairemont and her family. All she could think was that in a moment she would be alone with him again.

And she wondered what in the world she would talk to him about. He seemed to remove all thought from her head, all words from her lips. She didn't want to look a fool.

The servant returned with a wrap and Celia draped it over her shoulders before she took the arm Clairemont offered. Touching him brought a jolt of awareness through her, just as it had earlier in the evening, and she clung to his strong arm for purchase as he smiled at Rosalinde and Gray and then led her to the terrace.

Once the door had closed behind them, he drew in a long breath of cool spring air and took her farther down the long stone terrace, away from the parlor window. At last, he released her.

"I thought you might need some air," he said, his low, gravely tone hitting her in the chest. "You seemed tense."

Her eyes widened. "I did? Oh, I assure you, I wasn't."

He arched a brow. "I have a little talent, Celia—would you like to know what it is?"

Celia caught her breath. She could name a dozen talents she would guess he had, but none of them were appropriate to list, especially when they were alone together.

"C-certainly," she managed to stammer.

He moved a little closer. "I can read people. When I asked you what you and Rosalinde talked about, I saw your response."

Celia ducked her head. "Oh. Well, I certainly wasn't trying to drag you into my petty troubles. You needn't have gone out of your way to save me."

He took another step closer, and suddenly he slipped a rough finger beneath her chin. He lifted her face toward his and her heart pounded at how near he was.

"You couldn't stop me from saving you," he said softly.

"Do you *need* to be saved?"

She could hardly breathe at all now. He was really so very handsome and he smelled like pine and the world spun when he touched her. She'd never felt anything like this, even when she'd tried so hard to find it with Stenfax.

This was something magical.

"My—my sister and I were simply disagreeing on something to do with my grandfather," she admitted. "It wasn't serious."

"But if it were, if you felt threatened or unsafe, you know you could tell me."

She blinked, confusion at his statement momentarily trumping her body's reactions to his touch. "Unsafe? Why would I feel unsafe?"

His face went dark, and for a brief moment pain crossed over it. "There are many reasons a person might feel unsafe in their own home."

She swallowed. "It sounds like *you* might be the one who needs saving, Your Grace."

His eyes went a little wider at that statement and his stare grew wild and unfocused. It only lasted a fraction of a second and then it was gone, replaced by the calm and collected gentleman he normally displayed. But the flash made her wonder once more why he had hidden away for so long. What had kept him in the country?

"Are you offering, Celia?" he asked, his voice softer, rougher. "To save me?"

Her mouth and lips suddenly felt very dry, and she licked them before she spoke. "If I knew how, I would," she whispered.

He nodded slowly. "I believe you would."

The finger on her chin slid farther and he cupped her cheek in one big palm. His fingers spread over her skin and her heart stuttered with the action. He filled up everything in her sight, made her only aware of him and the fact that he was inching in closer, consuming all the space around her.

"I might even believe you could," he said, bending his head.

His lips brushed over hers. She had been waiting for this without even acknowledging it to herself. Waiting for him to touch her in a way no other man would dare do. And now he did and it was…perfect.

He was gentle in the kiss, his full lips only feather-light as they moved over hers. Until Celia let out her breath in a sigh. When her mouth parted, his tongue darted out and he tasted her, just as gently.

She was surprised by the deepening of the kiss, but even more surprised by her body's reaction to it. His arms folded around her and she didn't resist, he drew her closer and she didn't fight it. She fit against him like she was meant to do so, and opened further for his explorations. He tasted faintly of port, sweet and intoxicating, and he moved his tongue over hers, stroking and teasing.

Her body went almost boneless with the caress, but she didn't need its support—he was holding her now. Keeping her from falling. But also coaxing her to fall in a whole different way.

Warmth spread from where he kissed her and cascaded through her body, settling in the most wicked of places. Her nipples grew hard and sensitive beneath her silky gown, and between her legs there began a constant, pulling throb.

She'd never felt anything like it, and yet she was absolutely aware that this was *need*. This was *desire*. This was being swept away by passion.

Only she wasn't swept far. In an instant, he released her, steadying her carefully before he stepped away. His breath was short, his face flushed as he stared down at her.

"I'm sorry," he said, shaking his head. "That was wrong of me."

"Why?" Celia asked, her voice cracking. "I liked it."

He squeezed his eyes shut, mouthing some unspoken curse. "As did I," he said at last. "But I should go before I do something I can't undo."

Her eyes went wide. Before her engagement ended, she'd

been told a little about making love. Since Rosalinde and Gray's marriage, she'd gleaned far more. *That* was what he was talking about. He feared he would lose control and go too far with her. Right here. On the terrace.

Because he wanted her.

Her body thrilled at that fact and she took an involuntary step closer, reaching for this thing she had long denied herself, until the desire for it had changed her so entirely. This man personified the risks she'd never dared take, the feelings she'd declared were not meant for her.

"You told me I should call you Celia in private," he said, his voice still rough and needy. "You may call me—"

He broke off, as if he were searching for the name. She supposed she couldn't blame him. He was a duke, so he had likely been Clairemont and nothing else for many years.

"Aiden," he said at last.

She smiled. "Aiden," she whispered, letting it roll on her tongue. She loved the gift of it, though when she said it she didn't really feel like it fully fit him.

He nodded. "Goodnight, Celia."

"Goodnight, Aiden," she replied.

He bowed to her slightly, then moved back toward the house. She followed, her mind still spinning and her heart still racing. She'd gone into this night uncertain if this man liked her, if he judged her.

She ended it knowing the flavor of his lips and the intensity of his stare when he wanted something. And also knowing her own reaction when her body called for pleasures most ladies shunned out of propriety. Shunned out of fear of the unknown.

But she refused to do that. After that kiss, the unknown still seemed frightening, but it also felt like something she wanted. Something she refused to accept she would never have. She *would* have it.

One way or another.

CHAPTER SEVEN

Clairemont paced the parlor at Stalwood's home, waiting for the earl to join him. They had planned to discuss his meeting with Grayson Danford, so he should have been gathering his thoughts and impressions of the man. He wasn't.

Instead it was thoughts of Celia that kept pushing their way in. Over and over, he relived his conversation with her when he first arrived at the Danford home. She'd been shockingly straightforward in her worries about her past. And he couldn't help but think of later, when Celia's mouth had finally touched his. He could still hear her soft sigh when his tongue breached her, and feel her innocent and yet powerful reaction to a kiss that never should have happened in the first place.

But mostly his errant mind turned ceaselessly on what had happened *after* that stolen kiss.

He'd almost given her his real name. John, he'd almost said to her when he told her what to call him. John, a name he *never* went by or gave to anyone. John was a man who didn't exist, a ghost he wanted to forget had *ever* existed.

And yet *that* name had been on his tongue to give to her. He had almost surrendered some real and dark and hidden part of himself.

If he *had* done it, it could have been devastating to his case. He *wasn't* John Dane. To her and to the world he was currently Aiden Alexander Charles Morland Waring, sixteenth Duke of Clairemont. Just a hint of the truth could unravel the elaborate fiction he was telling and put himself and his case in great danger.

He'd never slipped up like that before on an assignment. He'd always fit himself perfectly into any role he was given and never once thought to bring any part of the real him into the light.

"What the hell were you thinking?" he asked out loud, slamming a hand down on one of Stalwood's side tables hard enough that his palm stung.

"The night didn't go well?"

He turned to find his mentor at the door, a smoking jacket around his shoulders, a pipe in his hand and a worried frown on his face.

Clairemont straightened and pulled at his coat to smooth it. "I—no, it was fine. Good evening, Lord Stalwood."

"Good evening," Stalwood replied, but he didn't look convinced of Clairemont's assertion as he pulled the door shut behind him. "*Fine*? You're here very early and you're beating on my furniture, so forgive me if I have a hard time believing you."

"I'm sorry for my outburst," Clairemont said, working hard to calm himself. "I know I'm early, but the night *was* truly fine. I merely excused myself with a slight headache in order to join you with my report."

Stalwood lifted both eyebrows, but didn't argue. "And your report is?"

"I met with Danford, just as we planned."

"And what do you think of him?" Stalwood asked as he poured Clairemont straight scotch and handed it over.

Clairemont frowned. He must look a terror if Stalwood was trying to appease him with the good scotch. He drew in a few breaths to center himself further and took a drink, hoping to erase Celia's sweet flavor from his lips. The liquor burned, but did nothing for his memories. He'd likely need four or five more to do that.

And he didn't intend on drinking himself into oblivion tonight.

"I'm not sure what to think about him," he admitted, at last finding his thoughts on his host for the night. "On the surface, he is a decent fellow, intelligent and even-minded. He seems to care for his workers and has a dream for the empire's future that could be considered admirable."

"A dream he's making fistfuls of money with," Stalwood pointed out.

"Yes, but he isn't ostentatious with his wealth," Clairemont said, thinking of the modest home Danford possessed. "It doesn't seem to affect him much one way or another. I get the impression he likes being able to provide for his wife, but that seems to be out of a true affection for her. He doesn't appear to be desperate for capital or willing to do anything to obtain it."

"So do you think he is cleared as a suspect in a nefarious partnership with the *real* duke of Clairemont?" Stalwood pressed.

Clairemont sighed. *That* was a more complicated question. He found he didn't want to suspect Danford because he actually *liked* the man.

And also because of Celia. Celia, the ultimate distraction to the game. If Danford and his wife were destroyed, she would be destroyed along with them.

"I don't know," he admitted. "It's too early to say. I'd have to get closer."

He said the last word reluctantly, for he knew the best way to do that. So did Stalwood, if his faint smile said anything.

"And the girl?" he asked.

Clairemont squeezed his eyes shut. "The girl?" he asked, though he knew exactly which girl.

"Celia, I think you said her name was. Danford's sister-in-law."

"Yes," Clairemont said on a voice that barely carried. He found himself gripping his glass so tightly he feared it would shatter in his hand.

"You flirted with her before. Were you able to continue that connection tonight?" Stalwood asked, apparently oblivious to his employee's struggle.

Clairemont set the drink aside so he wouldn't destroy the glass and clenched his fists at his sides instead. He felt reluctant to share anything more than he had to about Celia, even though he trusted Stalwood. And his friend trusted *him* to tell the truth.

"Yes," he finally admitted. "I have no doubt that Miss Fitzgilbert has an interest in the Duke of Clairemont. And her guardians seem to have no objection to a continuation of our affiliation."

"Excellent." Stalwood clapped his hands together. "Then it is settled. You'll court her. It takes care of your problem with added attention and gets you closer to Danford and whatever secrets you haven't yet ferreted out."

"Wait," Clairemont said, moving on his mentor. "You talked to me earlier about flirting, paying a bit of extra attention to Celia. That is a far flung thing from officially courting the woman."

"I got word today that Eccelson was pulled from the field," Stalwood said, turning from Clairemont, but not before he saw the earl's deep worry. "He was close to some important information, but his identity was compromised."

Clairemont blinked as shock rolled through him. He'd worked side by side with Eccelson on several cases over the years. The man was a true professional. "His identity was revealed?"

Stalwood nodded slowly. "He was working in Prussia, trying to undermine Napoleon's influence there. Suddenly he was revealed as an agent and he barely escaped with his life. He's injured and on his way back to England. I have hope he'll make it back alive."

"Shit," Clairemont said, scrubbing a hand over his face.

"Since Eccelson was mentioned by name in Clairemont's papers, we must believe he shared that information before his death. God knows how many others are in danger *without* our knowing."

The news hung in the room between them, heavy and

damaging. Clairemont's heart sank, his stomach turned.

"You're saying the lives of our agents are worth more than the reputation of one young lady," Clairemont said softly. The words were bitter, but he knew they were true. Life and death trumped foolish scandal every day.

And yet that didn't mitigate his guilt. He had looked in Celia's eyes and seen her hopes and dreams. He had felt her coiled passion, ready to be unleashed for the right man. What Stalwood was suggesting was to use that passion, to steal both it and her future.

Good work. This was supposed to be good work.

"This is for king and country, Dane," Stalwood said, and Clairemont flinched at the use of his real name. The reminder of what he had vowed years ago. "The work may be many things, but it was never meant to be easy."

"It *isn't* easy," he said, turning away to pace the room restlessly. "If I court Celia Fitzgilbert and this investigation falls apart, she could be tainted forever, especially considering her recently broken engagement. She might be ruined."

"Then you'll have to succeed," Stalwood said. "If you do so, then Clairemont will simply die at the end of our investigation. Miss Fitzgilbert will be left a tragic figure, but not a ruined one."

"And if she truly comes to...to care for me?" he asked, picturing Celia's upturned face on the terrace. She could love, that was clear.

"Then this is infinitely more tragic," Stalwood admitted. When Clairemont glared at him, he raised his hands in surrender. "It is distasteful, I don't disagree. Yet doing this could save untold lives, even save the country from losing this war. You cannot tell me those stakes don't make the risk to this young woman worth it. If you could freely tell her the potential for lives saved and know that she would not betray you, I'm certain she would agree."

Clairemont bent his head. He couldn't disagree with that assessment. The stakes were too high for sentimentality or honesty or honor. Those things were best left to men who had nothing to lose or to fight for. They could afford them.

"Fine," he said through clenched teeth. "I will seek to officially court her as soon as possible. But for now, I am tired and I'm going home."

Stalwood nodded and said nothing as Clairemont passed by him and back out onto the drive for his waiting horse. He swung up onto its back and thundered out toward the ducal townhouse just a short distance away.

Of course, it was a home he didn't belong in, ridden to on a horse he didn't own, wearing clothing that wasn't his. His entire life was stolen, even if it was in the name of the king. Perhaps it made sense that he would be just as mercenary when it came to courting a woman. Everything had its purpose in his tangled life.

But he still felt like utter shit about it.

Clairemont lay on the big, comfortable bed, staring at the fire as it burned down to nothing more than glowing embers. He had been trying to sleep for hours, but rest refused to come when he couldn't stop reliving his distasteful conversation with Stalwood and the vow he'd made regarding Celia.

Celia. He also couldn't forget his kiss with Celia.

With a grunt, he rolled to his back and stared up at the intricately carved ceiling instead of the dancing flames. The new position didn't help his spinning, distracted mind one bit.

The man he was pretending to be liked the finer things in life, that was clear, even in his naughty bedroom décor. The plaster on the ceiling had been carved in a series of bawdy images. Men and women were laid out above him, entangled in pleasures, their faces twisted in ultimate release.

He stared at the faces, the positions, and swallowed hard as his errant mind took over. What would Celia look like in the same positions?

He blinked at that thought. She was a *lady*—he shouldn't lower her by thinking of her that way. He had no right. But when he was staring at an image of a man's head buried between a woman's legs while she arched in pleasure, it was difficult not to do just that.

Celia would be sweet if he tasted her in the same way, he was certain of that. And probably hesitant if he touched her, for most ladies were not told of such things.

But once he passed her resistance, once she relaxed into pleasure, as she had done when he kissed her on the terrace, he was certain she would be responsive to each and every brush of his hand. Each and every touch of his lips on her stomach, her hip, her thigh…her sex.

He groaned at the thought and threw the bedclothes off. He slept naked and his cock was already at full mast. Release would help, he knew it would, so he took himself in hand and began to stroke.

Another image carved above him was of a woman straddling a man, her legs locked around his waist. Once more, Clairemont pictured Celia sashaying toward him, a wicked smile on her pretty face. Celia, lifting her skirts, placing herself over him, around him.

God, how he wanted her. To claim her, even though he had no right to do so. *He* didn't exist, he wasn't the man she thought he was, but that didn't lessen the pulsing, driving need in his loins, the overwhelming desire to grind down into her warm and willing flesh until she shattered in orgasm and milked the same from him.

His strokes increased in speed at that thought. His balls tightened to the exquisite sensation just between pleasure and pain. His entire body convulsed at last, and with a gasp, he spent, Celia's name a breath on his lips.

He flopped back against his pillows as his heart rate slowed to normal. When he could think rationally, he cursed once more at the untenable position he was in.

He hardly knew this woman and she already inspired such

dangerous, needy desires. If he were to enter this sham of a courtship, he could only image that would all get worse. Being close to her wouldn't be easy.

And he had to expect a great many nights spent just as he'd spent this one. Guilty, frustrated and alone.

CHAPTER EIGHT

Celia laughed at something Tabitha had said and they watched as Lady Honora spun by in the arms of yet another young man she cared nothing for. Both women shook their heads.

"Her inheritance makes her a favorite," Tabitha mused. "But she has no interest in a one of them."

"Perhaps she's holding out for love," Celia replied, her mind turning momentarily to Lord Clairemont...*Aiden*. In her mind, she had begun to call him Aiden almost exclusively.

In the two days since she'd last seen him, she had often found herself reliving his heated kiss on the terrace. His mouth had been so gentle, and yet so demanding. He'd drawn her into the kiss, taking her further than she'd ever gone before.

She almost felt awakened by that touch, like she had been sleeping before it, and now she couldn't go back to the way she saw the world before.

"Love?" Tabitha said with a laugh, yanking Celia back to the present. "Oh, my dear, you are too influenced by your sister and her handsome husband."

Honora returned to them with a quick smile for her dance partner, who then drifted away into the crowd. Once he was gone, their friend rolled her eyes.

"Sometimes they do not talk at all it is so discouraging. I feel like they think they are dancing with a bag of money rather than a person." Honora shook her head. "Now, how is Celia being influenced by Mr. Danford and Rosalinde?"

Celia's cheeks filled with heat at her friends' teasing. "I'm not. I was simply saying to Tabitha that perhaps you wished to hold out for love in a match rather than settle for someone who sees you as a moneybag."

Honora sighed. "It's a nice thought, but life doesn't work that way very often, does it? My father expects a good match and eventually he'll find one for me. I can only hope the gentleman won't have warts and he'll possess all his teeth and be able to string two sentences together. If he can't, I may be forced to bludgeon him to death the first night we're stuck together due to inclement weather."

Celia laughed at Honora's teasing, but inside she drew back from the truth beneath the playfulness. The kind of surrender Honora described didn't sound like a pleasant scenario at all, yet her friend seemed resigned. But then again, just six short months ago, Celia had also been resigned to marrying someone she wasn't connected to.

With a sigh, she found her former intended in the crowd. Stenfax wasn't dancing, but then he never danced anymore. He looked very serious and undeniably handsome.

And yet despite all his good qualities, she hadn't cared for him, no matter how much time she spent trying to do just that.

But with Aiden it was different. One moment with him and she felt like he'd taken a small piece of her with him. One kiss and she dreamed of him ever since.

"Ah, she's floating off," Tabitha said with a laugh. "Thinking of true love, no doubt."

"She *should*. I heard the Duke of Clairemont sent her flowers," Honora said, arching a brow in Celia's direction as if daring her to deny the charge.

"The duke came to my brother-in-law's house to see to some business with Gray," Celia corrected quickly. "He sent flowers to thank *all* of us for the evening."

Only she had commandeered those flowers for her own room, along with his note, which had specifically mentioned her.

How many times had she read the way he wrote her name? Ten? Twenty? One hundred and twenty?

Well, who was counting?

"He may be thanking you for another evening soon," Honora said, now lowering her voice to a whisper. "He's coming this way."

Celia moved to look over her shoulder, but Tabitha grabbed her arm with both hands. "Don't *look* at him," she hissed. "Great Lord, you have to make him work a little for your attention. Men love the struggle, the battle. You must give them one."

Celia pursed her lips. She'd always despised these little games. She wondered what her friends would think if they knew she'd forgone them in exchange for a passionate kiss just two nights before.

"Good evening, ladies."

Her entire body clenched at the sound of Aiden's voice, and a thrill went down her spine. Slowly, she turned and smiled. "Your Grace," she said. "How nice to see you again."

"Miss Fitzgilbert," he said, holding her stare a fraction too long.

She blushed to her toes before she stammered, "H-have you met my friends, Your Grace?"

He nodded. "Yes, I was introduced to both at the Harrington ball. A pleasure to see you again Lady Honora, Miss Thornton."

"Your Grace," the girls said in unison, and curtseyed slightly.

"You'll have to excuse us, my lord," Tabitha said. "Honora and I were about to go find her mother for an important discussion."

Honora blinked a moment, then nodded. "Oh, yes. Very important. Good evening."

Celia barely kept herself from rolling her eyes as her friends abandoned her to the company of the man at her side. But in truth, she was pleased to be alone with him. Her heart began to race as she faced him fully.

"They aren't very artful, I'm afraid," she said with a laugh.

He smiled. "In leaving us alone, you mean?"

"Yes."

"Does that mean that they believe you might wish to be alone with me?" he asked, leaning in just a fraction closer. Even though they were in public and the distance between them was entirely appropriate, she still thrilled at it.

"I would think any lady here would enjoy your company," she breathed.

"I'm not talking about any lady, Celia. I'm talking about *you*," he pressed.

She swallowed past a sudden lump in her throat. "I'm very happy to see you again," she admitted softly. "Is that enough?"

"Not nearly," he replied. Then he motioned to the dance floor. "Is your card open for the next?"

She nodded. "It is."

"Then will you do me the honor?"

Celia grinned, for her world seemed to lighten with his attention. "Yes. I'd very much like that."

He took her hand rather than offer his arm, an intimate gesture even though they both wore gloves, and took her to the floor. She felt the eyes of the ballroom on her as the music began and they spun around the room in each other's arms. Of course, the others *would* look. Aiden was the freshest catch in the room. Others would be jealous. They'd talk.

And Celia didn't care. When she was with him, none of it mattered in the slightest.

"You are very quiet," she said, searching his face as they moved.

"I'm counting in my head," he said with a self-conscious laugh. "I've never been very good at this."

She drew back. "Truly? You move very gracefully."

"It is a study in pain, I assure you," he said, and seemed to be speaking through gritted teeth, lending credence to his words.

"And yet you still do it," she said, tightening her fingers on his arm and hoping it would reassure him.

Instead he stumbled slightly before he caught himself. "It's expected," he explained. "And it was the only way to hold you without starting talk that would ruin us both."

Now it was she who stumbled at his words, but his strong arms kept her from falling. She stared up into his face, his handsome face, his focused expression, and saw so much of what she'd always secretly longed for. She saw passion, but also safety, security, *home.*

The last thought jolted her, and she turned her face in shock. She'd known this man for less than a week. These instantaneous feelings of connection to him were not right. They couldn't be real. She had to get them under control.

The song ended and she smiled at him, even though she knew the expression was shaky at best. He returned the expression and led her from the floor. But instead of returning her to her friends or to Rosalinde and Gray, he guided her toward the terrace.

"Will you come outside with me?" he asked.

She blinked, thinking of the last time he'd taken her to a terrace. He'd kissed her. And she knew she shouldn't let that happen again, lest he get the wrong idea about her. But she found herself nodding anyway.

They exited the hot and crowded ballroom and she took a long breath of cool air. He said nothing, but guided her away from the main area of the terrace, into a quieter and darker corner.

She tensed as they came to a stop and he turned to face her. In the dark, she couldn't read his expression and she wasn't certain what he wanted or expected now.

"Aiden?" she whispered.

She felt him stiffen slightly next to her, then he turned her away so that her back was to him. He lifted his hand and pointed into the sky. She followed the direction of his finger and caught her breath.

A great ball of light streaked through the sky above, its long tail trailing behind it in a stunning display.

"A comet," she gasped.

Clairemont smiled at the rapt awe in Celia's tone. Even though he couldn't see her face, he heard how thrilled she was by what she'd shown her and he almost puffed up physically at her excited reaction.

"Yes," he said, knowing he was too close and that his breath probably brushed the back of her delectable bare neck. "*The* comet. It only recently became visible."

"Oh, Aiden," she said, using that other man's first name again. But the tone of voice entirely belonged to him, so he softened to it a fraction. "It's *beautiful*. I've never seen anything like it."

"They are not entirely uncommon," he explained. "But this one is special. Normally they are not so bright. I thought you would like it."

She spun toward him, and he saw pleasure written across her face. "I do. Thank you so much for showing it to me. What a treat to see something so real in the midst of such frivolity."

He stared into her face, unable to stop himself from nodding. "I was thinking the same thing."

Her lips parted, for she clearly took the meaning of his compliment. She was just too beautiful in the dim light and he lifted his hand to cup her cheek. She made a soft sound and leaned into his fingers, and he was lost.

Without thinking, he leaning down and pressed his mouth to hers. Her lips parted immediately and he swept inside, tasting her and filling himself with her sweet flavor the same way he had two nights before.

He wanted to go further. To crush her against his chest, to back her into the darkness and show her what pleasures they could share. Instead, he stepped away, his breath heavy and his cock throbbing.

"I'm sorry," he managed to blurt out. "I-I shouldn't keep

doing that."

"Why?" she asked, face upturned toward him.

He shrugged. "You're a lady," he whispered. "I am not being a gentleman and that is what I *should* be."

She tilted her head. "I *like* it when you kiss me, Aiden. Unladylike or not, I liked it before and I liked it tonight. I won't lie and pretend I don't...or that I don't hope you'll do it again."

He groaned. Her utter honesty and fresh innocence were a dangerous combination. They could make a man forget all his duties. They could make a man throw caution to the wind and commit each and every sin he'd fought his entire life to avoid.

She could make a man feel alive. He so wanted to feel alive. With a curse, he leaned in and kissed her again. She smiled against his lips as she lifted her hands to his forearms and clung there. Her tongue darted out, gently tasting him, and his blood rushed hot and fast to very inappropriate places.

He pulled back. "You do test a man," he muttered.

She smiled. "I'm not trying to test you."

"Yes, and that's the biggest part of the test," he said, laughing despite his discomfort. "There is nothing disingenuous about you, is there, Celia Fitzgilbert? What I see with you is entirely what you are."

She blinked, and for a moment she looked a little upset. But then she turned away. "I try to be honest," she said softly.

He nodded. Certainly, she was that. Straightforward in a way he wouldn't have expected a woman in her position to be.

"I should go back in," she said, finally looking at him again. "My sister and friends will wonder where I've gone."

"I'll stay outside for a moment if you don't mind," he said, shifting in the hopes his erection would go away.

"Of course."

She moved to go, but he reached out and caught her hand. Touching her thrilled him every time, and he clung to her briefly before he said, "Celia, if I were to approach your brother-in-law and ask for permission to court you, would you...would you want that?"

She stared up at him, a small smile on her face, her eyes wide. "Yes, Aiden, I would very much want that," she said, and her voice trembled, revealing how happy she was at that question. The happiness, the anticipation, cut him to his very core.

But he had no choice.

"Good night, Celia," he said.

"Good night."

He released her hand at last and watched her reenter the house. When she was gone he finally breathed again. Now it was done. He had set the wheels in motion for the next phase of his investigation. And for her heartbreak, no matter how successfully this case ended.

And even though he hated himself for doing it, he also thrilled at the idea that Celia wanted him. And even if he hadn't earned her, he would have her for a little while.

That would have to be enough.

CHAPTER NINE

Clairemont feigned surprise when he found Grayson Danford at his club two days later, even though he had planned for this accidental encounter. He crossed the room, a smile on his face, and Danford pushed to his feet from the chair he was reading in and returned the expression.

"Your Grace," he said, extending a hand as Clairemont reached him. "How nice to see you."

Clairemont shook with him and nodded. "Indeed. I have been so far out of Society for so long, I didn't realize we shared a membership at Hopper's."

"Yes," Danford said, motioning to the chair beside his and folding his paper away. "Although White's and the like are necessary evils, I prefer it here. It's a bit less hectic. Certainly less political."

Clairemont looked around at the quiet room. Men were in the corners smoking and discussing politics and other topics. Some read in the adjoining rooms. It actually wasn't bad—certainly there was none of the peacocking he'd expected when he heard the word "club".

"It is. A bit more my speed, I admit," he said. "But I'm happy to see you, as I had hoped we could continue our discussion from the other night at your home."

Now Danford's welcoming smile fell a fraction and was replaced by wariness. "Yes, I think I know *exactly* what it is you wish to discuss. And here we can at last broach the topic freely."

The fine hairs on the back of Clairemont's neck began to
rise. Was this it? Would Danford finally talk to him about
whatever nefarious plots he and the real Duke of Clairemont had
hatched? Would he be able to break his case before he was
forced to damage Celia any more than necessary?

"What topic is that?" he asked, working hard to keep the
anticipation from his tone.

Danford arched a brow as if Clairemont should already
know the answer to that question. "Celia."

"Yes," Clairemont said, his excitement over the case
deflating but being replaced by all the emotions that
accompanied the topic at hand. He'd written her a letter that day.
In fact, he'd written her several letters in the days they'd been
apart. God knew why. It wasn't required and yet he'd found
himself doing it. And picturing her face when she read them.
"Celia."

"Rosalinde and I can see there is a connection between
you," Danford continued. "Though I admit I'm surprised to see
it so quickly. Not that I can talk. I believe I fell in love with my
wife the moment I saw her at an inn."

Clairemont stiffened. *Love.* He had never considered that
possibility. Did he feel desire for Celia? Most definitely, as two
nights staring at his naughty ceiling had proven. Did he like her?
He did. But love? That was too big a concept to even consider.
Men like him were not free to love. He wasn't even sure he *could*
love.

"Celia is a most unique woman," Clairemont said, his voice
rougher than he expected. "I won't deny that she intrigues me."

"And what exactly do you intend to do about that?" Danford
pushed.

Clairemont cleared his throat. "I understand that you are her
guardian now that she no longer lives with her grandfather."

A shadow crossed Danford's face at the mention of Mr.
Fitzgilbert, but he nodded slowly. "I have taken that role, yes."

"Then I would like to—to ask for your permission to court
Celia," Clairemont choked out.

He didn't know why this was so difficult. It was merely a move in a game of chess. And yet saying it out loud made it feel *real*. Like he could truly look toward some kind of future with Celia.

Which was pure balderdash, of course. It was Clairemont who was offering for Celia, not John Dane. Dane wasn't fit to clean her slipper.

Danford held his gaze for a long time, his expression entirely unreadable. At last, he folded his hands in his lap. "Has Celia told you anything about *our* relationship?"

"Your *relationship*," he repeated, suddenly having the urge to slam a fist through Danford's nose. What the hell did he mean by *relationship*?

"She was to marry my brother," Danford said softly. "And I was convinced it wasn't a good match."

Clairemont's brow wrinkled. He'd heard a great deal about the broken engagement between Celia and the Earl of Stenfax, but not this.

"Why is that? Are you warning me off her?"

Danford's lips pursed. "Of course not. In the past few months since my marriage, I have come to recognize how greatly I misjudged Celia at first. Though I cannot say I'm sorry she and Stenfax didn't marry."

"Why?" Clairemont asked.

"They clearly felt nothing for each other."

Clairemont felt himself relaxing at that statement. He'd observed Stenfax quite a bit in the past few days at parties and other gatherings. He'd truly begun to despise the other man for his having ever had a claim to Celia.

"What are you getting at?" he pressed.

Danford tilted his head. "She's been through a great deal."

Clairemont nodded. "Because of the engagement."

"Yes, but you must also know that her life was not easy before that either. Let me make myself plain. I will *not* see her hurt. Not just because Celia's heartbreak will devastate my wife, but because Celia does not deserve anything less than the best."

The sick feeling in the pit of Clairemont's stomach seemed to spread outward the more his companion talked. "And where does that leave my request to court her?"

"If I have your vow that you will not hurt her, then I will agree to a courtship," Danford said at last.

Clairemont stared at him. This protectiveness of Celia made him actually like the man more. And he didn't want to like him. Danford was a suspect in a vile set of crimes—Clairemont couldn't be *friends* with him. Nor could he say that he wouldn't hurt Celia and mean it.

He *would* hurt her. One way or another, that was going to happen before his case was done.

But he cleared his throat and did what he'd been trained to do. Perhaps born to do.

He lied.

"I will do everything in my power not to hurt her," he said.

That seemed to appease Danford, for he smiled for the first time. "Excellent. Then I approve the courtship, though whether or not Celia does the same is up to you, of course. Shall we drink to it?"

Clairemont nodded as Danford lifted his hand and motioned for a porter to bring then a drink. As they waited, Danford leaned closer, draping his forearms over his knees and examining Clairemont closely.

"You know, you aren't what I expected you to be after all our correspondence," he said.

Clairemont jolted at the statement, brought back to reality in a heartbeat. "No?"

"You were never interested in my personal life in the slightest," Danford continued. "In fact, you seemed quite irritated by my marriage and thought it might interfere with our business."

Clairemont frowned. That was the trouble in only having half of a correspondence. He only saw what Danford replied, not the duke's part of the conversation.

"Well, it hasn't seemed to," he said. "So I stand corrected."

Danford laughed. "And there's that, too. You were always so intensely focused on our investments and where your funds were flowing. And yet since your return you haven't harangued me at all about what is happening with the canals that are being managed by Perry."

Perry. Clairemont's ears perked up. He'd heard of Perry, of course, in some of the correspondence he'd read. Danford often mentioned him as the foreman of one of the canals being finished on the very southern tip of the country. It promised to be a profitable one, for it led directly to the sea and would ensure products could be moved from the middle of the country to a port with ease.

"I suppose I'm still adjusting to life in London," Clairemont said slowly, judging Danford's every movement, every flutter of eyelash and length of stare. "And things have gone so smoothly that I've let it go to the wayside."

"I wouldn't say entirely smoothly," Danford sighed. "I'm actually happy you're here so we can speak about the issues I'm encountering in person."

Clairemont focused so that he would recall every detail to write down later. "Go ahead. I'm happy to discuss any problems."

"You recommended Perry, and I appreciate that, for he does seem to know his way around the logistics of building such an endeavor," Danford said. "But Clairemont, I still question the prudence of putting the termination of the port at Withershank. It's a tiny town, not ready to handle the increased traffic the opening of the port will immediately create. I went down there to inspect the place myself right before my marriage and it was worse than I thought. But Perry insists he can hire men to manage it."

"You don't like his picks?" Clairemont asked mildly.

"I don't," Danford admitted, and nodded up at the servant as the drinks were brought.

He waved the man away and poured Clairemont a bit of sherry himself. When they'd taken their glasses, Clairemont couldn't ignore how Danford gripped his, almost white-knuckled. He truly did seem troubled.

"What's wrong with them?" Clairemont pressed.

"They're..." Danford hesitated. "I don't know how to describe it. There's just a wrongness about them. A roughness that I normally wouldn't hire. Now, I know you trust Perry—he's a relative or some such thing, isn't he?"

Clairemont nodded. "Some such thing," he said, unwilling to set himself into a lie until he verified it was the same one the real duke had told.

"Then I don't mean to make it uncomfortable," Danford said. "The canal system is wonderful. It's an easy way to transport goods that is safer and more efficient. And I won't deny that the profit is excellent. But these byways could also be used for far worse purposes. If we have the wrong people running them, they could be used for something like..."

He trailed off, and Clairemont leaned forward. "Like?"

Danford looked around, like he wanted to be certain they weren't overheard. "Like smuggling."

Clairemont was careful in his reaction. Danford seemed truly troubled at that statement and he wanted to believe that his attitude was real. But there was always the possibility that his companion had arranged for the murder or even murdered the real Clairemont himself. That all this was a complex ruse and that he knew full well that the Clairemont before him was false.

"It's a troubling thought that our plans are not going through as we hoped. I'll send word to Perry myself," Clairemont said.

"Good," Danford said, and looked truly relieved. "I would appreciate that. Now, we have our drinks so let us toast to happier things."

Clairemont lifted his glass. "To the future."

"To Celia," Danford said, smiling as their glasses clinked together.

Clairemont fought a frown as he sipped the sherry. He hardly tasted it over the bitterness on his tongue. To Celia, who he would possibly destroy. The idea made him sick.

But there was nothing to do but move forward in his plan, especially now that he had more information. And if he would hurt her, he had damned well better make it worth it.

Celia looked up from her sewing as Gray strode into the parlor. As he did so, Rosalinde got to her feet and moved toward him with a smile.

"Is my sister here?" Gray asked as they met each other and kissed.

"No, Felicity hasn't yet arrived. We didn't expect you for another hour," Rosalinde said, touching his cheek before she pressed another kiss to his lips.

Celia blushed as her mind flashed briefly to Aiden and his kiss, not only at this home, but on the terrace at the ball two days before. She had been thinking of those kisses far too much lately. They even kept her up at night, tossing and turning as her body reacted in ways she had never expected.

Aiden made her feel…needy. Achy. Hot. She tried very hard to be ladylike about the entire thing, but he didn't make it easy. After all, he had been writing her regularly when they didn't meet. The letters weren't untoward, but when she read them, she heard his words in his voice and every single syllable felt loaded with the physical connection they had built.

"I planned on being at the club a little longer," Gray said, breaking into Celia's scandalous thoughts. "But I suppose Felicity not being here is not such a bad thing. I have private news to share, which is why I'm early."

"News?" Rosalinde asked, drawing him to sit beside her on the settee.

"Shall I go?" Celia asked. "Let you two be alone?"

Gray laughed. "I don't think so. After all, my news involves *you*, Celia."

All at once, Celia knew exactly what Gray's news was. Aiden had asked him to court her, as he had promised to do two nights before. He hadn't mentioned it again in his correspondence since, but the pledge hung between them. Her heart began to pound and she set her sewing aside blindly as she stared at Gray.

It seemed Rosalinde had guessed the same thing, even though Celia hadn't mentioned Aiden's intention. Until he spoke to Gray, she hadn't wanted to breathe of it, in case Aiden's plans changed.

Now the color drained from Rosalinde's cheeks and she turned to face Celia. "What is the news?"

"I ran into the Duke of Clairemont at my club this afternoon," Gray said, but his deep voice sounded like it was coming from under water to Celia's ringing ears. "And he asked my permission to court Celia."

He smiled as he said it, and Celia returned the look even as she clasped her hands in front of her heart. It was done. Aiden had taken the step to officially pursue her. That meant the connection she felt was one from his side, as well. And now she shook with the power of it.

Until, that is, Rosalinde stood up and paced away. Celia saw her sister's face and it was not as pleased as she'd thought it would be considering their conversation about the man a few days before.

"You hesitate," Celia said, standing, as well. "Why?"

Rosaline faced her, but she shot Gray a look. A look that spoke volumes. Celia glanced between the two of them.

"What are you two keeping from me?"

"Nothing," Gray reassured her as he moved toward Rosalinde and took her hand. "I will admit that I wasn't certain of Clairemont when we were writing to each other. I shared that worry with your sister when you two met on the terrace last week."

"Why weren't you certain?" Celia asked. "You knew each other before, didn't you?"

Gray nodded. "In school, but that was a lifetime ago. I have certainly changed since then, and from his letters it was clear so had Clairemont. I was pleased to have him investing in my plans, but sometimes he wrote things...*implied* things...that made me question his character. That was fine in business, it's something I could simply keep an eye on. But when it comes to you—"

He broke off, and Celia stared at him. "You—you wanted to protect me?" she asked.

He smiled and released Rosalinde to take a step toward her. "You and I started on the entirely worst foot, Celia. I know I was judgmental of what I didn't understand and I know I hurt you with my interference in your engagement with my brother."

Celia nodded. There was no denying those things, even if she understood Gray's motives more now than she had then. He adored Stenfax and had wanted to protect him after he'd been hurt in the past.

"But I have come to admire and care for you, Celia," Gray continued. "As if you were my own sister. Which means, I'm afraid, you have inherited my protectiveness with my siblings."

Celia laughed. "Oh yes, your famous protectiveness. Felicity and Stenfax have both spoken of it many times."

"With rolled eyes, no doubt," Gray said with a laugh of his own. "But teasing aside, the fact is I don't *ever* want to see you hurt. If I can prevent it, I will move and heaven and earth to do so."

Celia blinked as sudden tears filled her eyes. She'd spent her life under the dubious protection of her grandfather, a man who had seen her as a tool. A man who had blackmailed her into nearly marrying what she did not love. She had never expected protection from anyone but Rosalinde.

Now hearing Gray say those words, lay claim to her as a sibling not because he had to, but because he cared for her. Well, it moved her. She reached out and he took the hand she offered, squeezing gently.

"But don't fear," he continued, pointing his comment both to her and to the teary-eyed Rosalinde, who watched them both with a broad and happy smile. "The more I talk to Clairemont, the more comfortable I become with him. He isn't the man I thought he might be, in the best way possible. So I gave him my permission to forward his suit, if that is your wish, of course."

Celia released his hand and nodded. "You don't know how much your support means to me, especially given our bad beginning. But I must say that I do want Aiden...Clairemont...to court me."

She blushed at her slip of using his given name so freely. That mistake didn't seem to escape Rosalinde and Gray, either, for they both stared at her, wide-eyed.

She ignored their looks and continued slowly, "I-I like him."

Rosalinde moved forward and stared at her intently, her bright blue eyes, the ones so like Celia's own, taking in every expression. Finally, she sighed. "You do?"

Celia nodded. "I do. Very much, despite our short acquaintance."

Saying those words out loud made the truth very clear to her. She really did like Aiden. And she could see that blossoming into something far deeper in the not so distant future. If it did and he went on that journey with her, that meant she would actually have the happiness she saw on her sister's face every day.

"I still worry," Rosalinde said with a sigh. "A sister's prerogative, I suppose."

Celia shrugged. "You and I weren't exactly lucky in love, not until you met Gray."

"No," Rosalinde said, stepping back into her husband's arm and settling her head on his shoulder with a contented sigh. "We weren't. But if I can find happiness, I know you will, as well."

"I want that," Celia said. "I want what you two have."

She bit her lip to keep from saying more. Yes, she was more than happy to have even the chance to fall in love and reach the joy Rosalinde had found. But there was more to her excitement about this potential match.

Aiden was a duke. A powerful one at that, despite his being gone from Society for so long. And she knew her grandfather would be attracted to that title and the power that went with it. But Rosalinde had reacted so poorly to her mentioning of reconnecting with Gregory Fitzgilbert, Celia hesitated to bring it up again. Gray despised her grandfather after his attack on Rosalinde. The two could easily forbid her from pursuing a new deal with him if she asked.

But if she didn't ask...well, she could always apologize later, couldn't she? If she decided to meet with him, if her plan worked out, Rosalinde would surely forgive her.

She smiled. "At any rate, there is nothing happening yet. He's asked to court me and he will. There are no bridges to cross yet when it comes to the future. I'll just hope for the best."

Rosalinde grabbed her and drew her in for a hug. "Absolutely. But I am happy for you that you like this man. When you say you want something like my happiness, I must tell you I pray nightly that you will find the same and more."

"More?" Celia laughed as she squeezed her sister tightly. "I don't know if there is more in the world."

But as they laughed, Celia couldn't help but think of Aiden again. It felt like she could find *more* with a man like him. Everything and more. She had always told herself she couldn't have it all.

But now she couldn't help but wonder if she could.

CHAPTER TEN

Clairemont stood in the parlor, staring out the window at the bright and sunny garden behind Grayson Danford's home. He'd been offered a seat by the butler who brought him here, but he'd not been able to stay in it long. He felt antsy and unsettled, and as much as he tried to chalk that up to his investigation, in his heart he knew it had more to do with Celia.

He faced the door just as Celia entered, her sister trailing behind her. As she looked at him across the room, her face lit up in a bright smile and the power of it hit him in the gut and nearly set him spiraling back. No one had *ever* looked at him like that before. Like he was everything.

He'd always been nothing.

"Hello, Your Grace," Mrs. Danford said, moving between the couple and breaking the spell between them. "How lovely to see you again."

The words were friendly, but her tone was a bit stiff. Clairemont blinked and forced himself to focus on her. There was hesitation in her eyes as she extended a hand to him in welcome.

He shook it. "Thank you for inviting me, Mrs. Danford. Will your husband not join us?"

Mrs. Danford shook her head. "Gray planned to do just that, but I'm afraid his meeting earlier in the day went long. He sent word that he'd be late, though we hope to see him before you depart."

Clairemont frowned, for he wondered who Danford was meeting with, but he didn't press. Already Celia's sister seemed uncertain of him, as outwardly friendly as she continued to be. He didn't want to raise her suspicions even more and perhaps block him from uncovering more.

And from spending time with her sister.

"Please, let's sit, shall we?" Mrs. Danford said as she motioned them all to the settee and chairs before the fire.

She took the chair and Clairemont settled himself in next to Celia on the settee. It was narrow and his larger frame barely fit, which forced his knee to bump hers when he moved.

Every time it did, it was a shock to the system. It seemed to affect her, too, for her pupils were dilated and her breath slightly short when she said, "Your letters earlier in the week reminded me that you haven't been in London for a very long time."

Clairemont nodded. The letters. There had been no reason in the world for him to write to her in the days they'd been apart, but he'd found himself doing so regardless. Sharing with her his impressions of London, giving her details on what he did and thought during the day. It made him feel like they were connected somehow.

And he liked it, even though he shouldn't.

"Yes, a very long time," he said.

"You've told me some of your activities, but I wanted to ask you how you find it overall, Your Grace?"

Clairemont saw Mrs. Danford gather up sewing from a basket beside her chair and turn slightly away. So they were to be given some small level of privacy despite the fact that they were being chaperoned. But not enough for more stolen kisses.

He supposed he should be pleased by that fact. Those kisses were wholly wrong and utterly distracting. And yet he kept taking them, savoring them, dreaming of them, regardless of the consequences to such an action.

"Aiden?"

The use of the name he'd given her jolted him back to reality. He shot Mrs. Danford a look, but she hadn't reacted to the use of what they all believed was his first name.

"I'm sorry, Celia, I was woolgathering," he said. "You asked me about London. I don't think it will come as a surprise that it isn't exactly my favorite place."

He said those words as an explanation for another man's actions, but they applied to him as much as the real duke.

She nodded. "I'm also not hugely fond of the city. It is always so crowded, the air is never fresh and it smells of…"

She trailed off and he shifted with discomfort before he whispered, "Smoke. There are too many chimneys. Too much smoke."

Her gaze lifted to his and she held there. He realized how much emotion had been in that one sentence. Too much. And she'd never know exactly why. He'd never be able to share that truth with her.

He laughed to play off the darker tone of a moment before. "But London is a necessary evil for men of rank. Still, I won't be sorry when I depart. But what about you? You grew up in London, didn't you?"

She smiled—he thought it was at the idea that he had done some research on her past. If she knew the real reason for his search, she would not be so happy.

"I did," she said. "When our mother—"

She broke off, and for a brief second she exchanged a pointed look with her sister. Then she took a deep breath and started again.

"When our parents were gone, our grandfather came and collected us. He brought us back to London to live with him. He had a country estate, of course, but we rarely went there. He was not like you and me—he thought London was where the action was and despised the country."

Clairemont nodded. Whenever she spoke of her grandfather, there was a tension there. He sensed it now in her sister, too. Mrs. Danford was now stiff as she continued stitching the fabric in her lap, her mouth a thin line. There was a story there.

One that had nothing to do with his case, and yet he wished to understand it nonetheless. Because it was Celia. And he yearned to know more. To be connected. Even if he knew it would end.

That realization pulled at him. He claimed to Stalwood and to himself over and over that this courtship of Celia was only to get closer to Danford and determine his involvement in the real Clairemont's schemes. His death. But there was no denying that these moments were all about *her*. Sitting with her wanting to take her hand was about *her*. Wondering about her past, wanting to heal whatever pain had been caused…was about *her*. There was no use pretending otherwise.

"Will you stay for supper, Your Grace?"

He jolted as Mrs. Danford's voice pierced through his fog. He turned to find her staring at him, her blue eyes focused very firmly on his.

"I—yes," he said. "I would enjoy that."

She nodded and set her sewing back in her basket. "Excellent. I will tell the servants to set a place for one more. Since we have time, perhaps Celia would like to take a turn with you around the garden?"

Celia stared at her sister. "Yes. The flowers are just beginning to bud, it's lovely outside."

He tensed. To be alone with Celia again? There was no way to refuse that opportunity. Especially since once supper started he would have to force himself to be focused on Danford.

"Why don't you get your wrap, Celia?" Mrs. Danford said, rising. Clairemont and Celia did the same. "We'll meet you on the veranda."

She sent Clairemont one last look before she slipped from the room. He turned to look at Mrs. Danford. "I assume you would like to speak to me about your sister."

"I'm not very good at subterfuge," she said, inclining her head. "Why don't we walk to the veranda, and I'll be direct."

He nodded. "Lead the way."

She did so, taking him down a hall toward a parlor that

backed toward the garden. They stepped outside. The afternoon sun was beginning to turn golden as it slipped toward dusk and he sucked in a deep breath of the fresh breeze.

Mrs. Danford smiled at him. "You like my sister."

He faced her. At least in this he didn't have to lie. "I do."

"That is good."

"And yet you have hesitations when it comes to me," he said.

"I do," she said, a hint of surprise at his observation in her tone. "I *must*. This is my sister, after all. But don't take my concerns as an attack. Not so long ago, she was equally worried about my prospects with Gray and told him so more than plainly. Now they are becoming friends and she knows I'm happy."

He forced his expression to remain benign. What this woman didn't know, could not know, was that he, unlike Danford, had no intention of marrying Celia. He *couldn't*.

"She is lucky to have someone on her side," he said instead.

"She's suffered some in her life," Rosalinde continued, moving a bit closer and repeating what Danford had implied earlier. "If you make her suffer more, even a fraction more, it will be *me* you must contend with. You'll *wish* it were Gray."

He held her stare evenly and nodded. "I understand you perfectly, Mrs. Danford. And I hope I will never deserve your wrath."

"So do I." She stepped away and smiled again. This time it was a warmer expression, as if he had passed a test and now she approved of him more fully. "Ah, and here is Celia."

He turned to watch Celia exit the house, a light shawl now wrapped around her shoulders. Once again she smiled at him and his world lit up like she was the sun through rainclouds.

"You two enjoy yourselves," Mrs. Danford said.

She entered the house and Celia edged closer to him. "If you don't want to walk in the garden—"

"No, I do, I most definitely do," he said, holding out an arm for her. She took it, sending lightning through his body. "Show me the best path."

Celia and Aiden walked through the winding paths of her sister's garden at a leisurely pace and yet she didn't feel very at ease. After all, she was alone with Aiden. Aiden, who awoke such feelings in her.

Aiden, who had been remarkably quiet in the ten minutes they had been strolling the small grounds. He smiled, of course. He asked a question if she stopped to show him a flower or point out a bird taking wing. But he wasn't engaging with her the way he normally did and that made her nervous.

She sighed. It had never been in her nature to take a risk. That was Rosalinde's way. Her sister had always flown headlong into life and love. She'd been hurt very badly by her openhearted nature. But she had also been receptive to the happiness she now had with Gray.

Celia had always watched Rosalinde's wild flights in both wonder and horror. What if she got hurt? What if she said the wrong thing? What if she fell instead of flew?

She could almost hear Rosalinde laugh at her internal monologue. Her sister would say she'd never know unless she tried. Her sister would tell her she would survive the fall, but standing on the edge was a slow death of regret.

Damned Rosalinde.

Celia shot a glance at Aiden again. He was watching her from the corner of his eye, interested, but withdrawn. And in that moment, she realized she didn't want to hide from the dangers he represented. Not if facing the unknown, potentially making a mistake, meant she could also find happiness. One was worth the other, it seemed, just as Rosalinde had always claimed.

So she took a deep breath and turned to face him. "You have been very quiet since we started our walk, Aiden. Is there something I have done to offend you?"

His eyes went wide. "Offend me? Lord, no. You could

never offend me, Celia. Even if you tried, I don't think you could."

She tilted her head. "Then do you mind if I ask why you are so withdrawn?"

He smiled and reached for her hand. She wasn't wearing gloves, even if she knew she should be, and his rough thumb stroked the sensitive flesh, sending ripples of sensation up her arm that made her dizzy.

"I have been told in no uncertain terms that I'm not to hurt you, Celia Fitzgilbert. It's a bit intimidating."

Heat flooded Celia's cheeks as she realized what he meant. Rosalinde had sent her off to find her shawl so she could harangue the poor man.

"Oh, Rosalinde," Celia sighed. She could barely meet his eyes out of humiliation. "I'm so sorry, Aiden. She is protective and often direct, though I suppose you guessed that after talking to her."

Aiden laughed, and the sound warmed her. "I guessed," he verified. "But I don't judge you *or* her for it. It's nice that you have someone on your side."

"Do you have siblings?" she asked.

She watched his face tense, and it took him a moment to respond. "No," he said at last. "I was an only child."

She sucked in a breath at the raw emotion on his face. He'd always masked his reactions very well, only letting her see what he wanted her to see. Now she felt pain radiate from him.

"Was it...*difficult*?" she whispered.

He jerked out a nod. "Yes."

She wanted to reach for him in that moment, to comfort him in his pain. But she wasn't certain he'd want that. And if he rejected her, that would be terrible. It seemed she wasn't yet ready to fully lead with her heart after all.

"I'm sorry," she said instead. "I understand *difficult*. I had Rosalinde, of course, but I wouldn't call our childhood a happy one."

He leaned in. "Both Danford and your sister implied the

same. Why is that?"

She drew a sharp breath. What he was asking her to reveal took trust. She thought of Gray and Rosalinde, who were so connected that he seemed to be able to sense her moods before she even knew them. That connection was born of trust.

And if she wanted it, she'd have to give. It was the best way to see if Aiden would receive, perhaps even share back.

"My—my grandfather wasn't always kind," she said, dipping her head as fresh heat rushed to her cheeks. "He resented us and made sure we knew it. Even as adults, he did his best to manipulate and even harm us for his own gain."

"Hmmm," Aiden murmured as he reached out and took her hand. His warm fingers closed over hers as he led her toward a bench in the middle of the garden. They sat, and to her surprise he lifted her hand to his chest, his gaze intense. "I'm sorry, Celia. Truly."

She could feel the steady beating of his heart, even through the layers of his clothing. She felt her own heart quicken at the intimacy of his touch and the connection born from her confession.

And suddenly she was no longer embarrassed by what she had admitted.

"It's all right," she breathed. "After all, these things are what make us, aren't they? I wouldn't be *here* if it weren't for my past."

His gaze grew more intense, more heated. "You wouldn't be here with me."

She shook her head. "No."

He edged closer and slid one hand against her cheek, his fingers splaying there. "Well, that would be tragic."

He leaned in, and she let her eyes flutter shut as she waited for the kiss she was so accustomed to. He didn't disappoint—his mouth brushed over hers and she sighed out pleasure and relief all at once.

He claimed her tongue with his, sucking gently, stroking firmly, and she relaxed against him, her arms coming around his neck as he slid her across the bench and held her. This time they weren't on a terrace where they could be interrupted at any time. Rosalinde would leave them be for at least a little while longer.

They were alone. And she wanted this so very much.

He might have sensed that surrender in her. Or perhaps he was also swept away by the pulsing passion between then. He deepened the kiss, tilting her head and driving harder with his mouth, his tongue. She moaned softly against his lips as pleasure mounted.

She found herself sliding one hand down against his chest, his side, and finally she gripped his thigh, searching for purchase in the rolling sea of new feelings and reactions.

The moment she did so, he jerked back, standing and stumbling away as his breath came hard and fast.

She blushed at the reaction. "I-I'm sorry," she gasped, trying to find her own breath.

"Don't be," he said, shaking his head. "But what you do to me…"

He trailed off, and she found her gaze dropping lower. She knew a little about what happened between a man and a woman. Rosalinde had told her the mechanics. Sometimes at night, she heard the reality, soft sounds of pleasure that drifted down from Gray's chamber. It had all felt abstract in those terms. Odd.

But now she found herself staring at Aiden and saw the proof of his desire for her. An erection that was outlined along the tight front of his trousers. She caught her breath at the sight. This was need, this was want, *this* was an instrument of pleasure.

"Yes, I see," she breathed. Her hand fluttered at her side as she fought the urge to reach out to touch him, trace him in the most inappropriate ways.

He made a soft groan deep in his throat. "You are testing me again, Celia."

She smiled up at him, thinking of the first time he had claimed she was a test. When he kissed her a second time and woke desires in her that pulsed beneath the surface now.

"Do I want you to pass the test or fail it?" she asked.

His eyes went wide and he bent toward her. He caught her cheeks with both hands and kissed her again, hard and fast, driven and passionate. She covered his hands with her own and kissed him back with just as much desire.

He pulled away, gray eyes glittering in the fading light as he drew her to her feet. "We should go inside before I do something your brother-in-law will kill me for. Or perhaps it is your sister I need fear more."

She took his arm with a laugh. Her whole body tingled, but it was more than a mere physical reaction that brought her to life. She actually felt excited about the prospects of her future. This man had gifted her with that.

And no one could take that hope away. No one.

CHAPTER ELEVEN

Clairemont lifted his gaze from his half-finished supper and looked down the table at his hosts. It felt like he was walking on a tightrope now and any wrong move could send him tumbling into oblivion.

It was a strange thing to feel so out of sorts, even out of control. Normally he was completely at ease in any situation a case took him to.

He'd participated in dozens of assignments during his career with the War Department. He'd played a role in every one of them, sometimes complicated roles with many things to remember. There had even been accents he had to keep consistent. So playing the part of a reclusive duke who no one knew much about shouldn't have caused him this much consternation. In fact, it *should* have been easy.

And yet it wasn't. This was swiftly becoming the most difficult case of his career. Worse, he was coming to realize that there was only *one* reason he faltered in his act, and that reason was Celia.

He let his gaze slip down the table to her. Outside she had asked him about his past and he had wanted to tell her everything. He'd wanted to spill out secrets no one in this world knew, not even Lord Stalwood, the mentor and friend who had plucked him from the desperate circumstances he'd grown up in.

In the garden, he'd wanted to take Celia's hands, look into her eyes and whisper to her about loss and poverty and abuse, to explain how he'd overcome it all. To explain how all of it had shaped him and how the memories of those dark times drove him, even to this day.

Except he couldn't. Because *that* wasn't Clairemont's story. And it was *that* bastard's tale he had to tell and live inside. His own skin, his own past, his own life meant nothing.

"Of course, you know perfectly well how surprised and fascinated people are by your return to Society," Danford said.

Clairemont blinked. Here was further proof he wasn't on his game, for he hadn't been paying any attention at all to the words of the very man he was meant to be investigating. Words that brought his situation, being another man, perfectly into focus.

He forced a smile as he took on the role of duke once more. "You know the *ton*—they're forever fascinated by the newest thing."

Danford laughed. "Indeed, *that* is true. Society as a whole seems to have the attention span of a gnat."

"Which can be useful if you're trying to overcome a scandal," Celia said softly. The eyes of each person at the table slid to her, and she shrugged.

Clairemont stiffened at the soft sadness in her eyes. Was she thinking of her broken engagement?

"Celia," Mrs. Danford breathed, her voice laced with pain for her sister.

"Don't all look at me that way," Celia said, suddenly laughing and breaking the tension of the room. "I didn't necessarily mean *my* scandal, which has been minor at worst. I meant scandal in general."

Neither of the Danfords looked completely certain of the veracity of Celia's statement, but Clairemont could see she didn't wish for the subject to be pressed. So he nodded.

"You are right about that," he said. "And it shall play into my hand if I'm lucky."

"What do you mean?" Celia asked, though there was no mistaking her brief smile of thanks that he had taken the attention off her with his words. He felt like his chest puffed when she looked at him that way.

Dangerous.

"My hope is that in a few weeks there *will* be a new scandal or something else that will divert their attention again and *I* will no longer be their focus." He shook his head. "I do not enjoy the role of prodigal son returned."

He sighed, for that was a totally accurate description of what he hoped. He still got far too many invitations and glances and unexpected visitors at his home. News of his courtship of Celia hadn't fully filtered into Society at large. Or perhaps it had and some of the more mercenary women just didn't give a damn. Until he was fully caught in a marriage knot, he was still catchable.

"I suppose you're right—it isn't much of a surprise that they chatter." Danford leaned back as a servant took his now-empty plate. "What surprises me more, to be frank, is that you disappeared from Society in the first place."

Clairemont kept his expression calm. He had spent months studying this very subject, trying to determine why the real duke had fled good company and holed himself up in his castle to plot against his own countrymen. From the man's diaries and letters, Clairemont had some vague thoughts on the matter, but there were pieces of the duke that would always be private. Stories he would have to concoct on his own.

This was one of them.

"My father's death was difficult," he said. "And I was given a great deal of responsibility at a young age. I suppose at first I was overwhelmed by it all. And later, as I stayed away longer and longer, it became harder to return."

He watched Danford's face for a reaction, a flutter that said he didn't believe him or that he knew better. But there was none.

"I must say it is a pleasure to have you back," Mrs. Danford said, drawing Clairemont's attention to her. "You've certainly made this season more…" She shot her sister a pointed look that made Celia's cheeks brighten with color. "*Interesting.* But if you don't mind my asking, what brought about your return to London this year over any other?"

"A man of my rank has a duty," Clairemont said. "I have avoided it far too long."

"And which duty is that?" she pressed.

Clairemont arched a brow. "To marry."

From letters and other records, he knew the real duke truly *had* been concerned with that fact. Only Clairemont had been more interested in bringing women to his castle to "test" them. He shuddered to think of what that would have entailed for those unlucky enough to be chosen, had he followed through with his plans. The female servants in the real duke's employ suffered enough under the man.

Celia cast him a quick glance, and he couldn't help but return her stare. Of course, testing *her* would be no hardship. He was certain she would pass any trial he concocted, from comportment to the pleasures they could share.

She blushed, almost as if she read his mind, and her gaze slid to her plate. But she smiled, a secret little expression that told him she was thinking of their stolen moments in the garden. How he wished he could have had more time with her. That they wouldn't be interrupted. That he had carte blanche to touch her as he wanted to do.

"I hope you do not *only* see it as a duty," Mrs. Danford said, intruding upon his thoughts.

He blinked. "Marrying?" he asked, trying to bring his mind back to the current moment.

She nodded, and he smiled once more at her protectiveness of her sister. Celia deserved that. She would need it even more once he was finished with her and her hopes were dashed.

That sobering thought brought his mood down, and he cleared his throat. "You and Danford seem to provide a great deal of proof that it can be a pleasure," he said.

Mrs. Danford beamed down the table at her husband and then the conversation shifted to other topics. Clairemont found himself looking at Celia once more, examining her features and wishing more than anything that he could plan a true life with her, not just use that idea as a way to further his investigation.

But he couldn't have that. Because at the end of this, he would no longer be the Duke of Clairemont. And he would never see Celia again. A thought that turned his stomach and made his chest ache.

"Thank you, Ruth," Celia said as her maid gathered up her clothing from the day to be washed and pressed. "Good night."

"Good night, miss," Ruth said with a smile as she left Celia's chamber.

Once she was alone, Celia returned to her mirror and stood before it, looking at her reflection. Although she'd seen herself thousands of times over the years, tonight she felt like she was looking at a stranger. In the garden, Aiden had changed something in her. His mouth on hers, his hands touching her, her realization of his desire for her...all that had shifted her to a new place. She couldn't go back.

And it seemed she might not have to. After all, before he'd left, he'd held her hand a moment too long, stared into her eyes just a little too intently. He wanted her as much as she wanted him. There was only one way that would end if he were a gentleman and she a lady.

Yet she wasn't completely thrilled at the idea of a future with him, not because she didn't want that, but because he remained a mystery in so many ways. Tonight he had withdrawn a fraction after supper. She'd felt his hesitation, but what was it born from?

The only thing she could think of was past. In the garden she'd felt his pain on the subject, and inside he'd seemed just as uncomfortable when he spoke to Rosalinde and Gray about why he'd hidden out in the countryside, why he had been so reluctant to return to his place in Society.

There was a great deal beneath the surface with this man. Sometimes she caught a glimpse of a roiling sea of emotion and heartache that he kept secret, quiet. She found she wanted to know it *all*. To share it every bit of it. To ease it all the best she could.

In the hallway, she heard the soft sound of voices. Gray's voice, answered by Rosalinde as they made their way to bed in the master chamber at the far end of the hallway. There was a tone to their voices, even if Celia didn't understand the words themselves. Whatever they said was born from deep intimacy. Love. Potent desire. Her sister let out a soft giggle and then the door to their chamber shut a bit too loudly.

Celia closed her eyes. Rosalinde had taken chances it had always come naturally to her. In fact, Celia knew that her sister and Gray had engaged in physical intimacy before they were wed.

For Rosalinde, making the decision to give herself to a man was a different situation, of course. She had been a widow when she met Gray, so there were fewer consequences to such an act.

For Celia, surrendering her body was far more dangerous, with many more potential consequences.

And yet she *wanted* to take that risk. She *wanted* to offer comfort to Aiden. She wanted to connect with him on a deeper level and help him see that it was safe for him to share his heart with her. She wanted to ease the ache he caused deep inside of her when he touched her or kissed her with such passion.

And yet being so bold as to take or even merely ask for what she wanted was terrifying. Celia had the barest bones of knowledge on what happened between men and women. She'd heard what she should expect when she was engaged to Gray's brother, the Earl of Stenfax. Certainly *that* would never be enough to properly seduce a man of experience like Aiden.

But she did want to get closer to him, to feel and understand the passion he inspired. To be his in every way that mattered. To make him hers in the same way.

She thrilled at that admission, made only to herself in her

head. Even thinking those words, imagining what would happen between them if she overcame her fear, made her body throb. Her nipples tingled, and low in her stomach there was a flutter of need and pleasure.

But the question now was how to suggest such a thing to him without risking rejection. And also if she could manage to be bold enough to enact any plan she did concoct.

CHAPTER TWELVE

"Your Grace, Lord Stalwood is here to see you."

It took a moment for the butler's words to register in Clairemont's head as he sat as his desk, staring at a ledger without truly seeing it. Tracing money had never been his favorite part of being a spy, but normally he wasn't too preoccupied to perform his duty.

"I am in—please show him here, Richards."

The servant bowed out and, in a moment, returned to announce Stalwood. He left them and Stalwood closed the door.

"No problems with the servants we hired, were there?" he asked.

Clairemont rose to shake his old friend's hand. "Not at all. The fact that the Duke of Clairemont fired his entire previous staff and brought on all new servants seems to have put the fear of God into them. I have never seen such swift and efficient work."

Stalwood smiled. "Well, the old staff got incredibly good references and have all landed on their feet."

"Then a happy ending for everyone, it seems," Clairemont said. "Sit, won't you? Would you like a brandy?"

Stalwood shook his head. "No, I ought not. I actually come bearing news about this fellow Perry that Grayson Danford mentioned last week."

At that, Clairemont took a step toward him. "Excellent. I have been wishing I could pursue that lead myself, but my situation here prevents it."

"Yes, these pesky duties of the titled," Stalwood teased.

"Even the falsely titled," Clairemont agreed with a frown. "Being a duke is stifling."

"You must be excited then at the prospect of ending the charade and going back to the field," Stalwood said. "And perhaps this information gets us that much closer to ending this."

Tension suddenly coiled in Clairemont like a tightly wound spring. "What have you discovered?"

"Perry is not in any way related to the *real* Clairemont," Stalwood began. "That was a lie on the duke's part, probably to subvert any questions Danford would have had about the man. Suggest a cousin as a good worker and there are fewer questions than if you suggest a stranger with a checkered past."

"It implies he doesn't want Danford to know something," Clairemont agreed. "And that bodes well for Danford's lack of true involvement or knowledge about the real Clairemont's conspiracies."

"It does. In fact, our agents can find nothing at all that concretely ties Danford to Clairemont's true schemes."

Relief washed over Clairemont at those words. He had come to much the same conclusion already after observing Danford over the past few times they'd interacted, but a gut feeling and actual evidence were two different things.

"He's being used," he said. "With his fingers in so many pies, he's the perfect person to invest in and funnel money or use his ventures to trade secrets or goods."

"Exactly," Stalwood said with a quick nod.

"So is Perry a contact or a lackey?" Clairemont asked.

"A lackey, we believe. The real Clairemont had some other partner, one he was trying to keep hidden. Perry appears to be the conduit, so that the two men never have to interact directly."

"Could this mystery partner be our killer?"

"Very possibly," Stalwood said, digging into his pocket to retrieve a paper with a long list of observations from the last few days. "There's been some odd activity down in Withershank since the real Clairemont's death. Shipment reroutes, changes to those employed at the canal port. It can't be a coincidence."

Clairemont looked over it briefly. "No, it can't be. And Danford is unaware of all this. Which would be the last indication to make me certain of his innocence."

Stalwood nodded. "I agree. We can set him aside as a suspect and I would suggest finding out who else is investing in the canal project specifically. It might be the most direct route to our next villain."

Clairemont set the paper down on his desk and walked to the window where he stood staring outside. He should have been thrilled by this development. Being stalled was infinitely frustrating. Now he could move forward. He could close this case and walk away, happy in the fact that he had served his country and saved lives once again.

But he wasn't thinking about lives. He was thinking about something else entirely.

"I shouldn't have moved forward with courting Celia until we had worked on Danford more fully," he said, shaking his head at the faint reflection of himself in the glass. "Now that it is clear her brother-in-law isn't involved, that means I will tear her apart for *nothing*."

"Not nothing," Stalwood said, moving toward him and grasping his arm to turn him around. "By building a closer relationship in his family, you will be better able to use Danford to help you with the truth. Whatever is happening, it still likely ties to Danford's businesses."

"But at what cost?" Clairemont hissed, self-loathing washing over him, coating everything about him.

"At what cost if you *didn't* pursue this course of action?" Stalwood retorted. He leaned in, searching Clairemont's face intently. "I'm worried about you. I've never seen you like this before, vacillating on a case. Or worrying so much about collateral damage when the stakes are so high."

"Celia isn't collateral damage," he said, shaking his arm away from his friend. Right now he didn't want to have this conversation.

Stalwood was silent for what felt like an eternity. "What *is* it about this woman?" he asked at last. "What has you tangled up so completely?"

Clairemont stared at his friend, then shook his head as his body sagged back against the window pane. "I-I don't know. I realize what my duty is, I swear to you I do. But it's complicated. Hurting her is…it is the worst thing I've ever done. I *hate* myself for it."

Stalwood watched as Clairemont paced away and poured the drink he'd hesitated to take earlier. Clairemont slugged it in one gulp and wished the burn of the liquid would consume him. It didn't.

"Do you remember the night I found you?" Stalwood said softly.

Clairemont lifted his head slowly, staring at the wall ahead of him with unseeing eyes. He must have been quiet for too long, for his mentor cleared his throat.

"Dane, do you remember?"

Clairemont winced at the use of his real name. If Stalwood was breaking character, he must think Clairemont was in a bad way. He wasn't wrong in that assessment. At the moment, he felt stretched so thin that he might break.

"Yes, I remember," he whispered, his voice cracking.

"You tried to pick my pocket," Stalwood said, even though Clairemont had answered in the affirmative.

"When you caught me, I thought I'd be transported for stealing from a titled gentleman." He turned to face the earl. "I was terrified. Why didn't you let them take me?"

Stalwood arched a brow. "It's been over fifteen years since that night and you've never once asked that question. Why ask it now?"

Clairemont shifted. "I need the answer now. When I'm failing in every way, I need to know, I suppose."

Stalwood's expression softened. He looked *fatherly*, and Clairemont took a long, deep breath. This man was his best and only friend. Seeing him like this…it meant a great deal.

"You are a good judge of character," Stalwood said slowly. "It is one of your best attributes, that judgment. But you're not the only one who possesses it. I looked into your eyes as the guard was hauling you off and I saw something there. Something deeper than a desperate street ruffian. Something deeper than your position or your anger toward me and the world."

"What did you see?" Clairemont whispered.

"A good man," Stalwood said, shaking his head. "A good man who could be taught to be even better. To be great."

Clairemont stared at him a long time, thinking about his past. Thinking about that pivotal moment in his life when he'd been offered a different way. Thinking about Celia and the lies he was forced to tell her as he drew her near.

"I don't feel like a good man now," he admitted. "I feel like a bastard. A cad. I feel as broken and violent as I did when I was that boy you saved from the street. What I'm doing to this woman is *wrong*."

"You care for her," Stalwood said softly.

Clairemont shut his eyes for a brief moment. "I'm beginning to, yes. God help me, yes. I don't deserve her, but when I'm with her everything falls away. It's never happened before and I don't know what to do. I would wager it will never happen again and I don't know whether to celebrate or mourn that fact."

"I am sorry you are in this position," Stalwood said. He rubbed a hand over his face. "I didn't anticipate it, though I should have. You're young, your life ahead of you. Of course a beautiful young woman, who by all accounts is lovely inside and out, would appeal to you."

Clairemont shrugged. "And yet what is there to do?" he sighed at last. "The situation is what it is. The best I can do is get through it quickly. To release her from this strange attraction and let her mourn the death of a man who never existed as swiftly as I can."

Stalwood nodded. "Yes. Unfortunately, that *is* the best

thing for her. To finish what you started and walk away before her heart is fully engaged. Before your own is."

Clairemont frowned. He feared it was too late for that. He swallowed hard and said, "I know. And I will. I don't want you to worry about me shirking my duty."

Stalwood slapped a hand on his back. "Dane...*Clairemont*...I never worried about you doing your duty. After all, I already told you I know you're a good man. Now, why don't we have another drink before I leave to prepare for this blasted ball tonight? I think we both earned it."

Clairemont poured two more drinks. But as they clinked their glasses together, he felt no pleasure. Duty or not, country or not, there was no joy in what he would ultimately do to Celia. Nor in losing her when this was over.

But Stalwood was right. The best thing he could do was make the pain as swift and uncomplicated as possible. Tonight at the ball he would speak to Danford. He would determine the other suspects and dispatch them promptly.

Then he would set Celia free. It was the only way.

Even before he was announced at the door, Celia recognized the moment when Aiden entered the ball. Where before she had been bored and distracted, now there was a crackle of excitement that worked through her. She turned as he swept into the room, all eyes seeking him as hers did.

Beside her, Celia heard her friend Felicity, the Viscountess Barbridge—and Gray and Stenfax's sister—chuckle. Celia turned to look at her.

"What are you looking so smug about?" she asked.

Felicity shrugged, but there was an impish quality to her quirked lips. "Nothing," she said in that tone she sometimes used that reminded Celia of her inexperience. Especially next to Felicity's sophistication.

"Your expression says it's far more than nothing," she pressed.

Felicity shook her head, blonde hair shivering prettily. "I was just thinking he is very handsome. And how desperately jealous everyone is of you now that news of his courtship is starting to circulate."

Celia frowned even though Felicity had said nothing unkind. "Yes, I've heard some of their comments, I assure you."

Felicity's teasing ended and concern filled her face. "You sound upset when you say that. What did you hear?"

"Oh nothing," Celia said, waving her hand to dismiss what she'd overheard just this very night. "Just some little comment about how I always stole the most eligible bachelors and a question about whether or not I could 'land' this one."

"Nasty biddies," Felicity muttered.

"I should have expected it," Celia said with a shake of her head. "After all, Stenfax was considered a great catch and he has hardly spoken to a woman since our engagement ended."

Felicity looked out over the crowd toward Stenfax, worry plain in her blue eyes. "Stenfax has his own reasons for that, I fear. I wager it has nothing to do with you."

Celia pursed her lips. "Well, no one else knows that. And it doesn't help when Clairemont reappears suddenly in London, sets everything on its head, and here I am being courted by him."

Felicity faced her with a determined expression. "So you are a bachelor stealer."

Her deadpan delivery of the line made Celia laugh despite herself. "Yes, you have me caught. I intend to tempt all the men and keep them to myself. Is that a harem?"

"A reverse harem," Felicity corrected her, and she was laughing now, too. "*Very* different."

"You are shocking," Celia said, squeezing Felicity's arm as thanks for brightening her spirits.

"You have *no* idea," Felicity said. "But if you're collecting a harem, you should get ready for the first piece. Here *he* comes."

Celia straightened and couldn't help her smile as Aiden came striding through the crowd, his eyes focused on her. This was the first time they'd been together in public since he had asked to court her, though his letters continued to come at regular intervals when they were apart. Still, it felt like half the room was holding their collective breath, watching to see how they interacted.

He reached her and she clenched her fingers, wanting to touch him, to be touched by him. He leaned over her hand, lifting it to his lips before he released her with a wide smile.

"Miss Fitzgilbert," he said, eyes twinkling as he used her formal address.

She smiled, and suddenly anything anyone said behind her back didn't matter one bit. "Your Grace."

He turned toward Felicity. "I don't believe we've met."

Celia faced her friend and found Felicity was watching him carefully. Before Celia could make the introduction, Felicity thwarted propriety and inclined her head in a cool greeting. "Viscountess Barbridge, Your Grace."

Aiden's eyes widened, and Celia knew he'd realized this was Stenfax's and Gray's sister. "Ah," he said, his tone now more neutral. "Well, good evening." Felicity nodded in acknowledgement of the greeting. "Might I steal your friend for a moment?" he asked. "To dance the next?"

"Of course."

Felicity smiled at Celia before Aiden offered an arm to her. Celia took it and allowed him to lead her to the dance floor. The music began and Celia shivered as the strains of the waltz filled the air. She couldn't help but be happy that she could remain in his embrace throughout the song.

They moved into the circling couples and she looked up into his handsome face, which was focused, and she realized he was internally counting once more. She smiled and he caught her gaze, held it and then, suddenly, looked away.

"What thought just came into your head?" she asked with a frown.

He arched a brow as he glanced back at her. "Thought?"

She took a breath. She could easily play off her question, pretend it away so that she wouldn't have to take a risk by pressing him.

Except he was worth the risk. She knew that as easily as she knew her own mind and heart.

"You were smiling and then suddenly you looked upset," she explained softly. "I wondered what in the world could have inspired such a shift."

His lips pressed together. "You *are* attentive."

Those words should have been a compliment, but they didn't sound like one.

"Do you want a lady who is not?" she asked.

He shook his head. "A lady who wasn't would likely be boring, indeed. Your intellect and your knack at observation are both bewitching, I assure you."

"And yet you don't sound happy," she continued. "Do you want to talk to me about why?"

"You are also singular," he accused with a laugh that didn't exactly sound jovial. Then he lowered his voice slightly. "The thought that went through my head is that I may not be the man you hope me to be. The man you *deserve*, Celia. I will hate to let you down."

She wrinkled her brow. "So you think you aren't worthy of *me*?"

She almost laughed at the notion. After all, she and Rosalinde were the granddaughters of a gentleman, but he wasn't titled. And no one save Stenfax, Felicity and Gray knew the truth about their real father. If Clairemont knew the facts of their parentage, perhaps he wouldn't be addressing his own worthiness, but hers.

She frowned at the idea.

"Now you are the one scowling," he said. "Perhaps I've struck on a topic you never considered."

The music was building toward the final notes, and she took a long breath. "Aiden, I assure you, I have never and would never consider you unworthy. Your title and whatever comes with it aside, I *like* you. I like being with you. I like the way I feel when you're near me. Now maybe those aren't ladylike things to admit, but they are entirely true. Nothing would change that. Not now, not in the future."

The music ended with her words and he stopped moving, staring intently into her eyes even as he held her a moment too long. Then he shook his head.

"None of us can predict the future, Celia. As much as we wish we could, it is not possible." He released her and guided her from the dance floor. "I should go talk to Danford now, as I have matters to discuss with him. Perhaps we can dance again later."

She nodded as he bowed and walked away, but it was a reflexive motion, not one born from what was inside of her. Right now she was a boiling cauldron of confusion. This man was meant to be courting her, which meant he was contemplating a future with her. She felt connected to him and she knew he felt the same with her.

So they should have been happy. And yet again she felt this disconnect between them. As if the closer he came to happiness, the more he built a wall between it and his heart. A wall that blocked her out, even as he drew her closer in public...in private.

Aiden was weaving his way through the crowd now, making a beeline for Gray and Rosalinde, who were about to take the dance floor for the allemande. She turned away from their intense smiles for each other, their connection that was so obvious even across the room.

She wanted that same connection so badly. And yet she sometimes wasn't certain that Aiden intended to allow it. With a sigh, she walked through the ballroom and outside onto the wide stone terrace. She needed air now, needed to get away from the crowd and her confusing emotions.

The night was warm for spring and the terrace was crowded, so she maneuvered her way to the stone staircase that led to the garden below. When she was hidden in the shadows, out of the prying eyes of those above, she stopped. She clung to the railing and stared up into the dark night. The comet Aiden had shown her just a week ago still lit up the darkness, and she smiled up at it.

"Making a wish?"

She turned toward the voice that had interrupted her reverie and smiled as the Earl of Stenfax came down the stairs toward her. Her former fiancé returned the expression as he held out an arm to her.

"Come, we could both use a walk," he said.

She laughed and took his offer, letting him guide her to the garden where they began to walk down a winding path to a gazebo in the distance. "How do you know I could use a walk?" she asked.

In the dimness she didn't see his smile as much as hear it in his voice when he said, "Standing there wishing on comets gave you away."

"I wasn't wishing on the comet—I don't think it works that way," Celia said with another laugh.

It was funny. When she had been engaged to the tall, handsome earl she had not been connected to him at all. They had struggled whenever they were forced to speak and she'd felt awkward and odd in his presence.

Now, with their engagement at an end, with him being the only person outside of Gray and Rosalinde who knew any of the truth about her past, that discomfort was gone. She actually *liked* Stenfax, even if she had no desire to be his bride.

"I'm not sure wishing on anything works very well," he said, taking them up the short set of stairs to the gazebo. Lanterns had been lit around its perimeter, casting a soft light into the building.

She sat on the bench that had been placed encircling the inside of the structure, and he took a place next to her. "Do you have something you need to wish for, Stenfax?" she asked.

He turned his face toward hers with a half-smile. "Is this your way of asking about Elise? Are you a spy for Gray and

Felicity?"

She examined his face closely. Stenfax had been engaged to a young woman named Elise long before Celia had even met him. When Elise threw him over for a better title, it had crushed the man. But recently the lady's husband had died, leaving her, the Duchess of Kirkford, free.

"Your sister and brother worry, you know that," Celia said softly. "They love you."

"Yes." Stenfax sighed. "I suppose Gray, especially, fears I will entangle myself in Elise—*that woman's* web again. That I'll be hurt as I was before."

"And *is* that your intention?" Celia pressed, truly interested and concerned herself. The last thing she wanted was for Stenfax to be hurt. He didn't deserve that. He'd never been anything but kind to her and never kinder than when they ended their engagement.

"She hasn't returned to Society as of yet," Stenfax said, staring straight ahead. His jaw flexed. "Her mourning period isn't even over until the fall. But when it is, I have no intention of seeing her. You may report that back if you'd like."

"I wasn't asking for your siblings' interest, but my own," Celia said. "You and I may not have married, but since our engagement ended I have begun to think of you as a friend."

He smiled at her. "A friend. I'd like to be your friend, Celia. Sincerely. And I appreciate your worry, as well as that of Gray and Felicity. But it is all misplaced. The Duchess of Kirkford holds no sway over me. She never will again."

But there was something in his tone that belied his words. Something in his expression, as well. Still, it wasn't Celia's place to push him or advise him.

"Now, as your friend, I suppose it is my turn to ask after you," Stenfax said. "What's this I hear about the Duke of Clairemont courting you?"

"Seems like your siblings are more a spy for you than me for them," Celia teased.

"It is in the grapevine, my dear," Stenfax said, holding up

his hands. "*Everyone* is raring to tell me how you have found yourself a duke."

Celia's lips parted and she turned toward him. "Oh, Stenfax, I didn't even think how the two situations might look alike to others."

He shook his head. "No one who matters thinks you threw me over for a duke. I'm certain they would be crowing to me just to see my reaction if you were being courted by a baronet or a shopkeeper, too."

"Well, if *anyone* is so bold as to suggest that I threw you over for a higher title, they will get an earful from *me* in retort," Celia said.

"What do you think of your duke?" Stenfax asked.

She lifted her brows. "Why do you ask?"

"I suppose curiosity as your former fiancé. And some concern as your friend."

"I-I like him, Stenfax, I really do," she admitted softly. "You and I, it should have worked, but neither of us felt that attraction, that connection that we should have as intendeds. But with him…" She trailed off with a blush.

"You feel it," Stenfax said, finishing her sentence. "You needn't feel badly about that, Celia. It is what I wanted for you when we parted. To find the love you richly deserve. If you have discovered it with Clairemont, then he is the luckiest of men."

Love. Celia let that word sink into her soul. She'd been avoiding thinking it, saying it, admitting it, but now that Stenfax had, it was like a seal was broken over her heart and she could see the truth.

She loved Aiden.

A thrill worked through her at the realization. One tempered by icy terror. She loved him but she had no idea if he felt or ever could feel the same. Oh, he wrote romantic words to her, he held her gently, he did all the things he should do and that had drawn her in and allowed her to fall in the most wonderful way possible. And yet she still felt a chasm between them she feared she'd never cross.

What if she risked herself and received nothing in return? What if they married and the feelings ultimately only rested on her side of the pillow?

"Why do you look so worried?" Stenfax asked gently.

Celia faced him, trying to keep the fear from her face and the tremble from her hands and voice. "It is...*complicated* with him," she said slowly. "Sometimes he withdraws and I'm not certain what he thinks."

"I watched him dancing with you earlier," Stenfax said. "If it helps, his body language reminded me of Gray's when he is with Rosalinde. It's like he's always looking for a way to lean into you. Or searching for a reason to touch you. He's been out of Society a long time. Rumor says he kept almost no company during that time. His hesitance may be uncertainty in how to behave, rather than a lack of feeling toward you."

She leaned forward, catching his hands as relief flowed through her. "Do you think so?"

"But certainly you must discuss this with him. You deserve to know what is in his heart long before you link your life to him forever. You *deserve* to be happy, Celia."

"Thank you," she whispered. "So do you."

He turned his head a little, and she frowned at his wordless denial that he could ever be loved or love again. But her worries about him were tempered by what he'd said about Aiden. The man might very well care as much as she did.

And that made her future look far more bright than it had when she exited the ballroom just a short while ago.

CHAPTER THIRTEEN

Clairemont hurried down the stairs away from the terrace and the prying eyes that watched him there. He needed air, he needed to think, he needed a break from pretending.

His dance with Celia had not gone as he'd hoped. Looking into her eyes, seeing her give of herself so freely, see all her hopes for their future, it was like a dagger to his heart. And he'd reacted by trying to reach out to Danford. Ending the case was the only way to save her from even more pain. The only way to save her from him and all the things he wanted and couldn't have.

But Danford had been busy with his wife, spinning around the dance floor, laughing together. When Clairemont had a moment to talk to him, Danford had looked him in the eye and told him to enjoy himself, *not* talk about their situation for tonight wasn't the time. Of course the man was right, but Clairemont was frustrated, not just by his inability to investigate but by his growing connection to Celia. Her joy only brought him terror. Her drive to care for him even if he didn't deserve her made him hate himself.

This was all an act. A lie. She was not his. She never would be.

He heard voices in the distance, a man and a woman. He looked toward the gazebo and saw the outline of two figures sitting there.

"Damn," he muttered. He'd hoped for a bit of privacy in the

garden where he could strip off the mask of Clairemont and take a few breaths as himself until he could pretend again. But now he would have to...

He stopped in his tracks as the woman in the gazebo laughed at something her companion said. That was Celia's laugh. He knew it too well. He had been obsessing over it of late. Dreaming of it.

Who was she with, alone in the gazebo? Some man.

He moved toward them, keeping to the shadows, watching his step so he didn't make a sound. As he got closer, his chest began to ache. He couldn't yet make out their words, but he could see then better in the dim light.

Celia was with the Earl of Stenfax. Her former fiancé.

He held back in the shadows and watched the man. Stenfax was handsome, there was no denying that. He probably had a head in height over most men in the ballroom. Certainly half a head over Clairemont.

He and Celia sat next to each other, though they weren't touching. That didn't mean there wasn't an intimacy to their proximity. From time to time they looked right at each other, as if what they had to say required eye contact.

Clairemont's hands began to shake. He'd just been reminding himself that his courtship of Celia Fitzgilbert was a lie, an act, a game. But in that moment, as he watched her with the man she had once pledged to spend her life with, it didn't *feel* fabricated.

It felt all too real. Celia was *his*.

Exactly as that thought torched through his mind like a wildfire, Celia caught both Stenfax's hands with her own. Possessive desire coursed through Clairemont at the sight. A primal need to stake a claim on this woman, to show this rival, to show *her*, that he was first in line for her affection, her touch, her attention.

It was wrong, so wrong, and yet he found himself coming out of the protection of the shadow and up the gazebo steps in one long step.

"Am I interrupting?" he asked, surprised by how calm his voice was when he was bubbling with the need to grab her and scream out, "Mine!" right into the face of the earl.

Celia released the other man's hands at once and got to her feet. "Aiden," she said. "What are you doing here?"

Stenfax stood, too, a bit slower than Celia had. There was a wariness to his expression, as if he recognized the true feelings in Clairemont's heart.

"He's come looking for you, Celia," Stenfax said softly. "And *that* is my cue to leave you. Good night."

He walked toward the stairs, and for a moment Clairemont considered not moving. He wanted to butt this man's chest with his own and wrinkle the earl's perfect cravat, his perfect face.

It took everything in him to step aside and let Stenfax pass. As he did so, the two men locked gazes, and Stenfax inclined his head like he was acquiescing a point before he strode back toward the house.

Celia remained standing, staring at him. There was confusion on her face as she observed him, apparently waiting for him to speak.

But what would he say? He knew the truth as she didn't. It should have mattered and it didn't. In that moment, *all* that mattered was the rolling tide of desire that cascaded over him like a wave on a rocky shore.

"Aiden?" she whispered, using that other man's name to address him. Once again, it didn't matter. Aiden, Duke of Clairemont, John Dane, abandoned son of no one…what they wanted was the same.

Her.

He reached out and took one of her hands. She had held Stenfax's hand in this one. He tugged her forward gently, down the gazebo stairs. In the dark he'd noticed a small gardener's shed in the corner of the garden, toward the back. Someplace with tools, but more importantly for him, privacy.

He wanted privacy to be able to reveal some part of himself. Not all, but part.

She let him take her across the lawn. She didn't hesitate, not until they reached the door of the little shed.

"Aiden?" she whispered again.

He shook his head as he tried the door and sighed in relief when he found it unlocked. He pulled her inside, into the darkness, and shut it behind them. It was dark inside, but through the small windows a sliver of light from the house above, the moon above and the lamps on the path just a short few paces away gave it *some* illumination.

Enough to see the hesitation on her face. She looked around at the tools hanging from hooks, the narrow open space, the door behind him. Perhaps she should have been afraid to be in such a position.

She didn't look like she was afraid. She licked her lips slowly and his cock began to ache.

"I didn't like seeing you with him," Clairemont whispered at last.

She caught her breath at that admission, her pupils dilating in the dim light and her chest rising with her reaction. She was surprised, but he could see there was some small part of her that liked this barbaric possessiveness.

"We—we ended our engagement months ago, Aiden," she whispered, her voice catching slightly. "Whatever you think you saw, Stenfax is nothing but a friend to me. It isn't like that between us."

He moved toward her in the small room, close enough that he caught a whiff of her honeysuckle scent and felt the warmth of her body heat. "How is it?" he asked. "Between you and him?"

She blinked up at him. "It's nothing," she whispered.

"And how is it between you and me?"

She caught her breath, and then she lifted trembling hands to cup his cheeks. "Everything," she murmured.

He crushed his mouth down to hers in response to that powerful declaration, and she didn't resist. She opened to him, mewling out a soft sound of pleasure and surrender. Blood rushed in his ears, his heart pounded out of control, his hands shook as he dragged her against him so he could feel every inch of her body pressed to his.

He wanted her so much. He wanted to strip her bare and make love to her, to claim her. But he couldn't do that. If he did that, he would utterly destroy her, and that was wrong.

But he had to do something to mark her as his. More than that to mark himself as hers. Something to give them both pleasure. Something neither of them would forget.

He pulled away from her mouth, panting as he looked around the tight space. Along one wall was a small portable bench, perhaps something the grounds staff sat on when working on maintenance. It wasn't big, but it would do for what he desired.

He kissed her again, backing her toward the bench. When they reached it, he let her go.

"Sit down," he said softly.

She blinked at him in confusion. "Wh-why?" she asked.

He smiled. "Because I want to touch you, Celia. I want to give you such pleasure. And it will be much easier to do that if you sit down."

Celia was shaking as she slowly lowered herself onto the bench behind her. She looked up at Aiden, uncertain what to do. Uncertain what she wanted to do. When he'd come into the gazebo and interrupted her and Stenfax, she hadn't been able to read him. He'd seemed angry with her, but now…

This was something entirely different.

He dropped to his knees on the dusty floor, and she gasped. "What are you doing?"

He didn't answer verbally, but leaned in for another kiss. He'd kissed her before, but this time felt different. There was more purpose to it, more demand. Like he had been resisting before but now he couldn't anymore.

And neither could she. When he said he wanted to pleasure her, she found it was all she wanted. She wouldn't resist. She couldn't.

He continued to kiss her even as his fingers glided along her collarbone, gently teasing the sensitive flesh there. His hands glided lower, lower, until he reached the neckline of her gown.

Only then did he pull back. "I won't ruin you," he whispered. "Will you trust me?"

She blinked. Ruin had been the last thing on her mind. If he was ultimately going to marry her, ruination didn't matter. But she nodded. "Yes, I trust you, Aiden."

His eyes fluttered shut with that statement, almost as if it pained him. But then he let the flat of his palm crest over her breast and gently began to massage.

She arched immediately. No one had ever touched her like this before. Oh, she'd felt an ache in her breasts, a tingling in her nipples, but this was different. *This* was heavenly.

She let her head loll back and surrendered to the sensation as he massaged then flicked her nipple through the thin fabric of her ball gown.

"I wish I could undress you," he growled as he leaned in to kiss her collarbone, "and take my time. But we'll be missed soon, so you'll forgive me if I don't savor this more."

His hand dropped lower as he spoke, over her stomach, her hip, and eventually he began to bunch her gown up her legs. She tensed as her calves were revealed, then her knees.

She pressed a hand to his chest. "Aiden?"

He lifted his gaze to hers. "I'll stop if that's what you want, Celia. I know I *should* stop, that what I want to do is wrong. But I want you so much. I want to make you quake with pleasure. I want to give you that and more."

She could hardly breathe as his words sank into her skin and her blood and her soul. She didn't understand what he was asking to do, but the idea of it made her legs tremble. Was she willing to refuse him out of fear? Or would she be brave?

In the end, need and curiosity won out. She shifted slightly, sliding toward him so he could lift her skirt even higher. He smiled up at her as he revealed her thighs.

Leaving the skirt bunched around her hips, he pressed each hand on her knees and gently pushed, splaying her open. She leaned back against the bench to balance herself. Heat flooded her cheeks as he stared at her. She was wearing drawers, but there wasn't much protecting her most secret and womanly parts now.

He grazed her thighs with his fingertips as he moved to the slit in her drawers. She tensed as he parted it, revealing her to him at last.

"What are you going to do?" she panted, staring at his face as he stared at her body.

He glanced up at her. "I'm going to make you come," he said. "With my mouth."

Her brow wrinkled. Her knowledge on this subject was limited at best. "Come?" she murmured. "What is that?"

He chuckled as he leaned in, his dark blond head moving between her legs. "You'll see."

He touched her first, tracing her outer lips with the tips of his fingers. His touch was warm and both soothing and arousing. The tension in her was coiled, ready to explode. She felt like she was fighting in a war, trying to control a situation that was wildly out of her command now.

As if he sensed that, he slowed his movements and looked up again. "Relax, Celia. Just feel this. It's gift. I promise I won't take more than you are able to give."

She drew in a long breath, closed her eyes and somehow did as he asked. She relaxed, muscle by muscle, limb by limb. As she did so, he began to stoke her, petting her sex, smoothing her flesh. It was a rhythmic action, and she found herself tensing and relaxing along with him.

And just as she became accustomed to that act, he gently parted her outer lips and revealed her to him entirely. Her eyes flew open and she stared down at him. He was watching that place between her thighs intently, his eyes glittering in the dim light.

He touched her again, but this time it was even more intimate. He stroked the entire length of her entrance, and she cried out as sensation mobbed her. His touch tingled, it throbbed, it made her lift toward him.

He stroked again, this time with more pressure. He held her down with the opposite hand, steadying her as he stroked and stroked with his fingers. And when she was gasping for breath, gripping at the bench with her fingernails, making wordless sounds of wonder and pleasure, he touched her differently.

His thumb pressed at the top of her sex, grinding at some hidden area that jolted electric pleasure through her. She lifted hard against his steadying hand and cried out softly. What was this sensation? This pleasure unlike any she'd ever known. It was…intoxicating.

He bent his head and she felt his breath over the sensitive flesh. She watched in shock as his mouth covered her. Liquid heat flowed between them as he stroked his tongue over her gently, tasting her, teasing her. She lifted to meet the stroke, gasping for air as she gripped the edge of the bench with both hands.

He flicked his tongue quicker now, replacing his thumb on that magical place, and she moaned as the pleasure doubled, tripled, grew out of control. It was like he was pushing her toward the edge with every kiss, but she wasn't afraid. She wanted the edge. She wanted to fall and fall and fall forever.

He sucked her, and her vision blurred as her body began to quiver. Her hips jolted out of control and wave after wave of untempered pleasure worked through her. She screamed his name, she thrashed her head, she struggled for purchase as he dragged her through the massive release of the pressure he'd built with his hands and his mouth.

Finally, just when it seemed like she might die from pleasure, her body slowed, the twitching ceased and he lifted his head to look at her.

He smiled, licking his lips as he smoothed her drawers shut, lowered her skirt. When she was fixed, he leaned up and kissed her. She tasted a sweet and earthy flavor on his lips. Her flavor.

"*That* was making you come," he whispered as he drew back.

She nodded shakily. "I-I see."

"I should be sorry I did something so bold," he continued as he got to his feet and dusted himself off. "But I'm not. I hope you feel the same."

She stared up at him. She could see the outline of his erection through his trousers—she knew he wanted to take her. She found she wanted that too. Oh, the release, coming, as he put it, had been wonderful, of course. But she felt *incomplete* somehow. As if she'd missed something.

"I do," she choked out.

He reached down, offering his hand. She was shaking as she took it. He drew her in, kissing her once more. He held her there, his arms around her, for what felt like an eternity. He looked into her eyes, seeking...she wasn't certain what. Then he released her.

"Come, we should return to the house. We'll be missed soon if we weren't already."

She nodded and let him lead her from the dark, secret outbuilding and back toward the brightly lit ballroom. Only as they neared the others, she wished she could hold back. Stay with him and only him.

She wished she could find a way to never let this night end.

Celia sat in Gray's carriage, watching as her brother-in-law helped Rosalinde into her place. He leaned into the door and smiled. "I see Stenfax getting ready to depart. Let me speak to him a moment, will you?"

Rosalinde nodded and Gray backed away, leaving the

sisters alone.

"The ball went well, I think," Rosalinde said, turning her attention back to Celia.

Celia blinked and forced herself to smile. The last hour of the ball she'd been fighting distraction as she thought of all the pleasures she'd shared with Aiden outside.

"Y-yes," she stammered. "It was a...a fine evening, indeed."

Rosalinde wrinkled her brow. "I received several congratulations on your being courted by the Duke of Clairemont, so it seems news of that development is traveling fast."

Celia nodded. "Yes, it seems so."

"I was sorry he left early," Rosalinde continued. "An ache in his head, he told Gray."

Celia pressed her lips together. She had no response to that. Aiden had slipped away without even a goodbye very soon after they returned. It was troubling.

"Where did you go?"

Celia swallowed hard at the question. "Go?" she repeated.

Rosalinde nodded. "You went outside at some point and I didn't see you for what felt like a while. Where did you go?"

"I was..." She trailed off as she tried to force calm. "I went to get air and bumped into first Stenfax, then Aiden."

Rosalinde's eyes went slightly wider. "There is an interesting combination. The former fiancé and the potential future one. They got along?"

"As well as can be expected. I explained to Aiden that there was nothing between Stenfax and I. Afterward we...we took a walk in the garden together."

Rosalinde, who had been examining a loose thread on her gown, now jerked her head up. She stared at Celia. "A walk in the garden," she repeated, accentuating each word.

Panic blasted through Celia as she straightened. "Yes."

Rosalinde bit her lip. "Celia—" she began.

But before she could finish her sentence, Gray climbed into

the carriage and took his place next to her, grabbing her hand as the footman closed the door and they began to move.

Celia had never been so happy to see Gray as she was in that moment. He smiled at the two women, and as he and Rosalinde began to talk, Celia settled back against the carriage seat.

Her mind wandered once more to those moments when Aiden had pleasured her so thoroughly. She'd heard the basics of what to expect when a man made love to her, but she'd never understood any of it until now.

Now that she'd experienced that thrilling sensation of buildup and release, she knew why women would risk it all for a night with a man. Why Rosalinde had surrendered to Gray even when they were enemies all those months ago.

She understood it all. But she had no idea what to do next. Something held Aiden back from fully committing to her, and that hurt her. But in many ways, it seemed her future was at last secure. Aiden wanted her, he was courting her, they would be together in the end. She would work hard to overcome those walls between them, and hopefully one day he would fall in love with her as she had fallen in love with him.

And with that more secure future, she did have one decision in mind to make. One thing she *could* do.

She glanced at Rosalinde. Her sister was staring at her, even as she talked to Gray. Rosalinde wouldn't approve.

But that wasn't going to stop Celia.

CHAPTER FOURTEEN

Celia hadn't been in her grandfather's home since the previous October, and yet when she stepped into the parlor to await his entrance the place felt exactly the same. Cold. Unwelcoming.

Exactly like the man who owned it.

She would never forget the surprise and near horror on his butler's face when he opened the door to find her there. When he learned she was unchaperoned, it was even worse.

"Are you *certain* you want me to see if he's in, Miss Fitzgilbert?" the older man asked.

She hesitated. The last time she'd seen her grandfather, he had been bent over Rosalinde, trying to choke the life out of her because she was attempting to break up Celia's engagement. Only Gray's swift and violent intervention had saved the day.

Celia would have no such guard today. And it was only the fact that she had what she believed Mr. Fitzgilbert might see as good news that she believed he would not strike out just the same way at her.

"Thank you, Cranston, but yes. Please do see if he'll receive me."

The butler nodded and stepped out, leaving her alone to ponder the prudence of her actions. She didn't have long, however, for within moments her grandfather entered the chamber.

She caught her breath when she saw him. In the months she

had been safely in the care of Gray and Rosalinde, her grandfather had clearly declined. He was thinner by at least a stone and a half, perhaps even two, and his shock of white hair was beginning to thin. His nose was crooked now where Gray had broken it months before. But his blue eyes, the ones she and Rosalinde had each inherited, were just as sharp as they had ever been. They focused squarely on her as he closed the door behind himself.

"I called Cranston a liar when he said you'd shown up here," he said. "Struck him across his bloody face."

She swallowed hard at that statement. "Well, you can see he was not lying, for I am here, Grandfather."

He looked her up and down with a sniff and then moved to the sideboard to pour a drink. "Without a chaperone, he said."

Celia pursed her lips. "I knew Gray and Rosalinde wouldn't approve of my coming here, so I...I pretended a headache, then snuck out and walked. Your home is only half a mile from theirs through good neighborhoods."

He faced her with a grin. "Are you not afraid your sister will put you out if she hears you broke her embargo and came to see me?"

Celia folded her arms. "Rosalinde would *never* put me out. She is not like *you*, sir."

"No, she isn't like me," he grunted. "*You* were always closer."

She turned her face as if his words slapped her, and in a way they did. The last thing she would ever want to be in this world was anything like Gregory Fitzgilbert. He was cold, calculating, unfeeling, cruel, along with a dozen other worse adjectives.

"So you snuck out of Grayson Danford's pitiful little manor and came crawling back to me," Mr. Fitzgilbert mused as he took a seat and stared up at her. He took a swig of his drink. "What do you want?"

He had not invited her to join him, but Celia sat anyway. She took a long, deep breath and met his stare evenly, although it was hard to do so. It was like looking into the eyes of a reptile.

A dangerous one at that.

"I am certain you must have heard that I am now being courted by the Duke of Clairemont," she said, in no mood to dance around the subject with him. The sooner she did this, the sooner she could leave.

His jaw set and his grip tightened on his glass, forcing her to tense in preparation for the storm that might follow. "Did you come here to brag, Celia?"

She shook her head. "No. There would be no point in that. I did not accept his suit because of you, nor to spite you. But you once wished me to marry a title, didn't you? You made a devil's bargain for me to do just that not a year ago." She drew in a deep breath. "Would that deal still stand?"

He pushed to his feet, and she flinched as he stalked around her to pace the room. He pivoted to look at her again, his smile predatory and smug. "You are talking about the bargain we struck that you would marry a title and I would tell you who your real father is."

"I assume you won't tell me out of the goodness of your heart," she whispered.

He stared at her a long moment and then tilted his head back for a laugh. "Why would I give away my leverage? I assume that means Rosalinde's husband has been unsuccessful in his searches for the man who all but stole your mother and saddled her with two children out of wedlock."

She shut her eyes at the cruelty of his description. In truth, her mother had fled this man's cold and angry household with a servant. No, she had never married the father of her children, but there was every reason to believe that their lack of vows had been a way to protect Celia's mother from being found by Fitzgilbert.

When she died, Fitzgilbert had swept in, stealing the children and telling them their father had died too. But since Celia had found out the truth, that the man lived, she'd hardly stopped thinking of him. Knowing he was out there somewhere, it felt like a hole in her heart. A hole that could only be filled with the truth her grandfather kept in his pocket like a miser with gold.

"Answer me," he said, his tone harsh.

Celia opened her eyes and stared at him evenly, praying her fear and loathing of him wasn't written all over her face. "Gray has not been successful," she said through her grinding teeth. "Your habit of abusing and discarding servants without reference has paid off. No one we've found can give us the information we seek. No one but you."

He chuckled but said nothing.

Her eyes narrowed. "I know that is exactly what you want to hear, so you may crow about it. But I am not here for you to celebrate your victory any more than I am to celebrate my own. I'm here to talk to you about the bargain. So I ask you again…if I marry this duke, if I take on the highest title I can obtain without catching a prince…will you honor your earlier promise to reveal our father's identity to me?"

Fitzgilbert rubbed his chin, pondering her request. "I have my doubts your bitch of a sister would agree to those terms."

Celia fisted her hands at her sides and swallowed back her defense of Rosalinde. "It isn't a deal between you and my sister. It's a deal between you and me."

He laughed. "How wonderful, so you will lie to her?"

"I will omit," Celia whispered, blinking back the tears that stung her eyes at the thought of such a betrayal. "It won't be entirely the same."

"As you wish, if it helps you sleep at night," Fitzgilbert chuckled. "And what of your *duke*? Would he be willing to offer me anything in the realm of influence, access?"

Celia held her breath. Clairemont had been out of Society so long, she wasn't certain he would hold as much sway as someone like Stenfax had, even if he was more elevated by his title. But she nodded regardless.

"I am sure I could soften him to you and your desires," she said.

Fitzgilbert returned to his seat across from her and set his drink aside, crossing his legs and steepling his fingers over his knee before he smiled at her. "And tell me, my dear, does he know you are a bastard?"

Heat flooded her cheeks both at his cruel question and at the answer she would be forced to give. An answer that burned within her the closer she got to Aiden.

"No," she admitted, her voice cracking.

Fitzgilbert's grin grew wider. Uglier. "And you and Rosalinde call *me* the mercenary. Good, Celia. Very good. You must keep him in the dark, for no duke would want you if he knew the truth. And it is only a duke that will do now that you have struck this bargain. If you fail in landing this one, don't think to come back to me with another earl or a marquess and expect that I will ever tell you a damn thing about your father. Am I making myself perfectly clear?"

She sucked in a broken breath. "Yes. Then do you accept the bargain? A duke for the truth?"

"Yes." He held out a hand. "Shall we shake on it?"

She stared at his offering and instead stood and moved away from him. "No need. I know how your bargains work, Grandfather."

He stood with her. "Of course you do. Now run along. I tire of your presence and *you* have much work to do. Don't fail me this time."

He pointed toward the door and she held her shoulders back as she trudged before it, trying to maintain as much dignity as she could. But in truth there was almost none to be had.

She had made a bargain with a demon. She had offered to trade Aiden for what her grandfather possessed.

She moved to the door and walked out into the sunshine, but there was no pleasure to be found in the warmth of the spring day. She took in big gulps of breath to clear her lungs of her grandfather's presence, but there was little use. He was in her mind now, and no amount of fresh air or clean water or distance could get him out.

She walked out onto the street and staggered blindly toward

her home. He'd said she was like him. And wasn't it true? If she was willing to lie to Rosalinde and to use Aiden to get what she wanted, wasn't she *exactly* like him?

She was about to turn down the next street when a carriage suddenly pulled up next to her. The door opened and she turned toward it. To her surprise, Aiden sat there, his eyes wide with astonishment.

"Celia?" he asked. "Are you…are you *alone?*"

She shifted, still reeling from her encounter with her grandfather. "I—yes," she admitted.

His lips pursed and he held out a hand. "Get in, please."

He said please, but there was no doubt he was ordering her to do so, not asking. She was too numb to argue and took his hand. He helped her into the carriage and a footman hopped down from the back to shut the door.

"Where to, Your Grace?" the young man asked.

Aiden stared at her, his gray gaze even and unwavering. "Drive around the block a dozen times, then ask me again," he ordered.

The servant nodded at the order, then shut the door. After a moment, they began to move. Only then did Aiden reach out to take both her hands.

He frowned. "You are cold as ice, Celia. What in the world were you doing?"

She swallowed. Her encounter with her grandfather was difficult enough, but now to sit face to face with the man she'd offered to betray for her own purposes? That was impossible.

"I needed air," she lied. "Just a walk."

He arched a brow. "Alone? Without Rosalinde or your maid to accompany you?"

She shrugged one shoulder. "I didn't want to trouble them."

His brows lifted and she could see he recognized she was lying. Of course he would. After all, he had always been capable of reading her moods. She waited for him to demand, to push, to rattle off some highhanded reasons why she should tell him the truth.

Instead, he slid to her side of the carriage and wrapped an arm around her, tucking her into his chest. She turned her face into his warmth, breathing in deep gulps of his scent and his presence. Somehow that calmed her, settling her shaking body and slowing her pounding heart. He stroked a hand over her hair gently as he held her, and she sighed.

"What do you need, Celia?" he asked, his deep voice reverberating through her.

She lifted her face toward his and froze. His mouth was just inches from hers, so close that his breath stirred her lips. She kissed him softly.

He made a low sound in his chest and his arms tightened around her. He tilted his head and claimed her lips with more fervor. She fisted the lapels of his jacket, leaning up into him as she opened her mouth to his touch, his taste, the feel of him.

And his kiss did what nothing else could. Thoughts of her bargain with her grandfather, her self-loathing that she might be anything like him, faded away. Left behind was just the simply throbbing need for this man. For the pleasure he'd already given her, for the pleasure she wanted even more of.

"Will you—" she whispered as she pulled back a fraction. Heat flooded her cheeks and she tried to duck her head, but he slid a finger beneath her chin and didn't allow it.

"What?" he said, his voice so low it barely carried.

"Touch me." Her voice broke. "Just touch me and make me feel good for a moment. That's what I want. *Need*."

His pupils dilated and he cleared his throat, looking around with his lips pursed. He was silent so long that she began to believe he wasn't going to answer.

"Are you trying to find a way to refuse?" she asked.

He shook his head. "No, I'm doing a math problem in my head. I told them to circle the block twelve times, we've gone around one and a half by my reckoning. If he stays at this rate then—"

She cut him off by sliding her hands up to his cheeks and drawing him in for another kiss. This time she took control, pressing her tongue between his lips, silencing any further words he might have said. It seemed to have worked, for he let out a long sigh before he drew back.

He locked gazes with her as he lifted a big hand to her breast. She gasped as he cupped her there, sliding his thumb back and forth over the nipple that hardened beneath her chemise and gown. He'd done this before, at the ball the night before. Now she wished they could do it without the constriction of clothing. She wanted to feel his touch skin to skin and melt with him like she was meant to do.

Just as her breath came short, he lowered that same hand, gliding his fingers down the apex of her body until he nudged her legs apart, settling his hand down against her skirts, between her thighs, where her sex pulsed in need.

"Normally I would try to be more artful in this," he explained, his tone clipped and filled with tension. "But we are short on time and I want to make sure you find...relief."

"That I come," she said, using that word he'd used the night before.

He let out a curse beneath his breath. "Yes, that you come."

"You could make me come like this?" she asked, and let out a soft moan as he began to move his hand against her. Even through her clothing, the question was answered.

"I could make you come in half a dozen ways," he growled. "How I'd like to explore each and every one of them. But for now..."

He ground the heel of his palm against her, and her body naturally lifted into him. She closed her eyes, letting sensation take over. She felt him watching her, heard his breath grow heavy as her moans echoed around them. It was amazing how quickly he could mold her body to his desires. A few strokes of his hand and the pleasure mounted, sending out tendrils through her entire being, making her reach and reach for sensations she was only beginning to understand.

"Come," he whispered against her ear. "Let go, Celia. I'll catch you."

She squeezed her eyes shut and her body began to convulse out of control as wave after wave of intense, heated pleasure ricocheted through her. She rode out the sensations, whispering his name, letting go of any fear or unpleasantness she had just experienced as she sagged against him in sated bliss.

He lifted his hand away from her and gently repositioned her skirts before he pressed a kiss to her temple and wrapped his arms around her.

"I could watch you do that all day. A thousand times."

She opened her eyes and smiled into the dimness. "And yet you have not had your pleasure yet. Will there come a time when I get to reciprocate?"

He made a low sound and shook his head. "Are you trying to kill me with those words? I promise you, Celia, I take a great deal of pleasure in this."

"But it isn't the same," she murmured, turning her face toward his.

He frowned, but was saved from replying when the carriage slowed. He kissed her once more, then moved back to his side of the vehicle. After a moment, the door opened and the footman poked his head inside.

"Where would you like to go now, Your Grace?"

Aiden looked at her, his gray gaze holding hers. "To the servants' entrance at Grayson Danford's home."

The young man nodded, and once again they were left alone. Celia's eyes went wide. Aiden had caught her in what could easily be seen as a compromising position. Ladies of her rank were not meant to go roaming the city streets without a chaperone. It was well within his rights to take her straight back to her sister and tell all. He would even be able to say it was for her own good.

"Why are you looking at me like I sprouted a second head?" Aiden asked with a chuckle.

Celia swallowed hard. "I was just trying to figure out why you would help me sneak back into the house without my sister knowing what I'd done."

He held her stare for a moment, then shrugged. "I assume that when you are ready to tell me what you were doing today, you will. Until then, you have the right to your own counsel. Though I will say that what you did could have been dangerous. Next time you want to sneak out, send word for me and I'll arrange it."

She wrinkled her brow. What he was saying was that he was willing to be her partner in crime. "You would do that?"

"Yes, and I wouldn't betray you by involving anyone you didn't wish, Celia."

Her stomach dropped. That vow not to betray her cut her to the bone. She had just done exactly the opposite with her grandfather. She'd already kept secrets from this man about her lineage. She'd promised Fitzgilbert that she'd keep doing that. That she'd use Aiden for her grandfather's self-serving purposes.

The carriage stopped in the alleyway behind Gray's home and there was a shuffling as the servants moved to open the door. Before they did, she reached across to slide her hand down Aiden's cheek.

"Thank you," she whispered. "Seeing you made today far better."

He smiled, and it changed the entire appearance of his face. She realized then how rare that expression was. But it made him look so much younger, so much less serious. How she longed to put that expression on his face daily and for the rest of their lives. But could she do that if she began that future with such deception?

"You will likely have a letter from me waiting for you. And tomorrow I am to call on you," he said. "I look forward to it."

She nodded as the servant opened the door and offered her a hand out. She turned and gave Aiden one last look. "Tomorrow," she said, and lifted her hand to wave.

He did the same, and she turned away, walking to the house. Her mind spun as she did so. She'd just done everything she could to obtain her grandfather's help, and now she was torn apart by the promises she'd made.

But Aiden would be there tomorrow. And by tomorrow she had to decide if she intended to follow the path she'd started with her grandfather.

Or if she might try a new path. One that took her toward the man she loved, but perhaps away from the father she so desperately wanted to meet.

CHAPTER FIFTEEN

Clairemont sat in Danford's parlor the next afternoon, waiting again for Celia to enter. He'd done this several times now, and yet this time felt different.

Yesterday had made *everything* different.

He'd been going from a meeting with Stalwood back to his townhouse when he saw her walking up the street. He had been shocked. Ladies did not roam about London unchaperoned. Even in good parts of the city, it was *not* done. Once he ordered his carriage to stop and verified it was indeed Celia, there had been no hesitation in what to do next.

He had to be certain she was all right.

He'd become accustomed to the loveliness of her face, but he'd never fully grasped what made her expression so appealing. But it was her light. There was a joy in Celia that bubbled just below the surface, bringing a brightness that flowed from within and warmed his cold and empty world.

But yesterday, when she climbed into his carriage, that light within her had been extinguished, replaced by a sadness and upset that made his stomach turn. He'd been desperate to heal her, help her, save her.

Of course, she had denied him that ability. She hadn't been ready to share whatever had caused her odd behavior. But he was a spy, and it hadn't taken much more than a flick of his wrist to find out that the place where he'd first seen her was just a stone's throw from the home of her estranged grandfather.

What was she doing with Gregory Fitzgilbert?

It couldn't be anything good, since she'd hidden it from her sister, hidden it from him. He'd searched far and wide for a reason for their estrangement, but a fight between Danford and Fitzgilbert at the time of Celia's broken engagement with Stenfax was the only information he could find.

Still, his intuition pricked. And he wanted so much to be able to help Celia.

The door to the parlor opened and Celia entered with Rosalinde trailing behind. Clairemont frowned. With her sister in the room, there was no way Celia would reveal anything to him.

"Good afternoon," Rosalinde said, smiling as Celia moved past her to sit on the settee. "I'm afraid I will not be a very good hostess, as I have a matter to resolve with the staff. But I shall return to you in…" She cast a quick glance at Celia, who was perched on the edge of the settee. Her expression was serene enough, but Clairemont could feel the tension rolling off of her.

Apparently, so could Rosalinde, for she shot him a meaningful look and said, "I shall return in half an hour, perhaps a bit longer."

His eyes widened. While he had heard that sometimes engaged couples were allowed periods to be alone, this was unprecedented. And judging from Rosalinde's face, it was brought about by Celia's distracted and unhappy demeanor.

"Thank you, Mrs. Danford," Clairemont said.

She nodded and slipped from the room, pulling the door almost entirely closed behind herself, yet another breach of conduct that Clairemont couldn't help to read volumes into. He pushed it aside, though, and turned his attention on Celia. Her gaze was focused on her clenched hands in her lap.

Slowly, he moved to sit next to her on the settee. He wanted desperately to touch her, but he held back, giving her a little space, at least until he got a better read on her demeanor.

"How are you today, Celia?"

She lifted her gaze. "I'm better, thank you."

There was something in her tone that made him doubt that sentiment. "Does Rosalinde know of your actions?" he asked, wondering if a falling out between the sisters had caused this malaise he now saw.

She shook her head. "No."

"I don't want to press you if you are reticent to share with me, but I must ask one more thing. Does the difficulty you're encountering have anything to do with what happened between us at the ball? Or yesterday in my carriage?"

He held his breath as he pictured both encounters. God, how he had loved giving her pleasure. But it wasn't his place or his right. And if he had hurt her with his actions, he would despise himself for the rest of his days.

Celia turned toward him, lips slightly parted, and did what he would not do. She took both his hands.

"No," she whispered. "Of course not. The connection between us is…it is incredible. I regret *nothing*."

He almost slumped in relief at her words. But she was still struggling. And once again he wondered if it had something to do with the strained relationship with her grandfather.

He lifted a hand and pushed a loose lock of hair away from her cheek with the tip of his finger. "You know, I understand a little about hiding pain. About struggle. I'm here and I'm listening."

She sucked in a deep breath and her eyes widened. It seemed as though she wanted to say something, yet she couldn't start.

He smoothed his thumb over her cheek. "Your grandfather's home was near where I found you yesterday," he offered, a statement, not a question or a demand.

Her entire body stiffened, and she turned her face. "You know that?"

"I found out." He pinched his lips together. "I'm good at finding things out."

Her hands were shaking beneath his, and he squeezed gently. When he did, she let out a shudder and said, "Yes. I-I went to see him. I went to make a bargain with him."

"A bargain?" Clairemont said, his eyes narrowing. That didn't sound good. But he didn't press. This wasn't the interrogation of a criminal. He had to be gentle if he wanted her to trust him enough to open up. He continued to stroke his hands gently, rhythmically.

"Yes."

"What kind of bargain?" he asked.

She was silent for what seemed like forever, but he could read her very well. She was in pain. And how he wanted to fix it, to comfort her. To keep her from ever looking so broken again.

This was protectiveness, and it overwhelmed his senses in a way he'd never experienced before.

"Tell me, Celia," he finally pushed, but as gently as he could.

The next breath she took was more of a sob. "If I do, you may hate me."

Those words raised his hackles. Her secret had something to do with him? Did that mean she knew something about his reasons for being in London? Was he in danger? Was she?

"I can't imagine that happening," he said, keeping his tone even while his body went to alert. "Why would you think that?"

She lifted her gaze to his at last, and there were tears sparkling in her eyes. "Because I've been lying to you, Aiden. I've been lying to you since the day we met."

The first thing that shot through Celia's body and soul the moment she said those words was abject terror. Aiden was simply staring at her, his eyes wide with confusion and hesitation. The second expression cut like a knife because it drew him away from her, though he continued to hold her hands.

And yet, even as she wrestled with that pain and heartache,

there was another emotion that made itself plain: relief. She had spent twenty-four hours reliving her grandfather's claims about her. That she was like him. That she had lied and should continue to lie in order to get what she wanted.

Those words had haunted her all of last night. But by confessing, she had erased them from her soul. She *wasn't* like Gregory Fitzgilbert. She wouldn't use the man she loved, she wouldn't trap him with a version of herself that didn't truly exist.

"Celia..." Aiden's voice was rough. "I don't understand."

"I know." She drew her hands away and got to her feet. Now was the time to give him everything. To lay herself bare and hope he could still feel something for her in the end. "And Rosalinde will be back soon, so I know I must explain quickly. Do you know anything of our story? Our past?"

He shifted slightly, and she recognized the answer. Of course he had researched her. As a duke, he would want a good pedigree in his bride.

"I suppose, though, that you only know the public version of who I am, who my family is."

"The public version," he repeated slowly.

"Everyone in Society believes that while my mother was spending an extended time with her aunt, she met and married a gentleman and they swiftly had two children, Rosalinde and me. But then she and her husband died in an accident, leaving us to our grandfather's care."

Aiden nodded. "Yes, that's the story I've heard. Is there another?"

She pinched her lips together. "Oh yes. There is *that* story and then there is the truth. My grandfather was and is a horrible, horrible man. Abusive to everyone he can reach, lashing out at the simplest slight. I don't know what my mother endured, but it was enough that she fell in love and ran away with a servant from his house."

Aiden stood. "A servant?"

His tone was unreadable beyond surprise, and she watched him closely as she continued. "Yes. They fled from my grandfather and never married. Gray presumes that is because the reading of the bannes might have revealed their location to Fitzgilbert and put them in danger. So, my first confession to you is that my father was no gentleman. And the second is that I am the *bastard* daughter of no gentleman."

Aiden's face was still indecipherable. He revealed nothing, but he never looked away from her. Like he was judging every nuance, every word, every motion.

"But you said you made a bargain with your grandfather. What does that mean?" he asked.

"This leads to my third...well, it isn't a lie exactly, but a betrayal." She turned away from his focused attention and tried to keep the terror and guilt from her voice as best she could. "My sister and I grew up believing our mother and father had died together. But when I came of age, my grandfather told me the truth. My father *didn't* die in an accident. My mother died birthing me, but my father lives still."

Aiden stepped toward her. "What? Then why would he let such a bastard take you?"

She spun on him. "I don't know. He was a servant with no resources and two daughters he hadn't married to claim. My grandfather was rich and powerful and cruel. I have to hope that Fitzgilbert simply swept in and took us, leaving our father little choice but to let us go. Either way, *that* is what truly happened. My father is alive and the only person in this world that knows his true identity is my grandfather. Long ago, he promised to reveal that identity only after I...after I..."

"What, Celia, what did he require you do?" Aiden asked.

She squeezed her eyes shut to calm herself before she opened them and looked him in the eye. "After I married a title. Hence, my engagement to Stenfax. He needed my grandfather's money, I needed his title for access to the truth. And he is a good man, but I never felt anything for him."

For the first time since she began pouring her heart out to him, Aiden smiled slightly. "And the broken engagement?"

"Another fiction," Celia sighed, realizing perhaps for the

first time, just how filled with lies her life was. "Rosalinde and Gray truly *did* fall madly in love."

"Anyone with eyes can see that."

"But Stenfax and I *didn't* step aside to appease my grandfather. Exactly the opposite, actually. Rosalinde tried to stop our marriage because she could see I didn't love him, nor him me, and she wanted me to have a chance at happiness, *true* happiness. When she did, our grandfather viciously attacked her."

Aiden jolted. "He attacked her? Physically?"

Celia began to shake as she remembered that horrible day just a few months before. "Yes," she whispered. "He tried to choke her to death in a rage. Gray's swift action is the only reason he didn't succeed. The claim of our stepping aside for the love of Rosalinde and Gray was made to reduce the scandal caused by the spectacle."

"Because people saw the physical altercation between Danford and Fitzgilbert," Aiden mused. "I wondered what would cause such a thing. But if your grandfather threatened your sister..."

"Yes. *That* is poking a lion. Gray would die to protect her. And I can't be sorry it all happened, for it allowed my sister great happiness. Besides, the breaking of my engagement was for the best. After all, I met *you*. But I...I...still want to know who my father is."

Aiden nodded immediately, although she couldn't believe for a moment that he actually understood that drive. Not when he had been raised with family and privilege.

"Of course you do," he said. "I assume Danford has looked into that for you since you came here."

"Far and wide. Stenfax has even helped."

He stiffened, and she took a step toward him. "I assure you, we are only friends. Better friends now that we aren't to marry. But neither of them has found out anything. My grandfather wove his lies and secrets so tightly that they seem impossible to pick apart."

"You need a different instrument to do so," he murmured, almost more to himself than to her.

"What?" she asked, cocking her head.

He moved forward. "You went to him because of me," he said. "Our courtship was enough to make you think you might have new leverage with a man so greedy for a title."

Her lips parted. He said those words and they sounded even worse coming in his voice. She covered her face with both hands.

"Yes," she admitted on a broken whisper. "That is exactly what I did, Aiden. I made promises that he would have access through you, that if you and I wed that it would mean he'd have *more* power than even if I'd married Stenfax. But the moment I did it, I know how wrong it was. He said..."

She trailed off with a sob that seemed to tear at her heart it was so painful.

"What did he say?" Aiden pressed.

She swallowed past the lump of emotion in her throat. "He said I was like him, and it was true. In that moment, I was willing to trade you for Fitzgilbert's secrets, and that was unfair. Cruel. I can't do it, Aiden. So I had to tell you everything, *everything*, even though I know it will likely change your opinion of me."

She dared to look at him. His face was a mask of pain and frustration, and her stomach flipped. He *did* judge her for this, just as he should. It was evident he was shocked and horrified by everything she'd said.

"Celia," he said after what seemed like an eternity. "I'm glad you felt like you could reveal everything to me, for it helps me understand your pain. Perhaps it will even help me ease it. But as for my opinion of you, this changes nothing."

Her eyes went wide and she couldn't help but take a staggering step toward him. "It doesn't?"

"Of course not." He reached out and touched her face, tracing the line of her jaw with a fingertip. "Don't you know how much I—" He cut himself off and his body tensed. "—care for you?"

She smiled, but the fact that he'd cut himself off stung. She'd hoped he would admit he loved her, as she loved him. But care was good. Care was something. Perhaps she could love enough for both of them.

"And you don't hate me for offering you up to him?" she asked.

"Of course not." Now he cupped her face in his palm, drawing her closer. He bent his head and his lips feathered across hers.

She wrapped her arms around him, drawing him closer, letting his warmth flow around her and comfort her. His reassurance and acceptance made her so happy that she thought she could burst.

He drew back at last and tilted her face up so she was forced to look at him. His expression was intense. "Listen to me, Celia. I will use all my resources to help you."

"But Gray—"

"I'm sure Danford did his best, but he hasn't the connections I do. But you must *never* go to Fitzgilbert again, do you understand? If he was willing to physically harm your sister, I must assume you'll also be in great danger if you are alone with him. So *promise* me, Celia. Please."

She nodded slowly. "I won't. I promise."

"Good." He dropped another kiss to her lips before he drew away, leaving her cold in his wake. "Now I must go. There are things for me to do and arrange now that I fully understand the situation at hand. I'll see you again soon, though."

Celia followed him into the foyer, and they watched as Greene went to call for his horse. In the brief moment they were alone, she sidled up to him and slid her hands through his.

"Thank you," she whispered.

He looked down at her. "For what?"

"For understanding. And for taking such good care of me, though I don't deserve it."

His lips pressed together, and he whispered, "Celia, you deserve so much better than me, I assure you. Good day."

He slid his hands from hers and hurried out to his carriage, leaving her alone in the foyer. But as she watched him thunder off into the street, she felt uncertain. He had reassured her, yes, but there was something in his demeanor that made her wonder if the future she'd dared to hope for was truly out of reach

CHAPTER SIXTEEN

Clairemont swung down off his horse and climbed the stairs two by two. It took everything in him not to rip the door before him off its hinges. Instead, he knocked, though it was not gently.

A man with a black eye opened the door and he looked Clairemont up and down. "May I help you?"

"I'm here to see Mr. Fitzgilbert," he managed through clenched teeth as he handed over his card. "Tell him the Duke of Clairemont is here and that I will *not* be kept waiting."

"Yes, Your Grace," the servant said, opening the door wide. "Will you adjourn to the parlor?"

He motioned to a room to the side. Clairemont strode inside and looked around. It was a cold room, both physically and due to its lack of trinkets or portraits. Oh, there was expensive furniture, of course, but nothing to reveal the character of its owner.

Not that Clairemont needed that extra information. He already knew what a bastard his host was.

"Your Grace."

Clairemont spun to face the voice at the door, and stared. "Mr. Fitzgilbert, I presume?" he asked, surprised to find such a slight, white-haired old man awaiting him. He'd built Fitzgilbert up to be a monster in his head.

In that moment, he realized he'd actually pictured him as the man who'd raised him. But this person was *nothing* like that brute. At least not on the outside.

"The very one." There was a joviality to his tone, but it was false. Clairemont saw the greedy glitter in his eyes, the needy longing he'd sometimes seen in men on the streets who would steal or even kill to get what they want.

Of course, those men were trying to survive. This man had that look merely because he wanted to advance in Society. Which made him a monster of a different sort.

"I wasn't expecting company," Fitzgilbert said, motioning to a chair before the fire. "Especially a duke to whom I have not been officially introduced. But I welcome you here. Would you like tea? Or perhaps brandy?"

"Nothing," Clairemont said, remaining standing. He had come here with the intention to use his skills and parry with this man, but now that he was here, his emotions were taking over. He was angry, he was vengeful, he was protective in a way he'd never experienced before. He clenched his fists at his sides and fought for control as he snapped, "And you needn't pretend as though you don't know exactly why I'm here. And on whose behalf."

Fitzgilbert's face pinched, and suddenly he looked very rat-like. "If you are referring to your courtship of my granddaughter Celia, yes, I am aware of that fact. If you came to seek my approval, I give it wholeheartedly. With provisions, of course."

Clairemont folded his arms. "Oh yes, Celia told me all about your provisions."

Fitzgilbert's eyes widened and he shook his head. "Stupid, *stupid* girl. She had just one duty. One duty on this earth, and she cannot even manage that."

Clairemont reached out and, without preamble, caught Fitzgilbert by the throat. Lifting him off the ground, he growled, "Disparage Celia's intelligence again and there will be nothing left of you but a stain on your rug. Do I make myself clear?"

Fitzgilbert clawed at his hands as he wheezed out, "Yes."

Slowly Clairemont set him down and then wiped his hand on his jacket. Fitzgilbert bent over, coughing and choking for breath.

"You're as violent as Rosalinde's husband," he said, his voice strained.

Clairemont shrugged. "You should know. I've done nothing more to you than you already did to your own granddaughter."

Fitzgilbert straightened, and he seemed to have regained some composure. "Celia told you all of it, did she?"

"Every. Single. Bit," Clairemont said, moving toward him a step and enjoying how Fitzgilbert flinched back. "If *I* had been in Danford's position that day, I would have killed you where you stood for daring to lay a hand on the woman I loved. If you ever think to touch Celia, *I* will not be stopped. Is *that* clear?"

Fitzgilbert nodded. "It is. But if you've gotten all that out of your system, we are still left with an interesting quandary."

"Yes. You have information that Celia and her sister need." Clairemont shook his head. "You're going to give it to me now."

"Or what?" Fitzgilbert laughed, and it grated on Clairemont's spine. "You'll kill me? Do that and you'll never know the truth. You *need* me, Your Grace. And if you want to obtain what I have, then the deal I made with Celia is the only way to do it."

Clairemont pinched his lips. "Once we wed, you'll tell her the truth."

"And not a moment before."

He turned away. What this bastard couldn't know, what no one could know, was that he had no intention of marrying Celia. He was only masquerading as duke. The crown was giving him leeway for the investigation, but no one in the War Department would *ever* agree to let him truly wed her in the guise of Duke of Clairemont. That would leave her as duchess in the eyes of the world.

A complication that would never be accepted, even as the vision of Celia as his wife burned a hole in his chest.

"If we were engaged, why would that not be enough?" Clairemont asked, turning back. "I would make sure you had the access you require, that you would be invited and included in whatever you wished in the future."

Both of Fitzgilbert's eyebrows lifted. "And risk that the marriage won't go through? Look at Stenfax. She had him caught. Was only days away from becoming a countess, and she failed. I don't trust this will go any differently until you slip a ring on her finger. Though your moonfaced devotion to her certainly makes me think she has a better chance at success this time around."

Clairemont stiffened. He'd always been good and hiding his emotions, but before an enemy he'd just revealed himself. A dangerous prospect.

"What can I offer you to give the information now?" he asked.

"Why are you so determined?" Fitzgilbert asked. "You intend to marry her, I assume. You are publicly courting her. Why not just do the deed and let the information come as it may?" He leaned forward. "Unless you have no intention of making her your bride? Did her telling you about her father turn you from your pursuit? Haven't had the bollocks to tell her you don't want to make a bastard daughter of a no one into a duchess? Is this your attempt at softening the blow?"

The control Clairemont had been fighting for throughout the meeting now snapped in two. He cocked back his fist and swung, connecting squarely across Fitzgilbert's cheekbone and sending him staggering to the floor.

"Did I soften the blow enough?" he growled as the older man struggled to get up. "Celia's history doesn't mean a goddamned thing to me, Fitzgilbert. But I *will* have the information I seek. How much you benefit from it will be entirely up to you."

He turned on his heel and stalked from the room, from the house, without looking back. Mostly he left to keep from unleashing the street tough inside him and killing the bastard in his own parlor. But as he swung up on his horse and began to ride, all the bravado, all the anger, melted away.

What it left behind was like acid in his veins.

Celia had confessed her past to him. She had done it because she couldn't bear to lie to him, to use him to further herself. And yet he was doing exactly the same to her. Worse, in fact. His lies could destroy her in every way. His lies would ultimately break her heart, there was no way around it.

Oh, perhaps he could help her by giving her the information she sought regarding her father, but would that lessen the blow when he was gone—dead, in her eyes? Would it make his life any less empty once he was back to being John Dane or whatever character was next in the long line of false identities that punctuated his War Department career?

He knew it wouldn't. And it was all because of one fact that had become perfectly clear today: he was in love with Celia Fitzgilbert. Entirely, completely and utterly in love with her. He wanted her in his life forever, to know her in every way and to share with her all of even the darkest parts of himself. He knew by instinct that her light would heal those things.

But she wasn't in love with *him*. No, she was in love with Clairemont. A man who didn't exist. A man John Dane would tear away from her in a blinding moment of pain and destruction.

A blinding moment that would kill some part of him just as much as it killed the false Clairemont. And he would never be the same. Not when he lost her at last.

And there was not a damn thing he could do about any of it.

Celia let her fingers dance over the pianoforte keys, but she heard the stumbles in the notes and winced. It was nearly impossible to concentrate lately and her playing suffered. As did her sewing and all other activities she attempted to participate in. Even Felicity had mentioned she was distracted when they shared tea this afternoon.

But now she was alone and happy for it. At least she could pound at the keys and try not to think about the subject of all her fantasies and fears: Aiden.

It had been twenty-four hours since she confessed everything to him about her past. He had sent her flowers that morning with a short note she supposed was meant to comfort her. But it wasn't one of his longer letters and she knew she wouldn't likely be comforted entirely until she saw him next.

Until she knew if his acceptance of her confession had been true or just a kindness meant to spare her feelings.

"Which song are you playing?"

Celia jerked her gaze to the door and found Rosalinde standing there, leaning in the doorway, watching her intently.

"What do you mean?" Celia asked, setting her hands in her lap. "I didn't think I was playing so poorly that the tune was unrecognizable."

"You weren't," Rosalinde said. "It is only that midway through one chorus, you switched to a different song entirely."

Celia gasped. "I did? Gracious, I didn't even notice."

"You wouldn't," Rosalinde said. She stepped into the room and held out a hand to her sister. Celia took it and let Rosalinde guide her to the settee. "You weren't paying attention, that much was abundantly clear." Rosalinde touched her cheek. "I have stayed silent long enough, Celia, I can do it no longer. Tell me what has been troubling you these past few days."

Celia dipped her chin. She and Rosalinde were too close to keep secrets. And she needed her older sister's counsel now more than ever it seemed. So she drew a long breath.

"What do you think of Aiden?"

Rosalinde smiled slightly. "I knew it was about him. What do I think of him…well, I suppose that depends upon whether or not he has hurt you in some way."

Celia shook her head. "He hasn't. Since meeting him, he has been nothing but wonderful to me."

"Then I will tell you that I like the man. When he spends time with the three of us, I feel as though he fits into our little family group. He seems intelligent, which is good, as someone who didn't match your wit would certainly bore you no matter how handsome he was."

"That is true," Celia admitted. "Though he *is* handsome."

Rosalinde laughed. "A bonus in his favor. But he also seems kind, and that puts my mind at ease. Most importantly, he appears to care for you. I have caught him watching you from time to time when you aren't looking, and there is an expression on his face that makes me think he would work very hard to make you happy."

Celia sighed. "There is a bit of sadness in him, as well. I see it around his eyes, his mouth. He hasn't opened up to me about it, but it is there. He isn't just some spoilt duke who never understood pain."

"Then he has depth," Rosalinde said. "Of course, none of how I feel about him makes any difference. The true question is how do *you* feel?"

Celia's hands had begun to shake and she clenched them together on her lap. She was about to say those words she hadn't dared to say out loud. Once she did, they would be real. They would be dangerously real.

"I am...in love with him," she whispered. The second she said it, her heart began to pound faster, but not out of nervousness or anxiety. No, this was out of pure joy. She smiled even as tears of wonder filled her eyes. "I'm in love with him. I know it's soon."

"Sometimes it takes years to know, sometimes just one night," Rosalinde reassured her, tears in her own blue eyes. "I'm so happy, Celia. There were times I questioned if I damaged you by encouraging you to break your engagement to Stenfax last year. But to see you now makes me so happy that you gave yourself a chance at love. You deserve nothing less."

Celia's smile faded a fraction. "I'll admit that these feelings are part of my distraction the past day, but there is...more. And I must tell you because it impacts you."

Rosalinde cocked her head. "What more?"

"When Aiden was here yesterday afternoon, I-I told him the truth."

Rosalinde drew back. Celia obviously didn't have to say more. Her sister fully understood what she meant by that comment. "I see. The *whole* truth?" she asked.

Celia managed a nod. "About Grandfather and the breaking of the engagement and about our origins. That we are bastard daughters of a servant whose name we don't even know." She shook her head. "I couldn't keep it from him. To pursue anything further without telling him felt like something Grandfather would do."

"A trap," Rosalinde said softly.

"Exactly."

"And how did Clairemont take the news?" Rosalinde asked. "He left so hurriedly and I wondered why."

Celia shrugged. "He was infinitely kind. He told me that none of it mattered. He said all the right things and it was a great comfort."

Rosalinde wrinkled her brow at those words. "That should make me feel better and yet it doesn't. Do you think he didn't mean those things?"

"I'm sure he did," Celia replied. "But just because he doesn't care about my origin doesn't mean it won't damage the bond between us. There was hesitation in him when I told him, I felt it."

Rosalinde folded her arms with a sudden, dark scowl. "Did I say I liked him? I meant that I think he's callous and self-serving."

"Oh, don't," Celia said, grabbing her hand. "Please don't, Rosalinde. You *know* it's more complicated for men like that. Even Stenfax hesitated when he learned the truth, although that isn't why our engagement ended. And Aiden is a duke, the last of his line. He must think of his title, his reputation."

"I suppose," Rosalinde said with reluctance. "Though if he loves you, I would think *that* would trump all else."

Celia shifted. Aiden had not said he loved her. He *cared* for her, which felt like cold comfort, indeed. Especially when her heart was swelled with love like a creek after heavy rain.

"Perhaps it will yet," she said, pushing those hesitations aside. "He said he would assist Gray in his search."

Rosalinde's eyes went wider. "He did? I'm certain Gray would appreciate that."

Celia sighed heavily. "I want to know who our father is, Rosalinde. So much that it makes my chest ache with the wondering."

"I know, Celia. And I want so much for both of us to have those answers. But not at any cost."

Celia flinched. Her sister didn't know she'd gone to Fitzgilbert. She wasn't about to share that fact, either. She would just have to keep her promise to Aiden and hope he would be able to help her.

"Do you think we'll ever know?" Celia asked. "Or that I'll ever reach the place you've come to?"

"What do you mean?" Rosalinde asked.

"You seem at peace with it," Celia explained. "I'm not saying you don't care, but there is an acceptance in you that I cannot say I feel."

Rosalinde hesitated and seemed to be searching for words. "It *isn't* acceptance. I would dearly love to know his name, to see his face, to ask him questions and to know if we ever had his love. But...but it's different now. Since marrying Gray, my heart is more filled. It isn't that the past doesn't hurt, but I have more faith in the future. And I hope, when you marry Clairemont, that you will experience the same shift."

Celia bit her lip, reminded that Clairemont hadn't yet spoken to her of marriage despite their courtship, despite the physical intimacies they had shared. "So do I," she whispered.

"Ladies?"

Both women turned as Gray entered the room. His face was somber, though he smiled as Rosalinde got up and came across the room to kiss his cheek. He took her hand and the two of them looked at Celia.

"You overheard," Celia said.

He smiled slightly. "I did. A little. Enough. I want so much to give you and Rosalinde that information you seek."

Rosalinde squeezed his hand. "And it sounds as though you'll no longer need to do that search alone. Lord Clairemont knows and has offered to help."

Gray's eyes widened as he looked at Celia "Yes?" Celia nodded. "I see. Well, with the two of us on the case, certainly we cannot fail."

Celia couldn't help but smile. He had faith. And she had to have it to. Both in Gray and Aiden's ability to find her father, *and* in the fact that Aiden did care for her. One day it would blossom into more.

She was certain of it.

CHAPTER SEVENTEEN

Clairemont swung off his horse and checked his pocket watch. He was late. He was never late. However today, punctuality had been intruded upon by unwanted thoughts of Celia. Unwanted dreams of her that had kept him up last night, and the night before, and the night before.

It had been three days since he saw her last. He'd tried to distance himself from her, he'd even stopped writing her as he had been doing. But he was still obsessed with her and what she'd told him. With what he'd encountered when he confronted her grandfather. His mind was a jumble.

One he had to clear before he reached the top of the steps and entered Danford's house. The gentleman had called him here to discuss business and Clairemont needed to be at the top of his game. Right now he wasn't, when all he could think about is whether or not he would see Celia. And what he would say to her after a few days' absence.

The door opened as he reached the top step, revealing Danford's butler. Clairemont forced a smile so his fraud wouldn't be as evident to everyone as it was to his own rotting heart.

"Good day, Greene," he said.

"Your Grace." Greene took his gloves. "Mr. Danford is expecting you and he—"

"Thank you, Greene," Danford said as he came down the stairs and entered the parlor. "I've got him now."

"Yes, my lord," Greene said with a slight incline of his head. The butler left and Clairemont turned his false smile on Danford.

"Nice to see you, Mr. Danford."

Danford clapped him on the back. "Seems like we're to the point where you can just call me Gray. I've never much like being mistered, especially by family and friends."

Clairemont stiffened. Were they becoming *friends*? He had always actively avoided doing that. Stalwood was the closest thing he had to one.

"Certainly, if you don't mind my dispensing with the formality," Clairemont said.

Gray motioned him toward the hall. "I have a feeling soon enough we *will* be family. Might as well get a head start."

Clairemont's stomach turned, but he did not deny or confirm Gray's words. "And where is Celia today?" he asked instead.

"Out with Rosalinde. They were saying something about bonnets, I blocked it out." Gray laughed. "But I know they have every intention of coming home for tea, so if we hurry through this business, we can join them. Perhaps even take a ride around the park if you've time."

Clairemont slowed his pace. What Gray was doing was folding him into the family. Accepting him as a brother would. And damn, but it felt good. Right.

But it was an illusion and he had more important matters to attend to. "What business is that?" he asked, trying to shift into spy mode.

Gray touched the handle of a door in the hallway and shifted to partially face him. "I've been thinking a great deal about what we discussed regarding the canal terminal in Witherhshank. I discovered that Perry was in town, so I arranged for him to join us today. Might as well discuss the concerns in person, yes? It's always better that way."

He said the last words as he pressed the door open, and Clairemont froze. Perry was here? Perry, who was one of the few people who had actually met with the *real* Duke of Clairemont before his death? He and the late duke looked somewhat similar, but he doubted it would be enough to fool a friend.

And yet he had no choice. Gray took a step into the room, then turned back with a look of confusion. "Aren't you joining us, Clairemont?"

He swallowed hard, shifted his weight so he felt the pistol hidden in the waist of his trousers and the knife in his boot. Then he nodded and stepped into Gray's office.

A man stood within at the fireplace, his back to them. Quickly Clairemont took in every detail. Perry was tall, wiry. He held his weight more on the left, which could indicate he kept his own weapon on the right. His clothes were not quite as fine as those of a man with a title, but he was well enough dressed. Clearly whatever mess he was involved in paid well and he enjoyed the fruits of his treachery.

The man turned slowly. He had a long, sloped nose and a thin-lipped mouth. He rather looked like the rat he was.

He glanced past Gray and his eyes settled on Clairemont, who held his breath, waiting, waiting for the response, judging what he would do once it came. Time seemed to slow as the seconds ticked by on the clock on the mantel.

Finally, Perry's eyes narrowed. "Who the fuck is this?"

Gray took a step closer and Clairemont bit back a curse. He was between Perry and Clairemont now, in a very dangerous position.

"The Duke of Clairemont," Gray said. "Your cousin?"

Perry's face pinched further. "Hell no he ain't. Just what the hell are you two about?"

He asked the question, but as he did so, he began to shift his position. Clairemont could see the moves on the chessboard and he dove for Gray, throwing him out of the way just as Perry drew a pistol from his waistband. He fired, and Clairemont felt the whistle of the bullet as it passed by him, just cutting through the fabric of his jacket.

He lunged forward and slammed his hand against Perry's wrist. The pistol fell away, discharging once again as it hit the floor. Perry threw a punch that connected, sending Clairemont reeling backward, and for a moment, he lost his grip on the man.

But Perry seemed in no mood to fight. Instead of staying or even trying to get his fallen gun, he raced out of the room.

"Damn it!" Clairemont cried out as he regained his balance and took off after the man, Gray hard on his heels. Perry shoved Greene aside as he tore through the foyer and slammed out the door, down the stairs.

Clairemont pushed his body, shutting himself off from pain, from fear, from anything except catching this man. If Perry had a horse, he didn't wait for it, but ran into the street and across it into the park that faced Gray and Rosalinde's house.

"We're going to lose him!" Gray called out from behind.

Clairemont jolted. He's almost forgotten Gray was with him. But he needed the help so he called out, "Go west, I'll go east. We can cut him off on the lower path near the lake."

Gray didn't argue but ran in the direction Clairemont had told him to go. Perry was far out ahead and frustration grew in him. He lunged over a low wall down onto a lower path and pushed his body to its limit. But Perry turned a corner out of the park, and as Clairemont followed, he disappeared into a large crowd of people on the street, waiting for an overturned cart to be cleared.

"Shit!" Clairemont cried out, slamming a hand through his hair as he looked up and down the street. But Perry was gone. "Shit!"

Gray ran up next to him, out of breath as he gasped, "He's gone?"

Clairemont nodded. "Yes, gone. For now."

Gray turned toward him, and Clairemont shifted his focus from one danger to the next. Gray's eyes were narrowed, his jaw tight, and he fisted his hands at his sides.

"I suppose I should thank you for saving my life," Gray snapped. "But right now the only thing I can think to say to you is, just who the hell are you?"

Clairemont dipped his head. There were times when a blown cover could be explained away. This was not one of them. Gray was too clever and too protective of his family to believe anything but the truth.

"Yes, I think you deserve that answer," Clairemont conceded. "Let's go back to your home. I must send a message to…well, I must send a message."

"And once that's done, you're going to explain yourself, *Your Grace.*"

"Your coat is shredded," Gray said as Clairemont watched him pace around the parlor fifteen minutes later. His message to Stalwood had been sent, he was certain it wouldn't be long before his superior rushed here.

He wasn't looking forward to anything about to come.

He glanced down at his coat and saw the damage to the fabric where Perry's first bullet had ripped through. "Yes."

"Are you injured?" Gray asked.

Clairemont wrinkled his brow. He hadn't thought Gray would give a damn considering everything that had happened. Slowly Clairemont shrugged out the coat, pushed the rip in his shirt beneath open and looked. There was a thin line of blood on his left bicep where the bullet had just danced along the skin.

"It's not bad. I've had worse," he said.

Gray said nothing, but turned to the sideboard and poured a hefty glass of scotch. He returned and handed it to Clairemont. "For the wound. Or for your courage. Whichever needs it more."

Clairemont dug into his pocket for a handkerchief and dipped it in the glass. He slugged back the remaining liquid before he rubbed the fiery alcohol across the cut. It was like rubbing salt in the wound and he sucked air through his teeth.

"Bloody hell, that hurts."

Gray glared at him. "Good. Now explain yourself."

Clairemont shut his eyes briefly. There was no avoiding this, not anymore. The ship had sailed on his lies, on his deception, on whatever bright little life he'd briefly allowed himself to have as Aiden, Duke of Clairemont. Now the pain was here.

Pain he had hoped to avoid for a little while longer. For Celia's sake more than his own.

"I'm not even sure where to start," he said. "Or how to make you understand."

"I have a feeling there is no way I'm going to understand," Gray spat, and poured himself a drink. He clutched it in his hand tightly. "But try, if you are capable of doing anything but lying."

Clairemont flinched. Lying was part of his game. Part of how he stayed alive. He'd never wished to be worse at it than now.

"You know the first part," he said. "I am not the Duke of Clairemont."

At the parlor door there was a loud sound. Clairemont leapt to his feet and both he and Gray faced the door. There, standing in the entrance, a hatbox at her feet where she had dropped it, stood Celia. Rosalinde stood behind her. But Clairemont only saw Celia. He saw the pain on her face. The confusion.

He hated himself for it.

"What do you mean, Aiden?" she asked, all the blood draining from her face. "What do you mean you aren't the Duke of Clairemont?"

CHAPTER EIGHTEEN

Celia stared at Aiden, waiting for his answer, waiting for him to say anything at all in response to her question. But it was Gray who stepped forward, not the man she loved.

"Celia, Rosalinde," he said slowly. "It's all right. I promise I'll *make* it all right somehow."

"Is that blood?" Rosalinde cried out.

Celia jerked her gaze from Aiden's face to his arm, where her sister pointed. She gasped as she moved toward him, forgetting for the moment everything except for the fact that he was hurt. He stepped back before he recovered the wound with his handkerchief.

"I was shot at. He stepped in the way and saved my life," Gray said.

Rosalinde made a soft sound of terror in her throat and flew across the room to her husband. "Shot at, Gray? What in the world? Are you injured? Who would do this? Why?" Rosalinde burst out, smoothing her hands over his face, his shoulders, as if to reassure herself that he was well.

How Celia wished to do the same to Aiden, but she didn't move again. She just stared at him, waiting for him to say something, anything. But he just looked at her, his expression dark and sorry.

"That's a lot to cover," Gray said softly, taking Rosalinde's hands. "I'm not injured."

Rosalinde spun on Aiden. "If you saved my husband, I'm

in your debt."

"No, you aren't," Aiden finally said, his voice strained. "I'm the reason he was shot at."

Celia's hands began to shake and she clenched them at her sides. "Enough of this. Answer my question. If you aren't the Duke of Clairemont, who are you?"

He bent his head, and there was such a look of pain and defeat on his handsome face that Celia longed to move on him, to wrap her arms around him, to smooth the lines from his face. But even though she didn't understand what was going on at all, she instinctively recognized that time was over. Whatever Aiden was going to say, it would destroy everything she'd hoped for. She didn't feel like she could draw full breath anymore.

"I'm sorry," he said, his voice soft in the quiet room. He lifted his gaze and met hers evenly. "It is complicated. I work for the War Department."

Celia shook her head. That meant very little to her. Was Aiden a soldier?

Gray moved toward him, eyes wide. "You're a spy," he said.

"For the crown," Aiden verified, his gaze still on Celia. "My mission had to do with the real Duke of Clairemont. I came to London to masquerade as him."

The room around Celia began to spin and she staggered on her feet. Aiden moved toward her, but Rosalinde rushed past, glaring at him as she caught Celia by the waist and silently guided her to the settee. Celia sank down there, covering her face with both hands as she focused on breathing. If this was a dream, she had to wake up.

But when she pinched herself, nothing happened.

"You owe us a great deal more explanation than *that*," Rosalinde spat. Her anger was clear in her voice even if Celia didn't lift her head to look at her sister.

"You lied," Celia moaned into her hands. "You *lied* to me."

"I did." There was something in his even tone that made her look up. She found him staring at her evenly, all the pain on his face seeming very real. "I know you have *no* reason to believe me now, but I hated every moment I was forced to do so. I had no choice thanks to my case."

"*What case?*" Gray asked, stepping toward Aiden.

Celia recognized the way his posture went on alert. She'd seen it before, but now she understood it better. He was preparing to fight. Gray didn't seem to care.

"Where is the *real* Clairemont?" Gray continued. "And why go to these depths, coming into our home and starting this courtship with Celia? Certainly that could have nothing to do with a case—it was only cruelty."

Aiden flinched, and for a brief second, his eyes fluttered shut, like he was trying to find some control over his emotions. Then he looked right at her again and said, "The real Duke of Clairemont is...he's dead."

Celia let out a low sob that was so loud and mournful it surprised even her. She swallowed hard past the bile that had risen in her throat and prayed she wouldn't proceed to be sick on her brother-in-law's office rug in front of the man she loved.

Or was he the man she loved? He looked like him, but now he was telling her he was a lie, nothing but a lie. That everything he'd said or done was a lie.

"Clairemont," came a hard voice from the door.

Everyone turned. There was a tall, thin, older man standing there, Gray's butler behind him. Celia recognized him as the Earl of Stalwood. He was a distinguished member of Society. And he was staring evenly at Aiden.

Aiden almost sagged in relief. "I had hoped you would be at home when my message arrived."

Stalwood jerked out a nod as the butler left them in privacy. He reached behind himself to tug the door shut. "Just barely." He glanced around the room, looking at each of them, and then he frowned deeply. He faced Aiden, their eyes met and a world of communication flowed between them before he said, "Report."

Aiden straightened up, his shoulders coming back, his tone

becoming clipped and precise as he said, "Perry was here, he recognized I wasn't Clairemont. Shot at Danford. He escaped after a foot chase through the park."

Gray moved forward. "Do either of you want to bloody well explain what the ever loving *fuck* is going on?"

Celia flinched at the redness of her brother-in-law's face and the harsh language she knew he would never normally use in front of her or even Rosalinde.

"You don't have to do this," Aiden said softly, his gaze on Stalwood. "You've never broken cover before."

"This case is not average, though, is it? It's more complicated, and I think, this is the best path. For the case. And for *you*."

Aiden's mouth thinned, and it was clear he was struggling even though Celia didn't understand why. Finally, he waved a hand as if in surrender and turned away.

"I'm sorry, Mr. Danford," Stalwood said, turning toward Gray with an incline of his head. "Clearly you have some information now that Clairemont's identity has been broken. That is why I've come. It's the same reason why I'm going to tell you now what very few know. I work for the War Department, as well."

"He's my handler," Aiden said softly. "He assigns and manages cases for me and several others."

Gray stepped back. He expression was bright with shock. "And are you truly the Earl of Stalwood or did you two kill *him*, as well?"

Stalwood frowned. "I *am* the Earl of Stalwood and no one from our department killed the duke, I assure you." He shifted and looked at Rosalinde and Celia. "Perhaps the ladies should step out."

Celia moved on him, her hands clenched at her sides. "I'm not going anywhere, my lord. You and this...this *man* engaged in a subterfuge that involved me more than anyone else. I have every right to hear the details as much as Gray does."

Gray folded his arms. "I agree. Celia stays if that is what

she desires."

She shot him a look of gratitude even as she reached back to find Rosalinde's hand. When her sister's fingers laced through hers, she drew a long, deep breath. "Now, Lord Stalwood, you and Aiden…Clairemont…whoever he is…you owe all of us the whole truth. Please start telling us now."

Clairemont stared at Celia, taking in the way she lifted her chin in defiance, how she held herself with such strength when he could see the tears sparkling in her eyes. He had never loved her more than in this moment, where she stood toe to toe with a wall of lies and deceptions and faced it down like a warrior woman.

Of course, he was also keenly aware that her tears had been caused by him and only him.

Stalwood cleared his throat and drew Clairemont's attention back to him. He had never expected his superior to reveal himself. But he was keenly aware that Stalwood was doing it for him, because of their long and personal relationship. He recognized the power of that and appreciated Stalwood's attempts to help him, even if he feared they would be fruitless.

"Very well, Miss Fitzgilbert," Stalwood said, "if your guardians believe you should be here, I won't dare to argue. First, let me restate that no one in my department killed the Duke of Clairemont. He was bludgeoned to death by an unknown party."

Celia flinched and Clairemont longed to go to her. To take the hand that held Rosalinde's and pull her in, soothe her. But she refused to look at him. It was like he wasn't there at all. She took her strength from her sister now. She no longer wanted him.

"Of course, we had to investigate," Stalwood said, and Clairemont forced his attention back to the very important matters at hand.

He wasn't surprised that Stalwood was giving Danford all the information now that he'd started down that path. They no longer suspected him, and since Gray already knew part of the truth, it was better to give him all and hope he would become an ally. Though judging from Gray's angry expression, Clairemont wasn't certain that was possible.

"Wouldn't that normally be the purveyance of the guard rather than the Department of *War*?" Gray asked, his voice still hard as steel.

Stalwood inclined his head slightly. "Perhaps under normal circumstances. These were not. What I am about to tell you must never leave this room. Not only was the Duke of Clairemont an important member of Society, but he was…let us say…involved in some damning activities that had attracted our interest for some time."

"You think the *real* Duke of Clairemont was involved in some kind of treason?" Rosalinde asked, her voice catching.

Clairemont shook his head and forced himself to speak. "Not think. *Know*."

"Then why not simply arrest him?" Gray snapped. "That could have saved everyone the pain that has been caused by your subterfuge."

Gray shot a glance at Celia, and Clairemont gritted his teeth. His whole body hurt from the tension and self-loathing pumping through him.

Stalwood came to his rescue by replying, "We were aware of him for some time, but couldn't directly tie him to his suspicions or get close enough to stop him. But it seems someone he was working with killed him. We didn't know who, but his vast correspondence gave us a great many suspects."

Gray stepped back. "His vast correspondence?" he repeated. "You mean with me?"

Stalwood nodded. "With you and some others, Mr. Danford."

"You suspected *my husband*?" Rosalinde asked, her tone filled with outrage. "The man would no sooner consider treason than he would think to cut off his own arm. He is working to *further* the Empire, not damage it. How dare you?"

Gray smiled softly at her. "I appreciate the defense, my love, and all you say is true." He turned his gaze on Clairemont. "But I suppose you had to explore all options. And do you *still* suspect me?"

"No," Clairemont said firmly, happy at least to be able to say that. It was the only place where he hadn't betrayed this family entirely. "After connecting with you and some deeper investigation, it became clear that you weren't involved in the schemes. However, we don't rule out that Clairemont and men like Perry were using your enterprises to manipulate and plot against king and country."

Celia slowly stood. She looked toward Clairemont but didn't meet his gaze.

"*That's* why you got close to me," she whispered.

"Oh, Celia," Rosalinde breathed.

Celia shook her off. "You needed to investigate Gray, and a courtship with me would put you in the middle of his home. I was merely a conduit by which to insert yourself."

She said the words so coldly that Clairemont had to physically restrain himself so he wouldn't turn away from her words and her demeanor. "Celia—" he whispered.

Stalwood stepped forward. "Miss Fitzgilbert, let me explain something. This man is my best agent. He has saved the lives of hundreds of men and women, both in the field and here at home either through direct or indirect action. He is a hero."

Clairemont dipped his head, loving the man for trying, but knowing he didn't deserve such praise. Especially now.

"That is well and good, but you will not convince me that manipulating my sister is an act of heroism," Rosalinde said with a glare that could have frozen Stalwood's heart.

Stalwood ignored her. His focus was still on Celia. "When the idea of courting you to further our motives came up, I assure you, he was entirely against the idea. *I* insisted."

Celia's jaw worked, like she was digesting that idea. But

still she didn't look at Clairemont. "Why?" she asked.

Stalwood folded his arms. "As you suggested, it was in order to get closer to Danford, yes. But also because the return of the Duke of Clairemont to Society caused a bit more of a stir than we anticipated it would. All eyes were suddenly on him, the attention so intense that it kept him from being able to fade into the background easily."

"And if he chose someone to court…" She swallowed. "*Me* to court, attentions would move elsewhere. Aiden would no longer be a catch."

"Yes." Stalwood tilted his head. "Miss Fitzgilbert, I apologize on behalf of the Empire for the pain that this has caused you. But I assure you, no one went into this lightly, nor without great dismay."

"Do you really think Perry and Clairemont were using my business, my canals, to work against the Empire?" Gray asked.

Clairemont nodded. "We have a great deal of circumstantial evidence to show it. And Perry's actions today all but confirm it to be true. They insisted on moving the terminal port of your ferry to Withershank, yes?"

"A questionable decision you and I discussed," Gray conceded.

Clairemont shrugged. "Not questionable if you intend to take over the town and divert goods and whatever else you're moving through the canals to the enemy."

Gray gritted his teeth. "Do you think Perry is the one who killed Clairemont?"

Clairemont considered the question and all he'd seen that afternoon. "No, he seemed genuinely surprised when he saw me and realized I wasn't the man he expected to find in your parlor." He shook his head. "Had he been the killer, he would have known for certain that I was an imposter and probably been more prepared for my arrival."

"I suppose that's true," Gray said. "Then you think they have a partner."

Stalwood was the one who answered. "We do. Clairemont

and I were going to do some research into your investors and associates, but you can make it easier on us by allowing us access to the information. Especially a list of anyone that Clairemont encouraged you to approach for involvement."

Gray shot Rosalinde and Celia a look, then turned his attention back to Clairemont. "I am disgusted by what you did to my family. And when this is over, you had best be ready to meet me at dawn to settle the damage you've done. But the idea that anyone would use *my* ventures to commit treason is appalling to its core. I feel compelled to help you in any way I can."

Clairemont pursed his lips. He deserved the duel that Gray was suggesting. He deserved far worse. "Thank you," he said softly.

Celia stepped toward him, and for the first time in what seemed like forever, she lifted her gaze to evenly meet his. Her blue eyes, which had always been so warm and welcoming and healing, were now cold as an icy sea. She was pale as the finest parchment when she raised her chin with a hint of defiance.

"We must *all* help," she said, her voice cracking.

Clairemont drew back, hardly able to breathe as he looked at her. "Celia?" he murmured.

Rosalinde stepped toward her and whispered the same. "Celia?"

She ignored her sister, and those icy blue eyes narrowed. "If our family were to suddenly cut you off, if our courtship were to end abruptly, it would draw more of that attention back to you, wouldn't it? It might even reveal your duplicity in some way."

Clairemont could find no words to reply, but Stalwood spoke for him. "Yes."

"It could hurt many. Perhaps even lead to the deaths of some."

"Soldiers and spies," Clairemont admitted past a suddenly dry throat. "Depending on whether the real duke and his partners are moving weapons or information."

"Or both," Stalwood supplied, his concern clear in his tone.

167

"Then the courtship will continue," Celia said at last.

As Clairemont's lips parted in surprise, Rosalinde reached out and grabbed her sister's arm. "Celia, you don't have to do this. No one could expect it of you."

Celia kept her gaze firmly on him. "But I *shall* do it. I shall do it for my country."

Clairemont's hands began to shake and he shoved them behind his back as he nodded slowly. "I appreciate that, Celia. I certainly don't deserve it."

"Call me Miss Fitzgilbert," she said, then turned on her heel and paced away.

Stalwood sighed. "It has been a trying day for everyone and Clairemont and I must go and do some work regarding Perry. He is loose on the streets and must be contained if we can manage it."

Gray nodded. "Of course. In the mean time I will gather all correspondence from Clairemont for you. And I'll look into my records and compile any information that might lead you to Clairemont's partner."

"Excellent." Stalwood moved toward the door, but before they could leave, Rosalinde approached Clairemont. She stood before him, hardly more than a wisp of a woman in comparison to his strength. Without preamble, she slapped him hard across the face.

Celia spun around with a gasp, and for a moment no one in the room moved. Clairemont's cheek stung, but he didn't recoil. He simply stood and waited for her to repeat the action. He deserved no less.

Instead, she reached out to touch his hand. "*That* was for hurting my sister. But I also thank you for saving my husband today."

With that, Rosalinde turned and left the room. Gray followed, and then Stalwood. Clairemont waited for Celia to step away, as well, but she hung at the door, staring at him.

"You told me a few days ago that if I needed to sneak away I should call on you to help me," she said when the silence had stretched between them for what felt like forever.

"Yes," he said. "I did say that."

"Then meet me tonight, in the same place you dropped me off after I saw my grandfather," she said. She moved for the door. "Midnight. Don't be late."

Clairemont stared at her retreating back, then hurried to follow her. Did she truly want to meet in private with him after everything he'd done, everything that had been said?

It was a very bad idea. But he would do it. She deserved the privacy to fly at him, to curse him, to give him the hell he had earned.

And he couldn't help but want to be alone with her one last time.

CHAPTER NINETEEN

Celia stood away from the door, but she couldn't help but stare at Aiden's retreating back as he made his way to his horse. His shoulders were stiff, rolled forward, and his pain was as clear as her own. Finally, Gray shut the foyer door and cut the image away.

There was a beat of a moment before he and Rosalinde turned together to face her. When they did, their expressions said everything, even before either of them spoke. Humiliation and pain flooded Celia, yet she somehow managed to keep her chin up.

"Oh, Celia," Rosalinde whispered, her voice broken with empathetic pain for her sister. "There are no words I can find to express it. I'm just so, so very sorry."

"Why?" Celia asked, shocked she could find her voice after everything that had just happened. "*You* didn't lie to me. *You* didn't create this situation at all. We are all victims of this investigation."

Gray's jaw tensed, and he hesitated slightly before he moved forward. "But none more than you." He cleared his throat and his discomfort was clear. "You and I were not always close, but I feel we have become closer recently. When I had you come to live with us, it became *my* responsibility to ensure that any man who courted you was worthy, and I failed in that."

Celia shook her head. "This isn't your fault, Gray. In the end we were all fooled by him."

She turned away from the sting her own words created. Fooled by him. That implied each and every thing between them had been untrue. Aiden...or whatever his name truly was...he had said as much.

Except there was a part of her that didn't believe him. When she had finally looked into his eyes and declared she would allow the false courtship to continue in order to help him, there had been something that lit up in his stare that told her some things had been real. That was why she was determined to meet with him. Alone, she could see better what his motives had been, beyond his case. Beyond his deceptions.

"What can I do?" Rosalinde asked, sliding up beside her. "How can I comfort you?"

Celia slowly faced her. "I love you and Gray so much for wanting to shelter me from these feelings. But I'm afraid I must simply feel them until they have lost their power. Right now I want to go upstairs and lie down for a while."

"Alone?" Rosalinde asked, her eyes brightening with tears.

Celia smiled sadly as Gray took a place beside Rosalinde and put his arm around her. At least her sister would have comfort and someone to remind her that this wasn't her fault.

"Yes, alone. For now," Celia said. "Perhaps later, perhaps tomorrow or the next day, I'll be more ready to talk. Right now I can hardly think of anything to say. I have to consider it more."

Rosalinde nodded. "I understand." She rushed forward and yanked Celia into a fierce hug that nearly squeezed the air out of her. "I love you."

Celia smoothed her hands over her sister's back and blinked at tears. "I know."

When she managed to escape Rosalinde's arms, she smiled weakly at the pair, then turned to go upstairs. What she had said to them was true. She did want to lie on her bed and simply digest everything that happened this afternoon.

But she also had plans to make for her escape tonight. And for how she would confront Aiden when there were no barriers and no one to protect either of them from the truth.

Clairemont swept his pocket watch from his jacket and flipped it open. It was after midnight now and yet he was still sitting in his carriage, watching out the window as he waited for Celia to join him. Had she been waylaid? Or had she changed her mind?

Worse, was she just toying with him, letting him feel a tiny fraction of the pain and embarrassment he had forced her to endure with his lies? Would she leave him sitting here, waiting for her?

If she did, he deserved no less. And he would wait here all night if necessary to pay the penance she required.

The servants' entrance to the house opened just as that thought filled his mind, and Celia stepped out. She was wearing a cloak pulled up around her face, but Clairemont recognized it was her from the way she moved with such grace.

He opened the door and moved to step out, but she motioned him back in. "I can manage," she said, her voice tight and cold.

She climbed up into the vehicle without his assistance. He frowned, but reached out to close the door behind her. In the dim quiet of the carriage he watched as she pushed the hood back from her face and caught his breath.

She was absolutely beautiful. Every time. Without fail.

"Are you certain you want to do this? To talk to me alone?" he asked.

She arched a brow. "We have things to discuss, and as much as I adore Rosalinde, she is too protective to allow us to be alone now to do so. So yes. I still feel this is our best option."

He leaned back to tap the wall. The carriage rumbled forward, maneuvering back to his townhome just a short distance away.

The few moments in the vehicle were quiet. If he had

expected Celia to launch directly into a condemnation of him, she didn't do so. Instead, she leaned her head on the window, staring out into the darkened streets with an unreadable expression on her face.

She never looked at him.

When the carriage stopped at the townhouse he had been staying in since his arrival in London, she straightened up and leaned forward. "I realize I never came here *before*," she said.

He flinched at that characterization. She had split their relationship into two sections. Before the truth and after. Before she despised him and after.

"No, I suppose you didn't."

"His?" she asked.

He nodded without needing clarification. "Yes."

She was silent a moment before she asked, "How did you manage the servants?"

"The real Clairemont was reclusive, remember. Most of his servants never even met him. But we hired a new group just in case. The old ones got very good references."

"Seems you found a way to make sure no one suffered," she said, turning her face.

He frowned. The unspoken words hung between them. No one had suffered but her. He pushed the door open and stepped out, then turned back to help her. She hesitated before she took his hand and barely touched him as she exited.

They moved to the front door, which Clairemont opened himself. She looked at him in surprise as they entered. "Or *did* you hire servants?"

"When you asked me for privacy to discuss everything, I gave them the night off. No one is home but us," he explained. "I hope that doesn't make you uncomfortable."

She glared at him. "*Uncomfortable* is not the word I would use, no," she said. "Where should we talk?"

He motioned to the parlor where he'd had his servants lay a warm fire before they departed for the night. Once inside, he closed the door behind them. He moved toward the sideboard.

"May I make you a drink?" he asked.

She turned on him suddenly. "What is your name?"

He froze in his spot, hand outstretched to the decanter of liquor. Slowly he faced her and leaned back against the sideboard. She was watching him, hands folded before her, gaze unwavering.

"It doesn't matter what my name is, Celia," he said softly.

Her expression, which had been so unreadable until that moment, twisted in a mask of anger and grief. "I haven't earned it?" she hissed out, fingers clenching in a fist at her side.

"You have likely earned it more than anyone I've ever known," he explained. "But if you knew it, you could very well be in danger."

"Why? How? It isn't as if I'd ever use it in public," she said.

He shook his head. "You would never mean to do so. But a slip can happen to even the best and most well-trained of agents. Or if you were questioned by a skilled interrogator, he would know you were lying if my real name was in your mind. So I can't give it to you because it is the best way for both of us to be hurt. You'll notice even Stalwood only ever calls me Clairemont."

"Stalwood," Celia repeated, the name like a curse. "And he seems to be so very important in all this, your *handler*, so I suppose that should appease me."

"Celia." He stepped toward her, but she held up a hand to ward him off. It took everything in him to accept her rejection and stay where he was, halfway across the room from her, unable to touch her or comfort her.

"What will happen to Aiden when your investigation is over?"

He blinked. "I-I don't understand," he said. "I've already told you the real Clairemont is dead."

"Not the real Clairemont," she said, pursing her lips. "Aiden. *You* as Aiden. You obviously won't go on being him, so what will happen to him? To the man I thought I knew?"

"The character," he said, understanding her now. Almost

wishing he didn't when he thought of the answer. "Well, he'll...he'll die, Celia. Probably not as violently as the real Clairemont did, but there will be an accident or illness that will take him. As far as Society, as the public in general, will know, he'll die. Since there are no heirs, the crown will take the title and his lands and that will be the end."

She caught her breath, tears filling her eyes. She blinked them back fiercely. "So I'll lose you."

He nodded. "Yes. But I promise you, Celia, we will resolve this as quickly as we can so as not to cause you more pain. I'm hoping to be finished in days now with Gray's help, weeks at most." She flinched, and he moved on her now, ignoring the barriers she'd put between them. "I'm sorry. You don't know how sorry. I did things I shouldn't have done, I went beyond the bounds of my role with you."

She looked up at him, her bottom lip trembling, her pupils dilated. "Yes, you did. You wrote me letters when we were apart, you touched me not just in my body, but in my soul. *Why?*"

He caught his breath. He'd spent his life being a liar. Tonight he couldn't bear to do it again, even if the truth made him vulnerable.

"Because it was *you*, Celia. You are wonderful and irresistible. I wrote you letters so that I would—"

He cut himself off and she lifted her hands in frustration. "You would what?"

"So—so that I would have your responses when I was gone. So that I would have a piece of you to remember that I had this time. It's the same reason I did everything else. I just wanted a tiny piece of everything that you are. I know it makes me a bastard, but I stole what I shouldn't have."

"You never stole anything," she whispered. "I gave it all. Freely and willingly."

The gentleness was back in her tone and he so wanted to sink into it. To forget that she knew the truth, forget everything but that she was here and they were alone and he wanted her one last time.

But that couldn't happen.

"You gave it under false pretenses," he said. "With your eyes shut by my lies."

She stared at him. Truly stared, and in that moment he knew that she saw him. Him, the real him. He was John Dane, not Clairemont, not Aiden, not a spy for the crown, not anything but John Dane. She saw him without knowing his name, and it felt like he didn't fit into his skin anymore. He felt revealed, defenseless.

They were close already, but she took a small step toward him and ate up even more of the distance. She was almost touching him now.

"My eyes are open," she whispered. "There are no more lies."

He could feel her breath and smell her skin as she eased ever closer. It was like torture, but he forced his hands to remain at his sides. "Celia," he whispered.

She reached for him, her fingers tracing the line of his jaw, her thumb smoothing over his lip. Her touch was like silk, gentle as butterfly wings.

"If I'm going to lose you, I want to have you," she whispered.

Then she lifted up to her tiptoes and kissed him.

CHAPTER TWENTY

Celia sank into the warmth of Aiden's touch as she traced her tongue along the crease of his lips. He tasted intoxicating, mint and male mixed together. He let out a low groan before he wrapped his arms around her and kissed her back with all the passion and fervor she'd come to expect from him.

She hadn't come here with the idea to make love to him. She'd been too angry, too tangled up in emotion and betrayal and hurt to consider such a shocking thing. But starting the moment she stepped into the carriage, what she *really* wanted had become more and more clear.

Him. She wanted him. Because the love she felt had nothing to do with his name or his title. It had everything to do with the way he looked at her and touched her and made her feel deep within her body, all the way to her bones. Like she was cherished, like she was perfect…like she was *his*.

When he said that he would leave her life forever, that the man she'd known would die, her course of action had become crystal clear.

She had to do this.

She lifted her hands up to wrap them gently around him and tilted her head to deepen the kiss. She molded her body to his, letting her breasts flatten against his chest, her knees press to his legs, let his hardness push against her stomach.

He let out a pained grunt and tried to pull away. "We can't," he said, his breath short as he caught both her hands in his and tried to hold her away from him.

"Why?" she whispered.

"You know bloody well why," he said, his tone raising and his face twisting in frustration. "I *know* you do. Don't make me say it."

"Because once you take my virginity, I'll be ruined," she said, providing the words he refused to say.

"Yes," he hissed out, but she could hear the sharpness of need in his tone and feel it in his touch.

She pushed back against him, testing his control by lifting on her tiptoes to brush her lips along his jawline. "I. Don't. Care," she whispered. "I want you. *You*. Tonight. Because we both know it's the only chance we have and I don't want to regret not taking this moment."

He turned his mouth into hers and claimed her lips, shaking off her hands to cup her cheeks. He drew her in, sucking her tongue, tasting her all over as if he couldn't get enough. But once again, he broke away.

"You'll regret doing this and I would hate that," he panted.

She shook her head. "I won't."

She said nothing else, but began to unbutton his jacket. She held his gaze as she slid the fabric apart and then pushed it from his shoulders. He squeezed his eyes shut, only grunting when she moved her hands to his cravat and slowly unlooped the intricate knots and folds.

"Don't do this," he murmured.

She ignored the plea and moved to unfasten his shirt. He didn't fight her, he didn't move, he just let her undress him. It wasn't easy. She had never served as valet for a man before. His buttons felt stiff, the fabric unruly, but at last she tugged his shirt tails free and parted the cotton to reveal a bare, tanned, thickly muscled chest.

Her breath hitched at the sight of him half-undressed. Her hands shook as she reached out to trace the planes of muscle that corded his stomach. He hissed out a breath and she lifted her wide gaze to his.

"You are determined?" he asked.

She nodded. "I *will* seduce you, no matter how poorly I manage it. I want you. I want this. I want tonight. And if *you* want to make up to me all the lies and manipulations, you'll give that to me. If you want to gift me something to make all this worthwhile, you'll allow me what I desire."

He pressed his lips together hard and she could see him pondering her words. Probably trying to find a way to deny them both what they wanted so much.

But in the end, she knew he wanted her. His hard body betrayed him. His hitched breath betrayed him. His dilated pupils betrayed him.

He drew back and held out a hand. She stared at it, uncertain what the offering meant.

"Come, Celia," he said. "A parlor is no place for you to surrender something so dear."

Her lips parted. He was yielding?

"Then where?" she whispered, her voice shaking.

"My room," he said as he drew her from the parlor and into the foyer. She followed him up the stairs, down a short hall and to a door. He sighed heavily before he threw it open and beckoned her inside.

A fire burned within and he took a moment to light a few lamps. She looked around. Like the rest of the house, there was nothing in this room that said Aiden. At least not the Aiden she knew. Everything was crisp and metal and hard edges. It wasn't inviting.

Well, *almost* nothing was inviting. There was a bed facing the fire, a big bed that was inviting, indeed. She was taking a step toward it when he turned back to her and shook his head.

"Oh no, not so fast."

She blinked. "Why? Isn't this…I mean, I know I don't have much experience in these things, but isn't it traditional to do this on a bed?"

"We're going to do a great many things on that bed," he reassured her, crossing back to her and placing his warm hands

179

on her shoulders. "But if tonight is all we have, we're taking our time. I want to remember this when I'm—"

He cut himself off abruptly and she frowned. "When you're gone. When you're no longer *my* Aiden."

He nodded as he slid a finger beneath her chin and tilted her face up. "No more thoughts about that. I want to give you pleasure, Celia. I want us both to forget tomorrow, at least for now."

She drew in a long breath to calm herself and nodded. "Forget tomorrow. I can do that. Especially since I want tonight so very much."

He turned her gently, forcing her to face away from him, and leaned in to kiss the back of her neck even as he began to unfasten the buttons along the back of her dress. A thrill worked through her as his fingertips brushed her spine, her shoulders, through her fine chemise. He parted the fabric and gently pushed, gliding it down her arms until it hung around her waist. Only then did he turned her back to face him.

She blushed. She was standing in front of him and he could see her chemise. No one but her maid or her sister had ever seen her this way.

"You are shifting your weight back and forth ever so slightly," he said with a soft smile. "Are you reconsidering your decision?"

"No," she croaked out. "I'm just hoping you aren't disappointed with what you see."

His eyes widened slightly. "With you? Never."

He took a step closer until he crowded into her space and lifted his hand. Slowly he traced the back of it over her shoulder, her collarbone, and finally over her chest. His knuckles slid back and forth over her nipples, and they immediately hardened as she hissed out a breath of unexpected pleasure.

Then he turned his hand, flattening it back against her shoulder, and slid it beneath the flimsy chemise strap. She held her breath, watching as he glided the scrap away and down her arm, bearing first one breast, then the other.

"You are," he whispered, leaning down to brush his lips just across the top of the swell, "so exquisite."

She took in a great gulp of air as she tangled her fingers in his crisp, short hair and held tight as his lips opened and he began to gently taste her exposed flesh. Lower and lower he swept his tongue until he brushed it over one nipple.

Electric heat flashed through her, and she found herself arching against him. He smiled against her flesh. "Since the first moment I saw you, I have longed to see you like this," he admitted.

She drew back. "You—you wanted me from the first moment you saw me?"

He swallowed hard before he nodded. "Yes, Celia. And that had nothing to do with my case. Nothing to do with anything but you. The more I grew to know you, the worse that ache became. And no amount of distraction or self-pleasure could make it less."

Tears suddenly stung Celia's eyes and she blinked them away so he wouldn't see how much his words moved her. Since his confession the afternoon before, she had been wondering how much of their connection was real and how much had been manufactured by him for the sake of his case.

Now his words freed her from the doubt that had plagued her. Slowly she hooked her fingers into her drooping chemise and gown and shimmied the entire contraption down her hips. She stepped out and stood before him in only her drawers and stockings.

"Would touching me make it less?" she asked, shocked by her own boldness and yet thrilled with how the erection hidden behind the placket of his trousers seemed to swell even larger.

"More at first," he said, reaching out to place a hand on her hip and draw her closer. "But then your body will be the only thing that can cure the need."

"And what of my need?" she asked, blinking up at him now that their faces were mere inches apart.

He kissed her gently. "I intend to take care of that as many times as you can bear."

Without another word, he swept his arm beneath her knees and lifted her. He pressed a kiss to her mouth as he carried her to the bed that had so fascinated her a moment before and laid her down. Her heart was beating like hummingbird wings as he tugged her drawers away, then her slippers, then unrolled her stockings.

And then she was naked, sprawled on his bed, his gaze burning into her.

"I do not deserve this," he muttered, she thought more to himself than to her.

She might have argued that point, but he didn't allow it. He bent to kiss her stomach and all her thoughts emptied. His mouth moved along her skin, down her abdomen, across her hip, and she tensed. He was going to kiss her sex like he'd done at the ball a few nights before. Her body contracted at the memory of the pleasure that had rushed through her when his mouth took her.

"Aiden?" she whispered.

He lifted his head from her thigh and said, "Did you like it before?"

She nodded immediately. "Y-yes. Very much. I couldn't stop thinking about it."

He chuckled, a masculine, possessive sound that rumbled through her whole body and made liquid flood the very sex they were discussing so intimately.

"And that was when I was rushed, knowing we had to get back to the ball. Tonight I have endless time to…" He looked back down, leaning in until his breath steamed across her sensitive flesh. "…explore."

She gripped the coverlet with both fists as his mouth lowered and at last he covered her in an open-mouthed kiss. Pleasure immediately burst there and she lifted into him with a wordless sound of relief and need. Unlike the last time, when he'd held her steady through his ministrations, this time he let her move and arch into his tongue.

He swept across her entrance, licking away the wetness that had gathered there and creating more through his wicked mouth. She turned her head into the pillow, gasping and groaning, but never more than when he let his tongue flick across her clitoris and a jolt of intense sensation would render her moaning and liquid.

But unlike that night in the out building, tonight he didn't focus his attention there. Oh, he teased, yes, ratcheting her breath higher and making her tremble, but he never focused, never drove her toward release.

"You are tormenting me," she panted.

"Indeed, I am," he murmured, letting the tip of his tongue circle her clitoris. "For when the release finally comes, I will make it so powerful, so complete that you will remember it when you are eighty."

His words gripped her just as he swirled his tongue around her yet another time, and in that moment the pleasure hit its crescendo. Waves of sensation smashed against her and she lifted into his mouth, crying out his name as her body convulsed against his seeking tongue.

He sucked her clitoris as she shattered and doubled the release an instant. But at last the waves slowed, her body twitched and she went limp on his pillows. He moved up her body and pressed his mouth to hers, letting her taste her own passion. When he drew back, he chuckled.

"*That* was supposed to be much more drawn out. Had I known that words could send you over the edge, I would have forced myself to remain mute."

She reached up to cup the back of his head, pulling him in for a second, deeper kiss. She sighed as they parted. "I will remember that even if I forget everything else, I assure you," she whispered. She looked upward, toward the heavens as she tried to calm her heart, and her gaze caught something unexpected on the ceiling above her. "Er, Aiden?"

"Yes?" he asked, his fingers smoothing back and forth over her shoulder in a rhythmic motion.

"Why is your ceiling covered with naked people?"

He shook his head and laughed. "The *real* Clairemont's ceiling is covered with naked people. For a recluse, the man was something of a libertine. He had that piece carved so he could look at all the things he wanted to do, I suppose. It is a bit distracting."

She wetted her lips as her gaze flitted over the erotic images. Men with women bent over, being taken from behind. A woman riding one man while she took another in her mouth. Women with women. Couples in every position one could possibly imagine and a few she wouldn't have thought were possible.

She cast a quick side glance at Aiden and found he wasn't looking at the images above, but at her. Judging her reaction. Heat flooded her cheeks.

"Can you really do all those things?" she asked.

"Can I? Or can anyone?" he asked with a chuckle as he wrapped an errant curl around his finger.

"Either one," she said, wondering at how her body felt hot and tingly all over again. Looking at those carved images while he touched her made them even more impactful.

"I've done a few," he admitted, his gaze holding hers. "I'd like to try at least three of them tonight with you."

"Which three?" She jerked her gaze back to the ceiling, trying to determine the answer.

"One we've done. Twice now," he said, his voice low and seductive.

She searched the images and found a few where a lady was being pleasured by a man's mouth. "I see."

"The others will be a surprise," he said, and leaned in to kiss her once more.

She closed her eyes, forgetting the erotic art, forgetting everything but his taste and how his rough tongue slid so gently over her own. How his hands gripped her with passion and smoothed her skin with tender care. Nothing else mattered at that moment. Everything else she trusted him to make right.

He broke the kiss at last and pulled away, backing toward the fire.

She sat up partially, watching him go. "What are you doing?"

"Removing the rest of my clothing," he said, his voice low and seductive as he finally shucked off the shirt she had opened what seemed like a lifetime ago.

She watched his muscles move beneath his skin and bit her lip as her sex began to tingle with need once more. How could he do this so easily to her? Whether he touched her or looked at her or just stood there being...being *him*...it seemed he was irresistible to her. A force that drew her in completely until she would give anything and everything to be in his arms.

His arms. Her gaze flitted to his arm, the one that had been injured earlier in the day. There was a dark red mark slashed across it, proof of how dangerous a man this was.

"Does it hurt?" she whispered.

He glanced down at the mark and then shook his head. "No. It's minor, I assure you."

She bit her lip. "But—"

"Shhh," he said, smoothing a thumb over her cheek before he stepped back.

He met her gaze as his hands moved to his trousers. Slowly he unfastened them and then glided them down his hips. She tracked as inch by inch of flesh was revealed and finally the erection she had been aware of so many times since he first touched her bobbed free.

She caught her breath as she sat upright. Rosalinde had told her a little about a man's...cock, she thought she'd heard it called. When she was to marry Stenfax, the idea of it was terrifying. Tonight, looking at Aiden, seeing the swollen, heavy, utterly masculine proof that he wanted her...well, it was still terrifying. But it was also exhilarating.

This man wanted her so desperately that his body hardened, rising like a divining rod meant not to find water, but to seek her out. It rose proudly against his stomach, and she stared blatantly.

"Is this the first time you've seen a man's cock?" he asked.

"Unless you count the ones carved above me, yes," she murmured. "I'm a lady, you recall. We aren't exactly taken aside and given intense lessons on the subject."

He nodded, but she thought she saw the flicker of a frown cross his face. He approached her slowly and let her get a closer look.

"May I...may I touch it?" she asked.

He was laughing and shaking his head at once as he purred, "Please do, Celia. I would like that very much."

She reached out and traced his length with a fingertip. She was shocked to find that the flesh over that steely, very male organ was silky soft. She cupped him with her palm and stroked once from base to tip.

"Goddamn, woman," he groaned, his head tipping back. "You will have me undone before we even begin properly."

She snatched her hand back, though she could still feel the weight of him in her palm, a phantom pleasure. "We haven't begun properly? With the removing of our clothing and your...your...*licking* me?"

He laughed. "Appetizers, all," he said as he took a spot next to her on the bed. He drew her closer, placing a hand on her thigh and lifting to drape her leg over his. The fine hairs on his legs tickled her smooth ones, and she found herself lifting into him with a soft sigh of pleasure.

He kissed her and she sank into him, surrendering completely to whatever he would do now. He would take her, of course, she knew about that. She also knew it would likely hurt the first time. And since the first time was the only time they'd ever be together, she wanted to take all the pleasure she could in the meantime.

And he gave it, in spades. He rolled her on her back, continuing to touch and kiss and stroke her. His thumb flicked her nipple even as his other hand kneaded her backside, pulling her body against him firmly. His cock pressed hard against her belly.

All of it was so good, so right, so utterly overwhelming. And she never wanted it to stop. She wanted to remain in this moment for the rest of her life. Where there was nothing and no one else in the world. Where the lies were gone and it was just the two of them.

His hand glided lower, lower, until he cupped her sex. She felt him spreading her open, teasing the sensitive flesh even as he kept kissing her and kissing her. His fingertips brushed her entrance and she moaned with pleasure at the touch.

When she did, he pulled back. His eyes were wide and his breath was short as he looked into her eyes. "Are you sure?" he said, his voice cracking.

She stared back up at him. "Sure? Of you? Of this?"

He nodded. "Once I take you, Celia, it will be irrevocable. Your body will be marked with proof that you are no longer an innocent. There may be consequences in the future, when you find another, when you marry—"

She lifted her fingertips to his lips. "Stop, Aiden. Stop. I thought we were forgetting about tomorrow."

He pressed a kiss to her fingers, then moved them away. "A wonderful thought in theory, but reality must still color what I do. I want to be certain that you truly want this before I continue."

She lifted up slightly, cupping his face gently. "I understand the consequences, I understand the impact it will have on the future. But I don't want you to stop," she said, calmly, evenly. "I want you to take me, to make me yours. Is that clear enough?"

He swallowed hard and she saw how difficult this was for him. He wanted her and yet he warred with his honor, with not wanting to hurt her. And she loved him for that, as deeply as she had ever loved him before.

He bent his head and kissed her once more, lowering her back on the pillows as he rolled over her, bracing his arms next to her head so that he wouldn't crush her with his body weight.

She wrapped her arms around him, smoothing her hands down the rippling planes of muscle on his back, gliding them back up his sides. He shivered as she touched him, making a little sound of possessive pleasure deep in his throat.

"Ready?" he asked, sliding a hand between them to position the head of his cock at the slickness of her sex.

She nodded before she squeezed her eyes shut and tensed in preparation for the pain.

"What are you doing?" he asked, nuzzling her throat.

"Getting ready," she said, opening one eye.

"You look like I'm about to stab you," he said with a low chuckle.

She rolled her eyes. "I've heard told it's nearly the same thing."

"No, sweet," he promised, kissing just the tip of her nose. "Not like that. Slowly, now."

As he whispered the last he pressed against her. To her shock, the narrow channel of her body stretched to accommodate him, welcoming him as he breached her. At the very beginning there was a ripple of pain, and she sucked her breath in through her teeth.

The moment she did so, he stilled, waiting, his breath held, as she grew accustomed to the merging of their bodies.

"Do you know how much pleasure this act can give?" he murmured, kissing her neck as he held still, cupping her breast and thumbing her nipple over and over.

Pleasure shot down her body, settled where his cock was buried, and she flexed out of instinct, drawing him in a few more centimeters.

"I don't know," she moaned.

"Let me show you," he said and thrust a bit farther. The pain was gone now, replaced by a strange, yet wonderful feeling of fullness. Of belonging. Of pleasure and beauty and ancient rightness.

She lifted against him, and he seated fully within her and held perfectly still once again. He kissed her and slowly circled his hips. His pelvis hit her clitoris and her eyes flew open at the wild spark of pleasure that lit deep inside her body.

"Yes, see," he said, circling again, again, so many times that she lost count.

She clung to him, rising to meet him, trying to force him faster, grunting out pleasure when he refused her body's pleas and instead slowed his pace. He was so good at this, like they were made to be joined, like she was made to accept him and surrender to his will.

And surrender she did, at last falling into the rhythm he created. When she did, every fiber of her being grew focused as pleasure mounted, growing as it had with his mouth. Yet it was a more intense sensation because he was inside of her. He was taking, she receiving, protecting, holding him in the most intimate of ways. And she wanted it to last forever.

But he wouldn't allow it. His thrusts grew more focused and purposeful and the pleasure that was growing within her increased accordingly until at last she was flying again, her body rocking against his as she cried out pleasure into the quiet room and dug her nails into his back to keep from vanishing in the swirling vortex of release and love that flooded her every sense.

In that same moment, he drove harder, his neck straining. Then he shouted her name and suddenly he was gone, turning away as he spent away from her body and collapsed back over her, smoothing his hands over her and murmuring her name again and again.

CHAPTER TWENTY-ONE

Clairemont smoothed his hands over Celia's bare back, loving how her beautiful dark hair fanned over his chest as she lay against him. In the aftermath of their incredible joining, it was impossible to deny how madly and deeply he loved this woman.

And equally impossible to deny that what he had just done was so wrong. They could never be together and yet he had selfishly claimed a piece of her because he was too greedy to let her go as he should. He had never hated himself more than he did in that moment.

She rolled over, resting her hands on his chest and her chin on the same hands. She smiled up at him, her eyes bright and free of regret.

"How did you become a spy?" she asked.

He tensed. He wouldn't give her his name, but she wanted his story. The story was far more intimate, and yet he wanted to share it with her, to give her a piece of himself that had never and would never belong to another, just as she had done with him. Her gift was physical, his was something else.

"I'm like you," he said softly, trying hard to find words he'd never sought before. "I never knew my parents. They died when I was not more than a baby. I had no other family and we lived far out in the country, where there was no orphanage, so the church took me."

Her smile had faded as he began to speak, and now her lips

parted. "Were they...*kind* to you?"

"Indifferent," he said with a shrug. "As far as I recall. I was very young, you see. And I left their care when I was just four."

"You were taken in?" she asked. "By a family?"

He swallowed hard as images of someone big and cruel filled his mind. "Not a family. I suppose that must have been what he told the vicar. Or perhaps he just bought me, I don't know. But he was a traveling chimney sweep and he needed an apprentice."

Her brow wrinkled. "At—at *four*?"

"That is the preferred starting age," he said, his lips thinning at her innocence of his world. "The chimneys are narrow and a small child fits perfectly in them."

"Aiden," she whispered, saying the name of a man who had never done such dirty, horrible work. Yet he was happy she did—it kept him grounded here instead of lost in memories of the early time of his life. "Was he at least kind to you?"

"He was not." Clairemont shut his eyes and could see him, Felix Freestone, rising up over him, a fist clenched, his eyes blurred with drink and rage. "He was cruel beyond measure."

"What did he do?" she asked, her hand coming up to gently trace his jawline. "What did he do to you?"

"Wouldn't you rather hear a lie?" he asked, his voice cracking slightly. "I could spin one for you that would make us both feel better."

She tilted her head, and suddenly there was a world of understanding in her eyes. "Part of the attraction of being a spy was living a life you could create. A past you could pull from whole cloth so you would forget the truth."

His nostrils flared at her observation. She was far too sharp and smart and wonderful for her own good. Certainly far too good for him. And yet she was here. And he loved her.

"Yes," he admitted.

She sat up slowly and edged closer. Her mouth dropped gently and she brushed her lips to his. "I would rather know the truth. Ugly and cold and hard as it may be, it is *yours*. It means a great deal to me if you are willing or able to share it."

His breath hitched as memories hit him hard and fast now. "When I didn't work fast enough in the chimneys, he would light newspaper at my feet. Once when he was angry with me, he left me up in a chimney for three hours and told me if the people who owned the home returned, he would let them burn the fire with me trapped inside."

Tears flooded her eyes, but she didn't allow them to fall. "Too much smoke."

He tiled his head in confusion. "I'm sorry?"

"You once told me London had too much smoke. Now I understand those words and the look on your face when you said them."

He drew back. He was shocked she remembered such a detail. But of course she would. She was Celia, after all.

She sucked in her breath harshly. "How could he do that to a little boy?"

Clairemont shrugged. "He had been an apprentice himself and this was how his master treated him. He was also a mean drunk who beat me when we got home."

"So you lived like this for your entire life?" she asked. "How in the world did you come to be at the War Department?"

"Not my whole life," Clairemont said. "The bastard had the good grace to drop dead when I was ten. I was so thrilled when it happened, I knew I'd go straight to hell."

"That's where he went, not where you would go," she said. "It was perfectly natural for you to celebrate his death."

"Well, I celebrated until a day or two later when I realized I had no one to feed or house me. I was on the street with no money and no prospects. I was too big to apprentice for another sweep, and collectors came and took my former master's horse and things as payment for a debt. I was left alone."

"Oh no," she whispered.

"Luckily we were close to London, so I came here," he said. "I hated it, but there were more opportunities."

"What did you do?" she asked. "At such a tender age?"

192

"I begged," he admitted, color flooding his cheeks as he tried to picture what Celia would have been doing at ten in comparison to him. Her life had not been easy either, but if she had met him then, she would have turned away from him in horror, he was certain.

Her gaze softened. "And then?"

"How do you know there was an 'and then'?" he asked, holding her gaze evenly.

"I know you," she said. "I can see it. You're afraid I will think less of you because of whatever you did. But let me reassure you—" She scooted closer and wrapped her arms around him. "—whatever you did, I will fully approve of. It kept you alive, it brought you here to me."

He looked around him slowly, at this comfortable room where he didn't belong. At the bed that contained a woman he certainly didn't deserve. In clothes that had been made specially for him. He hadn't had an empty stomach for years, nor gone without a roof over his head except for very specific instances where a case required it.

He had risen above his beginnings. And she said she didn't care how he'd done it. But then, she hadn't yet heard the truth. Perhaps that would change.

"I didn't know anything more," he began, trying to soften the words he would say. "I didn't have skills or empathy. Hell, I didn't have the ability to read. So I—I stole. For years I ran from hovel to hovel and I stole anything that wasn't nailed down. I got good at it, too, sliding my hand into a man's pocket and coming out with blunt."

He shivered at the thought of those nights when pocket full of coils had been cause for a celebration. Even now he sometimes sized up the men around him to see if he could steal from them. He never did it, of course, but he knew his marks. Like it was an old habit, like he somehow feared he'd need those skills again someday so he kept them sharp.

"Of course you stole," she said softly. "You had to eat."

He drew back. "How can you not judge me for that?"

"There were times, looking out my window at night, that I thought about running away," she said. "Certainly my situation with my grandfather was nothing like yours, but if I'd thought I was strong enough to do it, I would have tried. And I'm certain a young lady on the street must do far worse than steal to survive."

Clairemont gritted his teeth at the thought of Celia doing such a thing. It turned his stomach that her childhood had been so difficult that she'd considered surrendering herself to the dirty, harsh life he had been thrown into. It made him hate her grandfather all the more.

"I'm glad you stayed in your rooms, safe and sound," he said. "The street is no place for someone so lovely as you."

"It was no place for you, either, Aiden. An innocent child? You should have had a home, safety, security." She shook her head.

He threaded his fingers through hers. "There were many worse off than I was. Though I admit I was on a path of utter destruction. Arrest or death was my destination, and I knew it. I didn't care. I almost welcomed those ends, for it meant no more rainy nights in alleys or being chased by toughs."

"How did you escape?" she asked, her voice trembling.

"I didn't. I got caught," he said. "I was in a tavern in one of the better parts of town, pretending to sell newspapers I'd stolen. Really, I was just looking for a mark. I'd gotten cocky, you see, thinking I could take from a toff as easily as I'd taken from a drunk in the rookery. I chose one. This dandy, or at least I thought he was a dandy. He was dressed nice and that said dandy to me at the time. But when I brought my hand out of his pocket, he grabbed my wrist."

She lifted a hand to her lips. "Oh no."

"Oh yes. I'll never forget what he said to me, 'That was a good pull, boy. I almost didn't feel it.'"

Celia blinked. "I'm sorry, he was *impressed*?"

"It seemed so, but *I* was terrified." He squeezed his eyes shut, feeling every moment he described. "Especially when some others caught on and started screeching for the guard. I got dragged outside with the gentleman following, calm as you please. I was getting pushed around, people were yelling. Every time I tried to escape, someone else had me by the scruff of the neck."

"And the gentleman just watched?" she asked.

He nodded. "Just watched. But as the guard appeared, two massive men who looked like they could rip my arms off, the gentleman stepped up to me and started asking questions."

"What kind of questions?" she asked, clearly engrossed in the story.

And in truth, so was he. He often tried to forget his past, his story. Saying these words out loud brought back all of it, the good and the bad. There was something almost cathartic about the process.

"He wanted to know my name, but I wouldn't give it. So he started asking me about how long I'd been on the street. Whether I knew how to read. He said if I was truthful, he might be able to help me."

"So you told him," she said.

"Hell no, I told him to sod off," Clairemont said. "Excuse my language."

"I have a feeling your true language was worse," she said with a soft laugh. "But why did you do that? He was offering you an out."

"But I was certain it came with a price. Why would I let some dandy have one over on me? That was my thought. I refused him, even as the guard got closer and my fate became clearer. And then they called him 'my lord' and I knew my goose was cooked. I'd get transported likely, if not worse."

"You escaped?" she said.

"No, not at all. They were about to drag me off when the gentleman stepped in. He told them I hadn't taken anything. That he wanted to handle it himself."

Her lips parted. "What did *that* mean?"

"I wanted to know that myself. After a bit of negotiating,

the guard gave me up. Probably didn't want to have to deal with whatever they had to do to put me away and arrange for everything to do with my punishment. I was turned over to the man I'd tried to steal from. First thing I did was try to bolt, of course."

"Of course," she said. "I would have done the same."

"But he had me firmly and tossed me in a carriage, and off we went. Back to this palace in the middle of a part of London I'd never dared to look at, let alone go into."

"What did he want from you?" she asked, her hands shaking.

His had done the same that dark night. He remembered every moment so perfectly, all the horrible fates he had feared would befall him. And then he smiled.

"Once we were at his place, he took me into the kitchen and his servants brought me food. So much food. I'd never imagined one plate could hold so much. I gorged until I nearly vomited. And when I was done, he asked me if I'd come to work for him."

"As what?"

He arched a brow. "Well, *that* wasn't clear at first. I mean, there wasn't any work he had me do, really. He made me go to lessons and cleaned me up. It took over a year before he told me what I'd be doing for him."

"And that was?"

"The man was the Earl of Stalwood," Clairemont finished with a slight smile for Celia. "And he asked me if I'd like to be a spy."

She drew back, he mouth open in shock. "*Stalwood* took you in?"

He nodded. "Once I stopped fighting him, I became his ward. He taught me how to be a spy, but also how to be a man. A person. I learned to read, to write. At first I hated it, but ultimately I soaked it in. I loved it, and I loved the rest, too. And Stalwood was..." He trailed off and his voice caught. "He was the first flicker of kindness in a dark world full of hate and pain. I owe him my life, you see. Both the part of it that meant I didn't die and the part of it where I truly began to live. To see myself as worthy. So *that* is how I became a spy. A long answer to a question you may be sorry you asked now."

"Not at all," she said. "You told me more than I ever would have expected. And I understand so much more now about who you are. I suppose I hate Stalwood less, too."

He frowned. Of course she would despise his mentor. Stalwood had taken responsibility for using her in their plan. For manipulating her. He had a feeling the earl had done it for him. Yet another thing he'd never be able to repay.

"You shouldn't hate him at all," he said softly. "Whatever happened, my actions have been my own. If you hate anyone, hate me."

Her face fell slightly and she reached for him. She cupped his cheek. "I could not hate you. I might have wanted to when the truth came out, but it was never possible. And now that I've heard it all, I even understand it. As for Stalwood, he saved you."

"Yes, he did."

"And brought you to me. That trumps *almost* everything else." She laughed. "Not that he cares about my judgment of him."

"You would be surprised," Clairemont said. "He may seem stern and unfeeling, but there is a great deal more to him than that."

"I will take your word on it, as you know him best," she said. "I want to say something to you."

He nodded, bracing himself for the worst. Readying for when she would pull away from the damage he had just revealed to her.

"I'm so sorry for the pain you have endured," she said. "I ache for the child you once were, alone and afraid. I wish nothing more than to be able to comfort him, protect him."

"Of course you do," he said, picturing for a brief, wild moment, just that. Except the child he imagined her picking up to comfort wasn't him, but *his* son. Their son. He pushed the image away.

"But more than that, I am infinitely impressed by the man you've become, Aiden."

He flinched as she used that name that wasn't him again. It drove home the fine blade that he was nothing, still nothing, he'd never be anything more than nothing. That he was an illusion, not a man.

"The man who lies for a living," he said, getting up and walking away. He grabbed for his trousers and pulled them back on, keeping his back to her. "The one who just took your virginity."

"Freely given," she said, her voice soft in the quiet room.

"It doesn't matter," he snapped, facing her. It was impossible to look at her. She was so beautiful, gathered up in his bed, his sheets.

No, not his bed. Not his sheets. *Not* his woman.

"I have destroyed your future, Celia," he said.

Her eyes went wide. "Aiden, please! There could still be a future."

"What, for us?" he asked, laughing though there was no humor or goodness in what he felt. "Don't you understand? There is *no* Aiden. There is *no* us. There is *no* future. This night was stolen, something that we shouldn't have done, no matter how pleasurable it was." With every word, her face crumpled further. "When I'm gone, the best thing you can do for yourself is to forget me."

She lifted her chin slightly, but her defiance couldn't mask her pain. Unlike him, she wasn't as practiced at the act. He saw it there, as clear on her face as the fact that she foolishly cared for him. Him, a ghost. A phantom. A lie.

"And what will you do when you're gone?" she asked.

"Forget you."

He said the words. He even said them with strength. But they were a lie, the deepest and darkest one he'd ever told. He would never forget her. Her smile, her laugh, her touch, her body, how he loved her…those things would be with him every moment of every day until he finally breathed his last.

But she didn't know that. He made her believe it by the way he said those words. By the expression he forced himself to take.

The color drained from her face. "I see." She lifted the sheets to cover herself, and in that moment, he knew he'd lost her completely. "Well, then it seems I have all I came from. If you'll excuse me while I dress, you can return me to Gray's house."

He nodded, for he knew what she requested was best for her. It was, after all, what he had created by rejecting her. But it had never hurt more to walk away from anything than it did when he turned on his heel and exited the chamber. He shut the door behind him and leaned his forehead on the barrier, clenching his fists to keep from bursting back inside.

To keep from shouting the words he now only mouthed:

I love you.

CHAPTER TWENTY-TWO

Celia sat on the settee in Gray's parlor. Rosalinde was beside her, sewing quietly. Celia was also supposed to be stitching, but her piece sat on her lap, abandoned long ago. Instead, she stared out the window, toward the rainy garden behind the house. But even that she didn't see.

No, all she could think about was Aiden. She had not seen him, nor heard from him, in two days. Not since he had dropped her back off at Gray's house with a mumbled apology and goodnight.

But she had been reliving that night ever since. From the passionate joining that had made her soul and body sing, to his ultimate rejection that had sent her crashing to the ground.

Did she understand why he pushed her away? Of course she did. Not only did she understand his past now, but she knew that he couldn't remain in the role of Clairemont. He would be gone when his case ended. In some way, she thought he was trying to deal the harshest blows now so it would hurt less later.

Knowing that didn't lessen the sting.

The door to the parlor opened and Gray entered. He had a pensive look on his handsome face and he moved directly to Rosalinde to press a kiss to her forehead. Once he had done so, his expression relaxed a fraction. Celia turned away from their show of affection. How much she wished she could offer Aiden that kind of support.

"What is it?" Rosalinde asked, taking his hand.

He smiled down at her. "Am I so easy to read?"

"Only to me," Rosalinde said softly before she repeated, "What is it?"

"I've received a message from Stalwood. He and Clairemont are on their way to talk to me about any evidence I may have uncovered. They will be here momentarily." He shot a glance toward Celia.

She hardly noticed him as she rose to her feet. Her heart was pounding at the thought of seeing Aiden again.

Rosalinde frowned. "Why don't we go out, Celia?" she suggested in a falsely bright tone. "I know Mr. Banks gets his new fabrics in today. We could find a pretty silk or—"

"No," Celia said, surprised her voice could sound so even and strong when she was all but vibrating inside. "It's fine. Perhaps I can help."

Rosalinde moved toward her and caught her hand. She whispered, "I'm worried about you. Despite everything that has happened, I know you care for this man."

Celia didn't bother to deny it. Her sister knew her too well not to see through that lie. Instead, she shrugged. "That is why I *must* help. If he's seen coming here, it should be believed that he'd here to court. I must be there for that lie to be told."

The sound of a knock on the front door drifted in from the parlor, and Celia froze as they heard Greene welcome their guests. Then he appeared in the doorway. "The Duke of Clairemont and the Earl of Stalwood have arrived."

"They are expected, Greene. Please, allow them in," Gray said.

The servant stepped aside and the men entered. Stalwood came in first, but as he stepped aside, Aiden stepped into view. Celia's breath caught, then vanished as he turned his cool and hard gaze on her. The moment he did, it softened a fraction. Then he frowned and turned away.

She flinched. He was lost to her now. Already he pulled back, and it broke her heart into a thousand fragments.

"Good afternoon Mr. and Mrs. Danford, Miss Fitzgilbert,"

Stalwood said, filling what was now an awkward silence. "Thank you again for having us in your home and for your continued assistance in this unpleasant matter."

Celia kept her gaze on the earl since Aiden's continued refusal to look at her stung so badly. "Lord Stalwood, is there anything I can do to help?"

"No!" It was Aiden who answered, his tone sharp and bordering on cruel. "No."

Celia narrowed her eyes at him, and he did the same in return. "Might I have a moment with Clairemont?" she said, making the words a question though it was meant as a statement. If anyone refused her, she was going to insist.

But the room seemed to recognize this, for Stalwood, Rosalinde and Gray exchanged a look before they moved toward the door.

"We'll be in my office," Gray said softly. "Join us when you're finished, Clairemont."

Aiden didn't react or respond, but continued to hold her stare. Rosalinde was the last to leave the room and shot Celia a quick look before she tugged the door shut behind her.

Once they were alone, Celia took a step toward him. Immediately he took one of an equal distance back.

"Don't shut me out," she said softly.

He let out a ragged breath, his hand lifting at his side like he wanted to touch her but couldn't. Or wouldn't. Then he shook his head.

"This is madness. I must, Celia. I *will*." He turned and headed for the door. But there he paused, his hand resting against it, his head bent. "I'm ending this. All of this."

Then he threw the door open with such force that it nearly slammed back on the opposite wall and stalked away, leaving Celia alone with her pain.

She moved to the settee and sank back down, covering her face with her hands. She heard her sister enter, she recognized Rosalinde's soft footfalls. But Rosalinde said nothing, just sat down next to her and put an arm around her.

Celia kept her face covered, even as she leaned in to the comfort her sister offered. A comfort that would no succeed in making the situation any better.

When Clairemont stalked into Gray's office, both he and Stalwood looked up from the papers on his desk in surprise.

"That was quick," Stalwood said. "Is there any problem?"

Clairemont gritted his teeth and tried with all his might to forget the image of Celia's crestfallen face as he turned away from her. "No," he ground out. "What do we have?"

Gray glared at him, but then returned his attention to the desk. "I looked through all my correspondence with the real Clairemont, which I gathered here for you both. But I can tell you the only person he insisted I should include in my business was Lord Turner-Camden."

Stalwood arched a brow. "Turner-Camden?"

Clairemont shook his head as he exchanged a look with Gray. "Who is Turner-Camden?"

Gray folded his arms. "A marquess," he explained. "A very well-respected one at that."

Clairemont pinched his lips together. "It's probably nothing then. Cronyism is hardly treason."

"I would think the same thing except for something peculiar I noted in one of the letters about the marquess." Gray pulled out a folded sheet and pointed. "Clairemont refers to him as the Rooster once here."

Stalwood straightened up and took a long step back from the table, the color draining from his face. Clairemont stared at his mentor, seeing the same shock in him that he felt in himself.

"The Rooster," they repeated together.

Gray wrinkled his brow. "I thought it odd at the time and again when I read it. Does it mean something to you?"

Stalwood paced away, rubbing a hand over his face.

"Yes," Clairemont said, his throat suddenly dry. "The Rooster is a notorious traitor. He's traded in weapons and secrets, he's killed men by his actions and his own hand. We've been tracking him for years, but he's like a ghost. Could it be him?"

Stalwood faced them both. "I-I don't know. I have stood at a billiard table with Turner-Camden, chatted with him about the weather, and never suspected. But he is powerful. And rich. Far richer than his title and lands should have made him. It is possible?"

Gray shot a side glance at Clairemont. "Well, it goes to show we never truly know who we invite in."

Clairemont gripped his fists at his sides. "I deserve that, I suppose."

"You do," Gray agreed. "At any rate, I have more. Lord Turner-Camden has not been in Town yet this Season. Some sort of mysterious business has kept him away, though he's normally quite early in his arrival to London. But he has just arrived and..." Gray looked between the men. "He sent me a message this morning."

"What?" Clairemont said. "As soon as he arrived?"

"Apparently. It sounded urgent and he specifically mentioned he wanted to discuss the topic of the Duke of Clairemont."

Stalwood took a long step forward. "That *is* curious. It sounds like he has something specific on his mind."

"Indeed, it does," Gray said.

"So what do we do?" Clairemont asked. "What is our next move?"

Gray folded his arms and leaned back on his desk. "I know exactly what to do. I will invite him here to meet with me. And you'll be there."

Clairemont pressed his lips together. "The last thing we want to do is have me there. If he is, indeed, a killer, he'll know I'm not the real Clairemont and he might attack. That already happened once with Perry. And God knows what has already been reported to him if Perry is in league with them."

"Oh, he won't know you're here." Gray stepped around his desk and stopped at a bookcase there. He flicked out a hand to move a book and the entire bookcase opened up to reveal a narrow passage behind it.

"A secret room," Clairemont breathed.

Gray nodded. "Many men of rank have them. When I bought this home in London, it was from a penniless lord who liked to hide here from his creditors. I believe he also might have used it to sneak his mistresses past his wife. Either way, the passage is here, and if I move this book..." He pulled another book away and revealed an opening from which someone could observe the room. "You can even watch the meeting, undetected."

Stalwood looked at the set up with a smile. "The perfect solution to our problem."

"Except that Danford will be in danger," Clairemont said, thinking of Celia and Rosalinde. "Perry already shot at him. If Turner-Camden is involved, he could do worse, and escaping the passage to intervene won't be quick."

Gray shrugged. "This time I'll know to watch myself," he said. "And there isn't any choice, is there? Turner-Camden called for a meeting with me. It's our best option for quickly determining his guilt or innocence and ending this madness once and for all."

Clairemont let out a long sigh. There was no arguing the logic of the suggestion. He just didn't want to hurt Celia or Rosalinde any more than he already had. If Gray were injured— or worse—neither one could ever forgive him. He wouldn't deserve to be forgiven.

"I think Danford is right," Stalwood said. "But it's your case."

The case. Clairemont had to think of what was best for the case. And this was it. "Very well. Your plan is the best one. But I want you to do exactly what I say."

Gray looked annoyed, but he leaned back and glared. "I'm

listening."

The house was dark and quiet as Celia trailed through the halls, her busy, troubled mind keeping her from sleep. As she turned a corner, she was surprised to find Gray's office door was open and a narrow column of light from a lantern or candle fell into the hallway.

She'd thought Gray and her sister had retired hours before. She'd heard them talking, then soft sounds she now understood through her own brief but wonderful experience.

"Gray?" she said, stopping outside the door.

"Come in," came her brother-in-law's voice after a pause.

She entered to find him sitting at his desk. He stood at her presence, and she blushed. His shirt was half unbuttoned and untucked, his hair mussed by fingers.

"I'm sorry to disturb you," she said, not meeting his gaze.

"No," he said, coming around the desk. "You aren't. What are you doing up?"

"I couldn't sleep," she admitted, moving to the fire and fiddling with a few trinkets on Gray's mantel. A tiny portrait of Rosalinde, a figurine of a raven with its wing slightly outstretched, a small clock.

"An affliction I seem to share," Gray said, motioning to the two chairs before his fire. "You must have a great deal on your mind."

She took the seat he silently offered and was surprised when he sat at the one opposite her. He leaned forward, draping his forearms over his knees as he examined her closely. She was put to mind of the way he'd once looked at her when he thought she was a grasping title-hunter, after his brother. He'd searched her face the same way then, only now his eyes were much kinder.

"Aiden left this afternoon without saying goodbye," she said softly. "Without saying anything at all."

Gray leaned back, his lips pinching in what she could tell was frustration. It didn't seem to be aimed at her, though, but at Aiden.

"I see," he said at last. "What can I do, Celia?"

She sighed. "You and Rosalinde want to protect me, I know. I appreciate it. But I want to know what is happening. That is all that will put me at ease now."

Gray seemed to consider that statement. "You've earned the truth, I think. But I doubt it will put you at ease any more than it put Rosalinde at ease when I told her a few hours ago." He took a long breath. "Tomorrow I'll meet with a man who might be involved in the real Clairemont's treason, in his murder. And *your* Clairemont and Stalwood will be here, in hiding, ready to spring if anything of import is revealed."

Celia thought of the ugly red line slashed across Aiden's arm from the bullet meant for Gray. She shuddered. "That sounds very dangerous, Gray."

He nodded, solemn. "It is. You and Rosalinde will go out during the meeting."

She shook her head. "Oh no, please, let me stay."

Gray arched a brow. "I think not. Rosalinde demanded the same and I shall give you the same answer. I will not have you here with a potential killer in the house."

"But—" she began.

Gray lifted his hands. "God's teeth, you two are stubborn—there is no doubt you are sisters. No, Celia. That is final."

She flopped back against the chair. Truly, he wasn't being unreasonable. He wasn't even being unkind. She knew that her being here would likely only be a distraction to both Gray and to Aiden. Distraction could equal danger and she didn't want that.

"Do you think you might catch this potential murderer tomorrow?" she asked.

Gray nodded. "If the man coming here is truly the real Clairemont's partner, I think it is very likely we could catch him."

She caught her breath. "Then this will be…it will be over," she whispered, each word like a stab wound deep in her chest.

There must have been a tone to her voice, for Gray's expression softened greatly. "Yes," he said. "I suppose it will be."

She pushed to her feet and walked the length of the room. "He's already pulling away from me."

Gray stood and watched her. "But he must, Celia. You know that. It's what he feels is best for you. I can see the struggle in him, though. It's hurting him, too."

She spun to face him, finding hope in his words. "Do you think so?"

"I know it," Gray said. "It's killing him."

"And yet he still does it," she whispered.

"I'm sorry," Gray said, and nothing more.

"So am I," Celia said with a humorless laugh.

To her surprise, Gray moved across the space between them and wordlessly drew her in for a brief hug. This man who had been her enemy little more than five months before was now offering her comfort.

She looked at him. Really looked. There was hardness to Gray, but also kindness.

"You know, I understand a great deal more today than I did when we first met," she said. "And I thank you for loving my sister. For giving her such a wonderful life."

"It is my greatest pleasure," Gray said with a small smile. "I assure you."

Celia motioned for the door. "Well, go to her, then. I'm sure she's still awake, and if you're going to be in danger tomorrow, you should spend these hours comforting her, not brooding in here or fussing over me."

"What will you do?" Gray asked.

She shrugged. "Wait," she said. "Hope."

He nodded and squeezed her hand before he followed her direction and left the room. But alone, she knew one thing more than all others.

There was no real hope left for her. Except that Aiden would come out of tomorrow alive. Outside of that, her future and her fate were both sealed.

CHAPTER TWENTY-THREE

"Can you hear me?"

Standing in the hidden hallway behind Gray's desk, Clairemont exchanged a brief look with Stalwood in the dim light. "Yes," he replied, a bit louder than normal, since he wasn't sure Gray would hear him. "And see you."

"Excellent. Greene will show Turner-Camden in rather than inquire if I'm in residence, then he'll leave the house for safety. It should only be a few moments more."

Clairemont leaned in closer. "And Celia and Rosalinde are definitely out for the duration of the meeting?"

Behind him, he heard Stalwood clear his throat, but refused to turn. He knew his mentor didn't approve of his preoccupation in the heat of the battle. Why would he? A distracted agent was easily a dead agent. But Clairemont couldn't help it. Fearing for Celia's safety was as much of a distraction as asking after her. Perhaps more.

Gray glared at the bookcase. "I have told you three times, they are out and have been for some time. Rosalinde was been given strict instructions not to return for several hours. The servants will put Turner-Camden's horse in a specific place as well, able to be seen from the street. If my wife sees it there even after enough time has passed, they will not come back."

Clairemont let out a sigh of relief, even though he knew better than to trust Rosalinde and Celia with following orders. The sisters were of one mind when it came to watching out for those they cared for. He could only hope their desire to protect each other would trump anything else.

There was a sound in the hall, and Gray turned away from the bookcase and took his seat at the desk, cutting off all other communication just as Green stepped into the room.

"The Marquess Turner-Camden, my lord," he said, ushering a man into the room.

Clairemont leaned in closer to get a good look at the person. He was the only one who had never seen Turner-Camden before, and he couldn't say he was impressed. The man was short, squat and nearly as wide as he was tall. His clothing was dandified and he wore what looked to be a fortune in jewels on his hands.

"My lord," Gray said, and Clairemont was in awe of his calm demeanor. Gray knew this man could very well be dangerous beyond measure and yet he gave nothing away. "How nice to see you again. It's been too long."

"It has, Mr. Danford," the marquess agreed as he flopped heavily into the chair across from Gray's. "I'm so pleased we could meet so swiftly after my arrival."

"Your note sounded most urgent," Gray continued. "I trust whatever business kept you from Town earlier has been resolved to your satisfaction."

Turner-Camden's face pinched. "Not quite. But it will be soon enough."

Clairemont shot Stalwood a glance. Was the man talking about his assassination of the real Clairemont or something else entirely? Who was to say?

"Did it have anything to do with our business together?" Gray pressed, steering the conversation to the topics Stalwood and Clairemont would be most interested in. "With our partnership with the Duke of Clairemont?"

"Something along those lines," Turner-Camden drawled in a nasal tone that grated across Clairemont's spine. He didn't like this man. There was something that felt entirely wrong about him.

"His being back in London has created quite the stir," Gray

said, leaning back in his chair like he had not a care in the world."

"So I've heard." Turner-Camden leaned forward. "He is even courting your wife's sister, I've been told."

"Yes, he is quite serious about Celia, it seems." Gray shook his head. "But I have my...my hesitations."

Clairemont looked over his shoulder, and in the dim light he met Stalwood's eyes. His mentor looked just as impressed as he was by Gray's performance so far. The man could have easily been a spy, himself.

"Well, I had hoped to talk to you about Clairemont when I came here," Turner-Camden said. "As my note mentioned."

"Excellent. What would you like to discuss?" Gray asked.

Turner-Camden shifted in his chair and from Clairemont's angle, he saw the man's eyes narrow. He was sizing Gray up, analyzing him. What he saw or thought or would do next was anyone's guess, but Clairemont didn't like the change. He just hoped Gray saw it, too, and was prepared.

"I'd like your thoughts first. What are your *hesitations*?"

Gray waited a beat before he answered. "Well, to be honest, Clairemont has been...*odd* since his return to Society. He is not the man I recall he was when I knew him in our schoolboy days."

Turner-Camden straightened at that statement and his hand clenched slightly on the armrest of his chair. "I see," he ground out.

Clairemont leaned closer to the bookshelf, using everything in him not to burst out and interrupt the meeting. "Don't push," he said beneath his breath. "Don't push."

But of course Gray couldn't hear him. And it was obvious Gray thought he was close to something big. "You know him better than I do. He was the one who suggested you come on board in the canal project. So I thought perhaps you could tell me more."

Turner-Camden rose slowly and paced away, and Clairemont caught his breath. His view of the room was limited by the narrow opening in the bookcase. If Turner-Camden wasn't sitting right in the chair across from Gray, he could no longer be seen. Which meant Clairemont could now only judge what was happening by what he heard and what Gray did in reaction.

"You want to know more about Clairemont," Turner-Camden drawled from across the room. "Very interesting. You see, I came here today to get more information from you, Danford. I may not have been in London these past few weeks, but it doesn't mean I haven't been informed of what has been happening here."

Gray remained in his place at his desk, but Clairemont noticed how his shoulders stiffened. "I'm not sure I know what you mean."

"You've been spending a good deal of time with Clairemont for a man who questions his motives," Turner-Camden said. "And interestingly enough you've also spent some time with a very good friend of this Clairemont...the Earl of Stalwood."

Behind Clairemont, Stalwood drew a sharp breath. He had been a spymaster for decades and never had his identity revealed except by the very unusual circumstances with the Danfords and Celia. But Turner-Camden said his name like he knew something about him. And if Turner-Camden was truly the Rooster, he had betrayed too many spies not to take that seriously.

Gray rose slowly and Clairemont could see he was taking a defensive posture. Damn, but he wished he could see Turner-Camden.

"I'm not sure what the Earl of Stalwood has to do with anything. He and my brother are friendly and yes, he's been to my home a few times."

There was a long pause, and then Turner-Camden stepped back into view. He leaned both his hands on Gray's desk. "Mr. Danford, I didn't come here to determine anything about Clairemont. I came here to determine what I needed to know about *you*."

"Me?" Gray said softly. "What could you possibly want to know about me?"

"How involved you were in the schemes of Stalwood and…well, whoever the man masquerading as Clairemont truly is."

"What?" Gray asked.

"Please, don't pretend. My Perry saw it all."

The door to the parlor opened a second time, and Clairemont watched as Perry stepped inside. He had a gun lifted, pointed squarely at Gray.

Clairemont moved on the latch to exit the secret tunnel, but Stalwood caught his arm.

"No, wait," the earl said softly. "If you barge out now he'll shoot for sure. Let it play out a moment."

Clairemont gritted his teeth.

"Perry," Gray said softly. "You shot at me a few days ago."

"That's right," Perry said with a wide, ugly grin.

"Now, here is what we'll do. You're going to sign all the operations of the canals over to me," Turner-Camden said.

"And why would I do that?" Gray asked, with surprisingly little fear in his voice.

"Why do you think I bloody killed the real Clairemont in the first place? The canals are everything, Danford, and Clairemont wanted a bigger cut, a better position. He refused to see the larger implications, the bigger political picture. He was in the way and wouldn't see reason. And now he's dead."

Clairemont swallowed hard. The last piece of the puzzle had fallen into place. The real Clairemont had died because he cared about money and the Rooster cared about treason.

Turner-Camden pointed a finger at Gray. "Now do it. Or else you won't be the only one to die. Your servants will die, and Perry will wait here for your wife and your sister-in-law to return and *they* will both die. Slowly. Uncomfortably."

Once again, Clairemont moved for the door, but Stalwood grabbed his arm and held him back. "Wait, damn it."

Turner-Camden pulled a set of paperwork from his inside

pocket and held it out. "Now sign."

Gray took the papers and set them down on the desk deliberately. He made a big show of seeking out a quill and ink as he looked up at Perry and his gun, trained on Gray's head.

"When you came here a few days ago, you didn't know Clairemont wasn't the real thing, did you?" he asked.

Perry darted his gaze toward Turner-Camden and then back to Gray. "I don't have to answer your questions."

"No, you don't," Gray agreed, almost amiably.

"What is he doing?" Stalwood asked over Clairemont's shoulder.

Clairemont smiled slowly. "He's working the man with the gun. He's giving us, and himself, a fighting chance."

"Don't you wonder why *he* didn't tell you, though?" Gray continued as he dipped the pen in the ink and looked over the document, as if he were reading it before he signed. Like it was a normal business transaction. "After all, *he* knew."

Once again, Perry glanced away from Gray and toward Turner-Camden for a flash of a moment. "He didn't know nothing."

"Are you daft?" Gray asked. "The man just admitted to killing the real Clairemont. Of course he knew the man here in London wasn't the one he'd left bludgeoned on a floor in the countryside. You should hire smarter help, Turner-Camden."

"Do shut up, Danford," Turner-Camden said, but his gaze was shifting toward Perry.

Gray ignored him. "And if it was your partner here, that means he sent you to meet with me, *knowing* that the false Clairemont would arrive. Knowing you would be unprepared to deal with him. What if I had told the imposter about your visit before he reached my home? What if he'd come prepared while you were not? It seems that would have ended badly for you. I wonder why Turner-Camden would do that. Unless it's the same reason he killed Clairemont. He wants the entire canal scheme to himself."

Perry's mouth tightened. "That true, Turner-Camden? You

send me here not giving a damn if I ended up dead?"

"Shut up, Danford," Turner-Camden repeated. "Don't listen to him, Perry. He's the voice of a dead man."

"Yeah, but so was I if Clairemont had come prepared for me," Perry said, "And maybe this toff is right. After all, if I'd been killed, it would have proved to you that Clairemont was a fake just as much as if I'd come back to you with a report."

"Seems there's no honor amongst thieves," Gray said, signing the papers slowly, his voice still utterly calm despite the tenuous situation. "So who in this room is the bigger danger? Me, without a weapon, without a hope, or him? The man who wants it all and probably needs someone to frame for my death. I assume you'll make it look like a robbery, will you?"

Perry turned his weapon on Turner-Camden, and in that moment Stalwood and Clairemont burst from the secret passageway. Gray dropped behind his desk as the two men moved on Perry and Turner-Camden. Clairemont dove for Perry, hitting the tough with all his weight and sending his gun clattering away.

Meanwhile, Stalwood moved on Turner-Camden, slamming him to the ground with a well-placed punch and then rolling him to his stomach to tie his hands behind his back.

Perry struggled as Clairemont fought to restrain him, spitting up curses into his face as they grappled on the floor. But Clairemont was stronger, bigger, and he was beginning to get the upper hand just as the door to the parlor flew open once more and Celia rushed into the room, Rosalinde on her heels.

The distraction was all Perry needed. As Clairemont jerked his face toward her, Perry dipped a hand into his boot and came out with a knife. Celia screamed his name as Perry pressed the blade hard into his shoulder.

Fiery pain burst through Clairemont as he reeled back and threw a wide looping elbow, catching Perry across the temple. The man grunted and flopped back against the floor, unconscious.

"Oh my God, Aiden," Celia said, stepping toward him as Rosalinde rushed to Gray at his desk. The knife was still protruding from Aiden's shoulder and his face was dark with pain and emotion.

He ignored her, flipping the unconscious Perry to his stomach and hog-tying him at last. He stood up and spun on her, but if she expected the warm embrace that Gray and Rosalinde were now sharing, he disappointed her by glaring at her.

"What the hell are you doing here?" he snapped. "Both of you?"

Stalwood rolled his eyes at the couples. "I'll take Lord Turner-Camden out to the agents waiting behind the house," he said, "and let you all have a moment. We'll return for Perry briefly and to have that wound checked."

Aiden glanced at the knife in his shoulder as his mentor dragged Turner-Camden from the room. Rolling his eyes, he yanked it from his shoulder and tossed it aside. Celia's stomach clenched as blood seeped from the hole in his jacket.

"Aiden," she whispered.

He shook his head. "It's nothing," he insisted, despite evidence to the contrary. "Answer my question."

Gray had been holding Rosalinde, but now he pushed back, still gripping her arms. "Yes, what *are* you doing here?"

Celia folded her arms, her anger starting to rise at his dismissive behavior. "You told Rosalinde that when the horses were gone from the drive, it was safe. There weren't any horses in the drive."

"It's true," Rosalinde said. "We assumed it was over, but your villains must have come in a hack, for when we came in, we heard the commotion in the hall."

"So you ran *toward* danger?" Aiden shouted, his face turning almost tomato red as he stared at Celia. "Do you understand how utterly foolish that is? Do you understand that if you'd been hurt I would have—" He spun away from her and returned his attention to the still-unconscious Perry on the floor. "I would have died, Celia."

"But I *wasn't* hurt," Celia said. "You were. Now, will you let Gray guard this…this…*person* until Lord Stalwood returns and allow *me* to examine your wound?"

Gray moved forward, his hand still firmly in Rosalinde's. "Go ahead, Clairemont. I'll keep an eye on Perry. I assume in a moment my house will be swarming with agents of the crown who will relieve me of these duties."

Aiden pursed his lips. "Fine," he said.

Celia took a long breath. At least she would get a moment alone with him. Away from the others, she might at last be able to touch him and ensure he was all right.

Probably for the last time.

He turned his gun over to Gray and she stretched her hand out to him. He took it with a quick glance at the others, then followed her out of the room.

She probably should have taken him to the kitchen or another parlor, but she didn't. She led him upstairs and down the hall to her bedroom. He paused at the door.

"Celia," he whispered.

She ignored him as she all but dragged him inside. "Take off your jacket and your shirt," she said, walking away from him to the basin on her dresser. There she wet a cloth, trying to slow her racing heart before she turned back to him.

He was tugging the shirt over his head when she did. She caught her breath both at the sight of his bare chest and at the huge cut on his shoulder. A few inches lower…

"Stop staring, it's only another scar," he whispered.

She ignored him and crossed the room to him. There she stopped and looked down at him. She breathed in every part of this moment. The look of him, disheveled and handsome and half-naked in her chamber. The smell of his skin, the warmth of it as she placed one hand on his shoulder and gently began to wipe the wound with the other.

"You'll need stiches," she whispered, her voice breaking.

He nodded. "Stalwood will have it taken care of. I'll survive until then."

Her fingers traced the wound. "You could have been killed," she said.

He lifted his face to hers, and for the first time since she burst into the room, there was gentleness there. "Look at me." She did, meeting his eyes. He let out a long, heavy sigh. "John Dane."

She shook her head. "I-I don't understand."

"My name. It's John Dane," he repeated.

Her lips parted and the washcloth slipped from her fingers as she stared at him. He had refused her that answer before and it had hurt her. Now he said it and she recognized it for what it was. A gift and a goodbye.

Tears stung her eyes as she leaned down and pressed her lips to his. His arms came around her, dragging her into his lap as he drove his tongue inside with desperate, heated passion.

She shifted against him as the kiss deepened and felt the proof of his desire for her pressing to her thigh. She drew back and stared down at him.

"One last time," she whispered.

He closed his eyes and let out a long, pained breath. Then he nodded. "One last time," he repeated, and began to shift her skirts.

She reached between them for the flap on his trousers and managed to work the buttons free. He stood up as she did so, setting her on her feet. He kissed her as the flap fell forward and she cupped his erection in her hand. She stroked him once, twice.

He drew back with a deep groan. "I want more time," he murmured, and she wasn't certain he was only referring to this afternoon and the time they had to make love. "But they'll be expecting our return."

She stepped away and lifted her skirts, holding them against her thighs as she met his gaze evenly. "Then don't wait."

He squeezed his eyes shut, then grabbed her by the waist.

He spun her around, dragging her back against him as he walked her to the bed. He bent her at the waist, placing her hands on the edge of her high mattress. He lifted her skirts higher, pushing aside her drawers to slick his fingers over her sex.

She was wet there, ready, and he let out a low moan as he positioned himself at her entrance.

She braced for the twinge of pain she had experienced the first time, but as he slid home there was none of that. Only pleasure. She moved against him with a sigh and he cupped her breasts as he began to roll his hips against hers.

She pushed back with every thrust, closing her eyes to the sensations, memorizing them as best she could. She would never feel like this again, no matter what happened in the future. Because he would be gone and she would be empty.

He increased his thrusts and his panting breaths were desperate, almost like he could read her mind. His hands were shaking as he reached for one of hers and guided it between her legs.

"Touch yourself here," he ordered, pressing her fingers against her clitoris.

She followed the order, circling herself gently, then harder as the combination of her touch and his cock drove her to the edge. She turned her face into her arm as pleasure overtook her, whimpering against the sleeve of her gown. He followed fast behind, a few more long thrusts and then he pulled away, spending outside of her tremoring, clenching body.

Celia hadn't yet stood as John Dane smoothed the flap of his trousers back over himself and buttoned it with shaking hands. He pulled his bloody shirt over his shoulders and slung his jacket on without buttoning himself.

"I'm sorry," he whispered.

That made her stand up. Her gown fell down over her hips,

back into place, as she faced him, her flushed face saying more about what had just happened then anything else.

"I'm not." She moved toward him, hand outstretched. When she cupped his cheek, he couldn't help but lean into the warmth of her palm. "I'm not sorry, Aiden...*John*." She smiled as she corrected herself. "John suits you better."

He drew in a long breath. His entire life he had been attempting to escape the person who was John Dane. Now everything had changed.

"For the first time, it feels like it does," he admitted.

She leaned up and kissed him, her lips gentle against his. It sparked a flame in him, but he backed away. "I must leave, Celia."

She nodded, releasing him without argument. "When will *he*...Clairemont...die?" she asked, her voice cracking as tears filled her eyes.

Seeing them there, knowing they were for him, it cut him almost to the bone. He cleared his throat so his voice wouldn't be thick when he said, "That will be up to Stalwood. But I would say soon. A few days at most."

A sob escaped her throat and she moved on him, catching him as she lifted her lips. He grabbed her arms, dragging her close as their mouths merged. He tasted her tears, he choked on his own and he held her far too tightly as he drove his tongue against hers in defiance.

He wanted to stay. He wanted to be with her. But he couldn't. So he yanked out of her arms and backed up.

"Goodbye, Celia," he whispered.

She shook her head. "I won't say that to you."

He shut his eyes, his fists clenching at his sides as he struggled for control. For calm. For anything to help him survive this pain.

"Goodbye," he repeated. Then he flung open her door and left her without looking back.

CHAPTER TWENTY-FOUR

Two weeks later

Celia's gown was black. Perhaps it was inappropriate considering she had only been courted by the supposed Duke of Clairemont, not married nor even engaged to him. But black fit her soul as she sat in the parlor, staring blankly at the fire across the room.

The door behind her opened, and without looking to see who had entered, she sighed. "Hello, Rosalinde."

Her sister moved to sit in the chair beside her and touched her hand. "Half a dozen more cards of condolence arrived today."

"Put them with the others," Celia said. "I stopped reading them days ago."

"It must be hard to read their words of sympathy over an accident that never actually happened," Rosalinde said.

Celia turned her gaze to the ceiling. Three days after her last afternoon with John, the pretend Duke of Clairemont had suffered a tragic accident, falling down the stairs at his London estate. He had died instantly and been swiftly buried in a small, private service in the countryside that not even Celia and her family had been invited to.

And so it was over. Yet her part was still to be played. Everyone was watching to see her reaction. But grief wasn't hard to portray. She felt it keenly enough, even if it wasn't for the reason the world suspected.

"I know I should respond, but what do I say when I know the truth?" she asked.

Rosalinde nodded, offering sympathy when she could give no answers. "Tabitha and Honora also stopped by again this morning. They truly want to see you."

"I won't be able to lie to them," Celia sighed. "I'm afraid they'll see the truth in my eyes."

"I doubt that," Rosalinde reassured her. "They'll see your pain, as I see your pain. They'll put their arms around you and they'll never know the source. It might make you feel better to be around other people, rather than locking yourself in your chamber day and night."

Celia shot her sister a look. She could see Rosalinde was truly worried, but the idea that she could shake off the loss of John by simply seeing some friends was patently absurd.

"I appreciate your intention, but I can't. Not yet. In truth, I think the best thing for me would be to return to the north. I'm sure Gray is more than ready to go back to his business now that Turner-Camden has been arrested and things are complicated."

Rosalinde sighed. "He is. And I suppose that our return would not be seen as odd considering your 'loss'."

Celia nodded. "Excellent, is it decided then?"

"May I ask you something?" Rosalinde said, instead of answering Celia.

"Of course. Anything."

"Why must you marry a man with a title?"

Celia ducked her head. She hadn't confessed to Rosalinde about her visit with their grandfather, but now she felt compelled to do so. She'd seen the damage secrets and lies could do, even when done in the name of good.

"Grandfather," she admitted, her voice cracking.

"But your bargain with him for information about our father died when you broke your engagement to Stenfax, why would—" Rosalinde cut herself off and her eyes grew wide. "Oh Celia, tell me you didn't."

Celia shrugged. "When John began to court me in the guise of Clairemont, I thought perhaps we might still obtain the information we so desire. So I snuck out and went to Grandfather."

Rosalinde's lips parted. "You did *what*? That was dangerous, Celia. What if he had attacked you as he did me, with no one to save you?"

"But he didn't. At least not physically." She let out her breath in a long, shaky sigh. "Just as I suspected, the idea of being linked to a duke was too much for him to resist. He told me if I married Clairemont, I would get what I wanted. But then he said something that turned my blood to ice."

"What did he say?" Rosalinde gasped.

"That I was like him," Celia whispered, dipping her head. "Like that was something to be proud of. I was repulsed by the idea."

"And that was when you told Clairemont...*John Dane*...the truth about our past, our family," Rosalinde breathed.

"Yes."

Rosalinde was silent for what felt like an eternity, and Celia couldn't tell if she were angry or frustrated or just disappointed. At last Rosalinde took her hand. "Even if this had all worked out, you know Grandfather lies."

"I know," Celia whispered. "But I'm not like you. I have nothing to fill the emptiness that is in my heart. I thought I could fill it with John, but now that he is gone, I feel like if I could find our father..."

She trailed off as Rosalinde's eyes filled with tears. "I know. And I wish I could give that to you. To both of us. Gray hasn't given up."

"And John said he would use his resources. There is no reason not to believe he still might, even though he'll never be in my life again," Celia agreed.

"So your bargain with Grandfather ends up being meaningless," Rosalinde said.

"I suppose so."

Rosalinde leaned in. "Do you love him? John Dane. Not the character he played or the bargain he represented to you. The man he truly was."

Celia nodded. "I do. I love him very much. More than I ever thought possible."

Rosalinde traced her cheek with a sad smile. "Then let me give you the same advice you gave me on my wedding day not so long ago. Tell him."

Celia jumped up, trying to run from the thrill of possibility her sister's words represented. "How?" she asked, almost more to calm herself then to hear her sister's response. "He is gone. Dead to all who know."

Rosalinde pursed her lips as she rose to her own feet. "Come with me."

"Where?" Celia asked, confused by this sudden change in her sister.

Rosalinde grabbed her hand and all but dragged her from the room. "We're going to resolve this. One way or another. Right now."

Celia shook her head as the servant who had led her, Rosalinde and Gray to the parlor left to seek his master. "I don't want to see Lord Stalwood," she hissed.

"Celia, you cannot run from this," Rosalinde said, moving toward her. "If you love this man, at least you must take a chance."

Gray slipped an arm around Rosalinde. "Easy now, love. No need to push her into a corner."

Celia pushed past the couple. "You don't understand. It is easy for you."

"You know it wasn't always!" Rosalinde said. "You know how much we struggled to be together. And it was worth it in the end."

"Worth all of it and more," Gray said with a nod.

Before Celia could argue or point out that their situation was vastly different from her own, the door behind them opened and Stalwood stepped in.

"Mr. and Mrs. Danford. Miss Fitzgilbert," he said with a confused expression for them all. "I didn't expect you. Is everything well?"

Rosalinde shot Celia a look and Celia glared back. When it was clear the sisters were at a stalemate, Gray stepped forward with a sigh. "We are fine, thank you, my lord. There is no trouble, if that is your worry."

"No trouble? *That* is untrue." Celia turned her ire toward Stalwood. She couldn't help but blame this man even though her rational mind told her it was an unfair action.

"Celia!" Rosalinde burst out.

Celia turned on her. "*You* forced me to come here. You cannot be angry that I react how I react now."

"I forced you to come here because I know you are in pain. I hate to see you this way." Rosalinde waved her hand at the earl. "And this man could help you."

Stalwood was seemingly undaunted by the odd exchange being played out before him. "You have something to say to me, Miss Fitzgilbert?"

She took her time in looking at him. He had a rather kind face, actually. And knowing he had saved the man she loved from certain doom made it almost impossible to hate him as she wished to do.

She sighed. There was no escaping this humiliation now, so she might as well face it. "I want to talk to you. But may I have a moment alone?"

Gray and Rosalinde exchanged a look, as if they weren't certain leaving them was the best idea. But Stalwood waved them off. "We'll be fine. My roses are beginning to bud in the back and it's very pretty. Why don't you two take a stroll while I talk to Miss Fitzgilbert?"

Rosalinde let Gray lead her from the room with only the

briefest back glances at Celia. Celia ignored her, keeping her attention on Stalwood.

When they were gone, he crossed to a sideboard and poured a glass of sherry. He came back to her and held it out.

She stared at the liquor, then took it. "Thank you."

"You look as though you need it. I assume this mess with Clairemont's death announcement and Dane's departure has been difficult for you."

"It has," she whispered. "Is John…is John well?"

Stalwood's expression softened. "He is. After such a large and involved case as this, I tend to allow my agents time away. He is taking that time now, but I received word from him recently that he is fine." His face fell. "Well enough."

She moved forward at his hesitation. "His wound is healing? Is he having trouble with it?"

Stalwood's eyes widened at her focused attention. "His wound is healing, my dear. In truth, I think he suffers more from losing…losing you."

She caught her breath and turned away, uncertain how to proceed. Stalwood was offering her hope and the idea of taking it was terrifying to her core.

"He has lost a great deal in his life," she whispered at last.

Stalwood was silent a beat before he said, "Told you that, did he?"

She nodded as she faced him. "He told me about his parents, about that bastard who took him when he was a child, about his life on the streets."

Stalwood stared. "All that? I don't think he's ever told *anyone* all that before. I doubt I know it all, in truth."

"I can't believe that," Celia said, sipping her drink slowly. "After all, you are as close to him as family. You saved him."

"He was very much worth saving."

"I agree wholeheartedly." She tilted her head. "You—you love him, don't you?"

Stalwood flinched, as if saying those things out loud was uncomfortable. She supposed it would be. Most men, especially those of rank, were raised to avoid emotion at all costs. But when his expression cleared, he nodded.

"My wife died many years ago and we were never blessed with children. I couldn't bear to find another woman to take her place and present me with the heirs Society demanded, so I put all my energy into my work. My spies. But when John appeared...well, he was different."

"He was your ward," she said.

He shook his head. "No. He was my son. He still is, even if we never discuss it. You are correct that I love him. Am *I* correct that you love him, as well?"

"Yes," she whispered. Tears flooded her eyes as she stared at a man she had once seen as her enemy, but now was linked to through a man who'd told her she could never have him.

But standing here, it was clear how much she wanted John. She ached for him. Rosalinde had said she had to tell him. But would that matter? Would it work?

Was she brave enough to try?

Stalwood watched her emotions play over her face and sighed. "That certainly makes the risk I took in revealing my secret to you more worth it."

"You did it to protect him, even though it put him in danger," Celia said.

He jerked out a nod. "As I said, he is my son." He looked at her long and hard. "If you could have him, Miss Fitzgilbert, would you want him?"

She nodded without hesitation. "I would. If I could see him, tell him what was in my heart, if I could get past those barriers he places between us...I would very much want him."

"But you see the issues it would create," Stalwood said evenly.

"Issues?" she repeated.

"Not only will John put up barriers to protect you from yourself, but he will *never* be able to return to Society. His role in this case was far too public—he would likely be recognized and that could cause problems. Even danger. If you choose him, you would lose your standing."

She blinked. "Do you think I give a damn about standing?"

"I must think you do a little, based on your engagement to an earl and your courtship with what you thought was a duke."

She glared at him. "I have been accused of being a title-hunter before, my lord. Please don't insult me by doing it when you don't know me, nor the circumstances that led to either of those decisions. I don't give a *damn* about titles. I don't give a *damn* about Society. I only care about John. If I could have him, I would walk through fire. I would give up all that I have and all that I am."

Stalwood's stern face slowly brightened with a smile. "Then you are worthy of him, it seems." He sighed. "If you'd like, I'll tell you where he is."

Her lips parted in surprise. "You will?"

He nodded. "But I warn you, he won't make it easy for you. He wants to protect you from what he thinks he is and what he believes he'll always be. You'll need something to help convince him to let go of the past, let go of what he thinks he should do, and turn to you. I'll give it to you and the rest is up to you."

She moved forward, catching Stalwood's hand gently. He looked down at her in surprise and she smiled, the first glimmer of hope rising in her like a phoenix from a fire.

"I will fight for him, my lord."

"Excellent," he said, squeezing her hand. "He deserves nothing less, after all."

CHAPTER TWENTY-FIVE

Although it was only spring, the sun was still warm on John's back as he swung the axe and split another log in two. Without a shirt, sweat crept down his back and stung what remained of the wounds on his shoulder and his arm, but he ignored it. The physical labor kept his mind too tired to think. To remember. So he exhausted himself during the day and prayed for the nights—and the dreams that came with them—to end swiftly.

It never worked. The emptiness inside of him was too vast, too deep. He thought every moment of Celia. Dreamed of Celia. Saw her everywhere he went.

"John."

He froze. Now he was even hearing her on the wind. Except it didn't seem like an illusion. It truly felt like her voice creeping over to him, wrapping around him like her warm fingers had once done.

"John."

He turned, knowing now that the voice was not his imagination. There, standing out in the middle of the field, was Celia. She wore a pale blue gown that matched her eyes, and a bonnet dangled from her fingers so he could see the coiled beauty of her dark hair.

She dropped the hat and ran for him. And even though he knew he shouldn't, he dropped the axe and moved toward her at equal speed. They met in the middle, mouths crushing together with no finesse, but all the passion that existed between them. She clawed at his bare flesh, lifting into him as she flattened her body to his.

He was ready to surrender, ready to let his heart take over from his head, but there was a small part of him that screamed at him to stop. To pull away because she was not his. She never could be.

It took everything in him to listen to that voice. To set her aside gently and back away.

"What are you doing here?" he panted, trying to stay upright when his knees threatened to buckle in the face of her beauty.

She smiled at him, actually smiled, as if there was nothing to stop her. "I came for you, John."

It sounded so easy that he nearly moved toward her. Instead, he stepped farther away, holding up a hand to ward her off. "No, no. It's not possible."

She sighed, reaching for him still. "Let me come in. Let me talk to you. If you still feel it's impossible, I'll go."

He stared at her outstretched fingers, at her upturned face. If he let her into the cottage he had taken during his break, he knew it would never be the same. He would see her there and smell her there until the day he left.

He wanted that and feared it in equal measure.

But he couldn't refuse her. So he took her hand and led her to the house. Once inside, he found the shirt he had discarded to do his work. When he'd put it on he turned. She was standing in the middle of the big, open room, looking around with a smile.

"I like it," she said. "It's cozy."

"It isn't mine," he explained, going to the fire to stir it and adding a pot of water to make tea. "I'm only letting it until my next case begins."

Her mouth tugged down. "I see."

"How are you here, Celia?" he asked. "How did you find me?"

She shrugged. "Gray and Rosalinde brought me. They left me at the end of the lane. They won't return for a while now."

He blinked. "They knew you were coming to find me and they left you alone?"

"I think they assume my intentions are far less honorable than yours will be," she said with a light laugh.

He couldn't help his own small smile. "They don't know at all, do they?"

They couldn't. All he wanted to do was lay her down on the rug in the middle of the room, to strip her bare and make love to her until she was shaking with release, begging him to stop, begging him to never stop. Claiming her until there was nothing left but him.

He turned away. "And *you* found me how?"

"Stalwood," she said softly.

He spun on her. "No."

She nodded. "Yes."

He swallowed back a salty curse. He was going to have to have a stern conversation with the earl when he next saw him. To send Celia to him was unkind. Bordering on cruel. How could Stalworth do it?

"I love you."

She said the words so calmly, so softly, and yet there was a certainty on her face that spoke of her strength. Her determination. He couldn't help but stare. *Was* this all a dream after all?

"Did you hear me?" she asked, taking a step toward him.

"No, Celia," he said past a bone-dry throat. "You—you love an illusion."

"You know my mind now?" she asked, her tone laced with annoyance. "You may think you do, but you have no idea. I love *John Dane. You.* And having just been in your arms, I assure you, you are no illusion. You are wonderfully real, though you're wearing too many clothes at present."

He shook his head. "You are playful with something so serious."

She folded her arms. "You're right. My love for you is entirely serious. I'm glad you recognize it."

He slammed his hand down on a tabletop. "Damn it, Celia. Stop saying that. Don't waste something so precious as your love on a man like me."

She moved again, and he hadn't the strength to step away. She reached him but didn't touch him. She only stared up into his eyes and said, "What I feel is not a waste. I love you. And what's more, *you* love *me*."

With her eyes, she dared him to deny it. Dared him to be strong enough. But he wasn't. Not when her scent filled his nostrils, not when he could feel her warmth that was more powerful than a dozen suns. Not when she seemed so certain.

"I do love you," he choked out, hating that his eyes filled with tears when he said it. He'd never said it to anyone in his life, never once before. Now it filled him to the brim and made everything tilt sidewise so he had to fight to remain upright. "But if I got down on a knee now and offered myself to you, it would be an offer of *nothing*. No title, no grand amount of money, no big house on a hill."

She wrinkled her brow. "I'm not sure where everyone got the idea that I am some title-hungry money-grabber, but I assure you it is not true. If I were to have you, *all* of you, that would be more than enough for me. None of the rest ever meant anything to me."

"And what about your grandfather's secret?" he asked.

"You *must* be reaching if you invoke him as a talisman against me. You told me already not to go back to him. Even if I did, I have no duke now. If I could land one, I know Grandfather could very well be lying. He might *never* give me the information I seek. I would have to surrender a happy future for an empty past."

He shut his eyes. She was determined and what she offered was so fucking tempting. A life he'd never believed he deserved, a future he hadn't dared plan for.

But it was all a risk and he found he was...afraid. He, who had faced down villains so vile they would make an average man's stomach turn. He, who had escaped a past of violence and poverty.

This slip of a woman and all she offered *terrified* him. Made him desperate to find a way to turn her aside so he wouldn't run out of excuses to keep running from something so powerful as her love.

"And the War Department?" he asked. "What would you think of that life? It has already endangered you once."

She dug into her pelisse pocket and handed out a note to him. It was folded and he recognized the handwriting across the face even before she said, "From Stalwood. He told me to give you this once you tried to use the department against me."

He took it and slowly unfolded it. He read it, stared at her and repeated the reading, this time out loud. "'John, you are hereby discharged from the service of the king, with great honor and a generous lifetime pension to follow. Be happy, John. Be free. All my love, Walter.'"

He read the last line over and over, *feeling* his mentor's love in the shaking handwriting. Seeing how Stalwood had taken away his last refuge from true happiness. Loving and hating him for him at once.

"He let you go," Celia said, her surprise plain on her face. "I didn't know."

"He didn't tell you?" he asked.

She shook her head. "No. He said this might help you decide. I-I would say I'm sorry to take this from you, but—"

"If I refused you, I know he would take me back. He's setting me free to give me a future." He folded the note and put it aside on the table. "He's sending me to you. Even though he should know damn well it's impossible."

"You keep saying that," she said, lifting a hand to cover his heart. Immediately the rhythm there doubled. "But it's not true. The love is all that matters, so it isn't impossible unless you chose to make it so."

"What would you have me do, Celia?" he whispered, not to argue with her, but because he truly didn't know. He'd never known himself, never been anyone but a lie, a ghost, a tool.

She smiled as if she understood. "Make a new start with me. As John Dane. Whoever he turns out to be. Make a life with me. Love me, and more than that, allow me to love you as you grow into the man you will be next. Please."

The "please" was what broke him. She was offering him everything he'd always wanted and never dared hope for. She was offering him herself, and he knew that would be enough, more than enough, to sustain him for the rest of his life.

"I-I love you," he whispered, daring to say the words out loud once again, but this time not as a curse. He expected them to still be bitter but they were infinitely sweet on his tongue.

Pure joy brightened her face even as she asked, "But do you want to be with me?"

"More than anything," he admitted. "Though I fear I'll let you down."

"You couldn't," she whispered as she wrapped her arms around him and drew his lips to hers.

He sank into her, knowing that the war was over, the battle won…or lost, he supposed, since he had fought her so long and now he was giving in. But he reveled in the losing, for it meant such happiness, such joy. For the first time, he let himself look forward to the future and he was surprised by how wonderful it felt.

He drew back with a gasp as he was filled with happiness. She smiled.

"There's John Dane," she murmured as she slid her hands into his open shirt and glided it from his shoulders. "There's the man you'll become."

"And what is that?" he whispered, not fighting as she tugged him over to the very rug he had pictured taking her on and drew him down onto it.

"Happy," she said, kissing him. "Free. Mine."

"All yours," he agreed, laying her back and covering her body with his at last.

Her hands smoothed over his flesh, kneading there, taking and giving all at once. Her gown buttoned in the front and his fingers flew over the fastenings, loosening it even as he kissed and kissed her. She sighed as he parted the dress and let his mouth draw away from hers to kiss the column of her throat, then the arch of her collarbone, the smoothness of her chest.

He pulled at the dress, taking it down her arms as she arched her back for access. The chemise came with it, baring her from the waist up.

He stared at her, beautiful in the streaming sunshine from the window, the jumping light from the fire behind her. She was perfect and glorious and his, all his, for the rest of his life.

He bent his head and captured one tight nipple, licking and gently biting the flesh until she cried out and her hands tangled in his hair. He pushed her dress lower and followed the rolling fabric, kissing the flat plane of her stomach until he was forced to draw away and use both hands to pull her dress over her hips. Her drawers followed, then her stockings and at last she was naked on the rug, staring up at him not in fear, not in worry...

But in pure love and welcome. She was home, and he covered her with his body, setting in the V of her legs where he fit so perfectly. She smiled against his neck.

"You are too dressed," she whispered, tugging at his pants.

He smiled. "I am, I know. But I am too comfortable to ever leave."

She laughed, a happy sound, a beautiful sound that filled his ears with pleasure. "Take them off and I will find you a more comfortable spot to rest."

He chuckled as he got up. "Who knew you were such a negotiator?" he asked as he kicked off his boots and pushed his trousers off in record speed.

She leaned up on her elbows to watch him, licking her lips as his erection bobbed free and he stood before her naked.

"You are too beautiful," she muttered as she reached for him.

She caught his length and he sucked in a breath. "Isn't that my line?"

"I'll steal it," she purred, drawing him closer and rubbing

her thumb over the sensitive head of his cock. Pleasure poured through him, making his cock twitch even as his whole body relaxed into liquid pleasure.

"Steal all you like. Everything of mine is yours now."

"I only want this," she said.

He lowered himself back over her and she opened her legs wider, watching him carefully as he positioned himself at her dripping entrance.

Their gazes held as he slid inside, inch by inch, take by take. When he was fully seated, her body shuddered around him and she gripped him with her internal muscles.

"Great God," he moaned as he began to rotate his hips above her. She lifted into him, her body clinging to him, but she never looked away, holding him hostage with her hooded, heated stare.

He drove harder, judging his motions by the catch of her breath, the way her skin flushed. She was close to the brink and he couldn't wait to join her, especially since his body was so very ready to claim her, *truly* claim her, at long last.

He slid a hand between them and found her clitoris. With a flick of his thumb, he tossed her over the edge and she screamed as she fell, her nails digging into him, her body milking him.

He couldn't wait any longer. He felt the impending release and growled out her name as he poured himself deep within her, drawing both their orgasms out as long as he could.

Then he collapsed to the floor beside her and gathered her to his chest.

"Now," he panted. "You are truly mine."

"I was yours the moment I saw you," she gasped back. "And I will be yours until the stars die out."

He looked down at her, fitted comfortably in his arms, and knew she meant it. All of it. He knew, and it gave him strength and power and all the hope in the world for tomorrow and the rest of his life.

EPILOGUE

June 1811

Celia had only been a wife for a short time, and she still loved to see her husband come down the stairs to breakfast. His hair had grown out in the month since they reunited. He'd also grown a beard. She loved them both, loved that he looked a new man as well as acted and spoke as a new man.

And yet John was still, at his core, the person she'd fallen in love with. His gaze found hers and his hooded expression spoke of all the pleasures they had shared the night before in their bedroom above.

A smaller bedroom than the one she'd shared with him when he was still pretending to be a duke. In actuality, everything was smaller now. Their home, their staff, her wardrobe—all had shrunk as they began together. Yet her life felt *bigger*. Fuller.

"Rosalinde and Gray return to London today, yes?" he asked as he took a spot at the table beside her and grabbed her hand to lift it to his lips.

She smiled as a maid brought him a plate of food. "They do. We'll see them off in about an hour."

"Do you wish you were going with them?" he asked, his tone even but his eyes concerned.

She shook her head. "Not at all. London holds no sway for me. I'm happy here in my home. We're close to Gray and

Rosalinde and you're in it, so that's all I need. Honestly, I don't think Gray would go, himself, except that he seems concerned for his brother. Something is going on with Stenfax, I fear."

John said nothing, but pursed his lips at the mention of her former fiancé. She laughed at the foolishness of that notion.

"Still jealous, are you?" she teased.

"No," he said, his expression gentling. "I think I've made you mine quite thoroughly."

She stood and slid into his lap, wrapping her arms around his neck and pressing a kiss to his lips. "And that was just last night."

He laughed, but his eyes still held worry. "No, it isn't Stenfax who concerns me. I have only been working as Gray's partner in his businesses for ten days. I am being left in charge and I can't help but wonder if I'll cock it up entirely."

She nodded, understanding him entirely. "Gray wouldn't have left things to you if he didn't think you could handle it. He trusts you."

"Somehow, after all the lies, yes," John said. He threaded his hands into her hair, cupping the back of her head gently. "This new life, it is all because of you, you know."

She smiled. "And are you happy with it, my love?"

"Happier than I could ever express," he whispered. "And I am also truly, madly, deeply in love with you."

She leaned down so he could kiss her again, drowning in the power of his love and all the joy it brought her. This was her husband. This was her life. This was her bliss. Forever.

Coming next from USA Today Bestselling Author Jess Michaels:

A wedding that cannot happen…

A man who is not what he seems…

A woman who betrayed for love…

And a couple who can never be.

It will all happen during one year of passionate Seasons. Turn the page to read an exclusive excerpt of Seasons book three — One Summer of Surrender, coming November 8, 2016.

Excerpt of
One Summer of Surrender
SEASONS BOOK 3

Elise's heart was racing so fast that it felt like she would collapse. She stared across the room and couldn't believe what she was seeing. This was a dream she'd had so many times that she wished she could pinch herself now to prove it was real.

Only she knew it was. Lucien was here. Just a few feet away from her. And he was so utterly beautiful. He was tall, impossibly tall, with thick, dark brown hair and dark eyes the color of rich molasses. He had a strong jaw and full lips that she had pictured moving over hers a thousand times in the three years since she'd seen or touched him last.

"Answer me," he snapped, his hard, harsh, broken tone shattering the spell between them. "What the hell are you doing here?"

As he asked the question a second time, he started across the room at her in long, certain strides. He looked like a bull racing across a paddock toward an intruder and she should have been afraid. But she wasn't. Not even a little. She stood her ground without effort and sucked in a long whiff of his scent as he crowded into her space and all but pinned her to the door behind her.

"What do you *think* I'm doing here?" she managed to ask, pleased she could talk at all, let alone sound as cool and detached as she somehow sounded.

His jaw tightened, the muscle along it twitching and she had a powerful urge to lean up and kiss him there, feel him move beneath her lips. But she didn't do something so foolhardy.

"Why?" he finally shouted.

Before Elise could answer the door behind them flew open and Vivien raced in, a guard behind her.

"What is going on in here?" she cried.

Lucien glared at Elise one last time, then pushed past her toward Vivien. "What the hell, Vivien?"

Elise remained facing away from them, but flinched at his anger and his familiarity with Vivien. He was here, after all, and he had obviously been looking for someone to take as a mistress. Not her, of course, not her. But someone.

"Isn't this what you wanted?" Vivien asked.

Elise spun around to see his face when he answered her. It twisted in pure horror. "Is that what she told you?"

Elise gasped. "No!" she burst out. "I had no idea it was you I was being led to meet."

Vivien nodded. "I didn't tell her a thing, nor did she ask for you. But I assumed…I assumed…"

"What?" Lucien fumed, raising his hands in animated fury. "Why in God's name would you assume I wanted *this*?"

Vivien lifted both eyebrows. "You showed up here after over a year away from my club, on the very night your former fiancée appeared looking for a protector. I assumed you were hoping to match with her. The coincidence-"

"Is just a coincidence," Lucien snapped.

Rejection stung every part of her, but Elise lifted her chin as he turned to look at her at last. His dark gaze flitted over her and his pupils dilated.

"Get out."

Elise wrinkled her brow. "Are you speaking to me?"

He shook his head very slowly. "Not you. Vivien. Get out."

Other Books by Jess Michaels

SEASONS

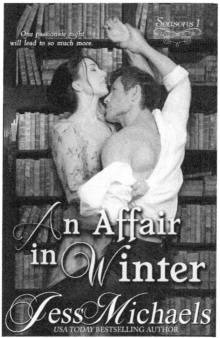

THE WICKED WOODLEYS

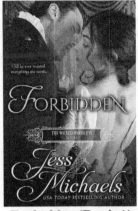

THE NOTORIOUS FLYNNS

THE LADIES BOOK OF PLEASURES

THE PLEASURE WARS SERIES

About the Author

Jess Michaels writes erotic historical romance from her home in Tucson, AZ with her husband and one adorable kitty cat. She has written over 60 books, enjoys long walks in the desert and once wrestled a bear over a piece of pie. One of these things is a lie.

Jess loves to hear from fans! So please feel free to contact her in any of the following ways (or carrier pigeon):

www.AuthorJessMichaels.com

Email: Jess@AuthorJessMichaels.com
Twitter www.twitter.com/JessMichaelsbks
Facebook: www.facebook.com/JessMichaelsBks

Jess Michaels raffles a gift certificate EVERY month to members of her newsletter, so sign up on her website: http://www.authorjessmichaels.com/